THE
BIRD
THAT
FLIES
HIGHEST

THE
BIRD
THAT
FLIES
HIGHEST

BRAD JOHNSON

*Dear Bob —
Thanks for all
your support.
Fly High!*

Rutledge Books, Inc.

Danbury, CT

Cover artwork by Aimee Peterson

Rutledge Books, Inc.
107 Mill Plain Road, Danbury, CT 06811
1-800-278-8533
www.rutledgebooks.com
info@rutledgebooks.com

Manufactured in the United States of America

Cataloging in Publication Data
Johnson, Bradley T.
   The Bird that flies highest

   ISBN: 1-887750-99-1

   1. Adventure stories. 2. Conspiracy stories - fiction

813.54   98-66871

CHAPTER 1

SECRETARIES AND ASSISTANTS BUSTLED BEHIND MIRRORED GLASS ON the top floor of the eight-story building in downtown Baku, Azerbaijan. The concrete structure, which at one time housed Stalin's Transcaucasion Intelligence Commission in early twentieth century communist Russia, had been transformed into an eclectic architectural collage, mixing high-tech composite metals, brilliant tinted glass, old-world concrete, and protruding steel support bars. Behind the glass, a young male assistant sporting worn jeans and a white collared shirt slapped thick manuals in front of the hundred or so shareholders and bankers:

THE AZI-GROUP: 15th Annual Shareholders Meeting
Fiscal Year: September 1, 2012 — August 30, 2013

Passing the young assistant, a forty-something security guard in blue uniform moved mechanically from row to row, scanning the ID tags of the impeccably dressed guests. He shot the infrared beam across the hologram tag of a noble-looking, fair skinned young man sitting in the far corner of the auditorium-style room. A green light flashed twice and the guard smiled.

"The famous BNG Bank. One of the AZI-Group's finest."

"Indeed," said the chubby banker with a British accent. "What's going on outside?"

The guard showed a certain satisfaction at being more informed than the hotshot executive, whose boyish face pressed against the window and gazed at a mass of humanity collected in the narrow street.

"Two protests. The environmental group, Human Race, and a religious group."

"Let me guess," the banker hypothesized, his breath fogging the window, "Human Race wants us to close the old oil rigs in the Caspian Sea?"

"That's correct, sir."

"And what about the religious folks?"

"They're supporters of Baruch. You know, the spiritual guru."

"And what would they be protesting?"

The security guard's eyes cast a look of bewilderment as, peeping over the head of the executive, he focused on an attractive, middle-aged woman speaking passionately to the crowd. He mumbled to the banker, "They're claiming that the AZI-Group is somehow responsible for Baruch's disappearance. You know, the conspiracy-mongers."

"They look to me to be westerners. I bet you there's not one local in the lot," the banker remarked, noting the stark contrast of the aggressive protestors' white skin and apparent affluence set against the darkness and poverty of the slow moving Azeris - the people of Azerbaijan—walking the streets.

"I don't know what their deal is," the security guard commented, "but the bottom line is that Jim Anderson and Haig Abku own Baku."

Scanning the next executive's ID and moving toward the center of the conference room, he looked back over his shoulder and added, "When you live here long enough, you realize the locals, let alone protestors, don't have much say in anything."

The guard scanned a final ID, gave a look around the filled room, and then motioned the dozens of assistants to exit through the back Security Personnel Only door. When the last one had left, he sealed the room with military efficiency.

The auditorium possessed a quiet energy, awaiting the team of well-dressed men and one woman being escorted through the bright hallway on the eighth floor. Another blue-suited security guard whispered, "All clear. Out," as he opened the double walnut doors and watched the ten officers of the world's largest virtual corporation enter the auditorium.

◆ ◆ ◆ ◆ ◆

"Any further questions regarding the meeting protocol, by-laws, or the likes are found on pages 5-15 in the manual in front of you."

With her usual British charm, the graying veteran of the International Law Department, Marleen Breighton, finished an eloquent fifteen-minute explanation of previous business, governing laws, and the meeting format. This routine, a formality that every executive in the room had heard more than the Beatle's *White Album*, heightened the tension of the shareholders, most of whom had that 'yeah, yeah—get off the stage' look.

"Any procedural questions I can answer before moving on?"

"Can we proceed now?" the smartly dressed, chubby banker from BNG Bank yelled sarcastically.

"Yes, we most certainly can," Marleen Breighton replied above the laughter of the room. She paused, waiting for the noise to disperse, and then continued in an earnest manner: "The nineteenth century introduced to an agrarian world the age of industry. The technological advances of the twentieth century gave the world's population a glimpse of increased efficiency and a higher standard of living, made possible by a new model of business management based on information. There is a new business paradigm for the twenty-first century—the virtual corporation. The man about to take the stage created the first virtual corporation and has since redefined what it means to be a global power."

Letting silence fill the room for dramatic effect, Marleen Breighton turned to the panel of company directors. "Without further ado, it is my pleasure to present the CEO of the planet's most successful corporation, Mr. Jim Anderson."

The shareholders rose to their feet and applauded the tan, six-foot two-inch balding executive who had accelerated their stagnating share price from $125.12 in 2008 to $165.00 at the close of business on August 30, 2013. He took the podium in a confident, rehearsed manner.

"I would like to welcome you, the shareholders, to our fifteenth annual meeting at our new headquarters in the capital city of Baku."

The hundred bankers, institutional investors, and proxy holders in the room held over 85 percent of the AZI-Group's stock; therefore, Jim Anderson felt no hesitation referring to this small group as 'the stockholders'. Turning to a stately, dark skinned man in the front row, he broke into an aside.

"Speaking of our new home in Azerbaijan, let me thank Haig Abku, the president of our Oiltron Industries group, for working with the national and local governments to find a solution that allows us, the AZI-Group, to operate in a true free-market environment."

Jim Anderson motioned for his colleague to stand and take a bow. Clapping loudly into the microphone, he waited for Haig Abku to sit down and then proceeded.

"I remember my final year at graduate school...a number of years ago," Jim Anderson said, patting his shiny head to the delight of the crowd. "In my final thesis I predicted that the next century, this century, would see a single corporation controlling over 5 percent of total global business. While I did graduate, the head of the business school dismissed my hypothesis as just that."

Pulling a piece of paper from the inside pocket of his suit coat, he continued, "So I wrote a letter to that professor last week. It reads: Dear Professor Peterson. That I so underestimated the potential growth of what I call the virtual corporation has caused much embarrassment. Enclosed is our latest shareholder report noting that the AZI-Group now accounts for 7 percent of all business activity worldwide. Sincerely, Sir Jim Anderson."

After the chuckling stopped, Jim placed his bifocals on the bridge of his nose and turned to his prepared notes. "When I took over the helm in 2008, this was a fine organization. But this wasn't a *powerful* organization. Without power—petroleum, gas, electricity—our world doesn't work. That's why my first priority was to develop the Energy Division of the AZI-Group. Having now effectively integrated Oiltron Industries, I will lead the energy division and the entire AZI-Group into a new round of expansion."

Jim grinned at the applause from the shareholders. He knew the majority of the shareholders cared only about one thing: money. Those clapping hands were merely pawns for governments, bankers, and a dozen other power brokers. They were, in fact, Jim's competitors, because the richer he made them, the more powerful they became.

Haig Abku, president of Oiltron Industries, the energy division's largest holding, had helped Jim prepare today's presentation.

"Tell the investors how they can make more money and assure the bankers that this growth creates more debt," was Haig Abku's sage advice.

Jim's discourse went on to discuss the results of the various divisions—banking, media, high-tech, insurance, defense—all of which had underperformed compared to the explosive energy division. Jim wound down into his final summary, using Haig Abku's strategy of 'restating the positive and marginalizing the rest.'

"The last five years have forced me, as CEO of your company, to focus on developing the most powerful energy division on this planet. Now we have the time and resources to parley that into further expansion and growth in all areas of *your* company, of *our* company, the AZI-Group."

Jim's powerful closing line brought a standing ovation from the starry-eyed shareholders. As he returned to the one empty seat on the platform, Scott McNally, the burly, redheaded president of the Media Division, World News Network, entered from a side door and grabbed the microphone.

"As the president of WNN, I've been asked to mediate the open discussion portion of the meeting. I see the gentleman in the back of the room would like to ask a question...."

CHAPTER 2

"World News Network welcomes our viewers from around the world. Global Business magazine recently called him 'The spiritual revolutionary'. Millions of people consider him a prophet. Yet he has never before appeared live on global satellite."

Amy Laurance, the feisty twenty-five-year-old reporter who had romanced viewers with her compelling beauty, held up a picture of the glossy cover showing the AZI-Group, Bates/McMillan, and other powerful virtual corporations as tiny human bowling pins. The virtual corporations recoiled in fear as a giant bowling ball with the name 'Baruch' prepared to steamroll them. Setting the magazine on the glass tabletop and gently pulling her suit coat into place, the sexy young reporter flashed a million-dollar smile, but spoke in a serious tone.

"He is a man many love; a man many love to hate. I present to you the man known simply as Baruch."

The camera captured the sharp facial lines, deep-set eyes, and soft, dark complexion of the thirty-nine-year-old Austrian. He winced and said with childish surprise, "A spiritual revolutionary? Should I start wearing battle fatigues?"

The small studio audience exploded into laughter.

Amy Laurance waited for quiet and started the interview.

"First, let me thank you for taking the time for this first-ever live interview."

"Ms. Laurance, yesterday I spoke to almost a million 'spiritual revolutionaries' in New York's Central Park. Cicero, St. Augustine, Spinoza—they have said it all before. The real news is that the I am appearing on the very medium I despise."

"But this is your first public interview?"

Baruch answered matter-of-factly, "I've been tried and convicted on the evening news, but never interviewed."

Amy Laurance tried to get in her next question, but Baruch continued his thought not so much in an arrogant way, but more as if he had a mandate.

"You see, Ms. Laurance, interviews are not real. When I sit with a friend before the fireplace and contemplate the beauty of a spark, that's real. What you and I are involved in is a charade that oils the media machine. You control the questions, then splice the video at corporate headquarters. Just like everything in the world media, things always end up nice and tidy in a pretty package."

The lights of the converted talk show set crashed on Amy Laurance.

"But there's incredible diversity in the media, is there not?"

"The media has incredible *coverage*, Ms. Laurance. But like the Roman generals who conquered cities by drowning the citizens in pleasure, so does the media lure people from reason by making comfort an addiction."

Amy Laurance looked straight-faced at the TelePrompTer.

"You often speak of faith. In fact, during your Central Park speech you said, 'The ages have shown that there is no energy, no compelling force, greater than faith.' Is this the cornerstone of your philosophy?"

Baruch leaned slightly forward, moving closer to Amy Laurance.

"So you call it a philosophy? Isn't it funny that we call our own beliefs religion and those of others philosophy?"

The audience was dead silent as the handsome Austrian stared into the camera.

"Faith is the cornerstone of mankind. Without faith you will accomplish nothing. Without faith, life is devoid of common nature. Without faith, there will be no life."

"Could you explain what you mean?"

Baruch had an inspired look in his eyes. "A young lady ascends the same staircase every day. She develops faith that it's reliable. One day, a certain step breaks and the young lady is injured. She is told the next day that the step was repaired and, in fact, she can see it was repaired. Yet every day she skips that particular step. Each step becomes suspect because of the failings of the one. She has lost faith."

Baruch used this speaking technique frequently, finishing a point with a series of monosyllabic words.

Amy switched directions.

"Your main target has been the media. Why is that?"

"The media is not my target. Words, especially truths, fall more burdensome on some. If a police officer yells 'thief' on a crowded street, it's always the thief who will run."

"Are you saying, Baruch, that all corporations are thieves?"

"That's an interesting question, Ms. Laurance. Let me ask you: can a group of five hundred 'good' employees be part of an evil corporation? If a corporation is evil, then, necessarily, the components of that very organization must be evil as well. People, Ms. Laurance, are thieves, not corporations. The real question is do evil people create an evil corporation or does, for example, your corporation manifest itself in evil people?"

Baruch took a sip of water from his glass and added, "Just a thought."

When Baruch touched a sensitive area, he often finished with the harmless words 'just a thought'. Such passive behavior from a powerful figure seemed odd, almost contradictory, to Amy. She skipped to the next question on the TelePrompTer.

"Some call you a New Age messiah."

"You call me a philosopher!"

He said this with a smile framed by a studious gaze that only heightened Amy Laurance's contempt for this prophetic sage who had it all. When her boss, Scott McNally, told her that Baruch had chosen her instead of Greg Lancy for the interview, Amy figured she had been chosen because she was a rising star. It was clear to 40 million viewers who the real star was.

"Is it correct that you're not affiliated with any organization?"

"Yes."

"You have no group that stands behind you?"

"Only the people." Baruch flashed a warm smile.

The TelePrompTer went blank—and so did Amy. She shuffled her notes for a painful second or two before finding another question.

"Based on what you've said, many feel that you despise corporate America; that you wish to destroy America, maybe the world, as we know it."

Baruch laughed.

"I can't create, nor can I destroy, Ms. Laurance. I am trying merely to clean up the spiritual waste caused by your company. Virtual corporations have tarnished the jewels of humankind: our beliefs, our emotions, our compassion."

Amy jumped back to the TelePrompTer: "How do you plan to accomplish this? What is your deepest desire?"

"Michelangelo was once asked how he sculpted David. He answered that he simply removed everything that wasn't David. I look to change the object of our twenty-first century desires by removing everything that isn't the truth. Just look at this, Ms. Laurance."

Baruch swept his arm around the room.

"Tens of millions of people watch tonight seeking this thing we call truth."

Baruch moved closer to the camera.

"My friends, I will tell you the truth. From the time you wake up until the time you go bed, the virtual corporations play with you like a kitten plays with a ball of yarn."

Pressing his temple with his right index finger he urged, "Learn once again to think your own thoughts. I say this not as a messiah, a philosopher, or a prophet." He paused and looked at Amy. "I say this as your friend."

"If you're not a prophet, the churches would like to know who you are," Amy interjected.

"I am your last chance to save yourself."

The sincerity and depth of one telling glance undid the evil typecast that corporations, media groups, and churches had collectively laid on this young sage. Amy suddenly felt like she knew him. Her emotions paralleled the solemn tenor of the audience.

"Baruch, why is it that you accuse the media of so many evils? Doesn't the media serve any function?"

"We human beings accuse each other every day. Each time we lock the door, every time we engage an alarm. We hide our money in vaults. We've reduced our fellow humans to the lowest common denominator—a bunch of untrustworthy thugs judged guilty by the locks on our doors."

Amy looked confused. "And how does this relate to the media?"

Baruch hesitated, like a parent choosing the right words to explain a complex thought to a child. "It relates to the daily life of every human on this planet. In every person burns a deep faith. But we are taught distrust; we are taught fear; we are taught hate. I don't believe without hate there is no love—or that one must cheat to understand honesty. Today, we take refuge in our keyboards in order to avoid our neighbors. Is this an accident, or a victory of mechanical technology over human technology? Faith opens new possibilities. I attempt to stoke the fire that burns in every individual. But the media destroys faith, thus destroying mankind."

Amy looked briefly at the audience and saw only mesmerized faces.

"So what is it you wish people to have faith in....you?"

"Corporations, governments, and religious institutions are constantly fighting over power, splitting the same hair over and over. Someone gains power, another loses. I want people to understand that they possess a very different currency called faith. Unlike power, faith is infinite; therefore faith is dangerous. Haven't you seen the media trying to secularize this country, this planet, for over four decades? The virtual corporations understand that faith is the ultimate power. But unlike the Manhattan Project's scientists who were able to split the atom, neither the virtual corporations nor governments have figured out how faith can be converted into power. So they use the only tactic their feeble minds know: they can't have it, so they choose to destroy it."

"Is that your secret, Baruch? Have you figured out how to bottle faith?" she asked.

"My secret is that I would do anything to free my fellow man. I care about my fellow man more than you will ever understand."

Amy swallowed noticeably. "And what about the government? They're not on your hit list?"

"During the Cold War, governments were dangerous because they commanded obedience. Today, governments are given too much credit and too much blame.

You see, Ms. Laurance, now that your employer, together with Bates/McMillan, corners the financial institutions, the government lost what little power it had. Jerry Bates, Mike McMillan and Jim Anderson are the centers of power. In other words, you, Ms. Laurance, not the government or me, command obedience."

"So you believe there's a media conspiracy to gain control?"

"Ms. Laurance, life is a progression of conspiracies. Some are simply better than others."

Baruch lifted himself from the recliner and wiped his forehead with a handkerchief. He said apologetically, "Ms. Laurance, I must draw this discussion to a close. We won't change anything tonight. I've imposed on your network enough and I believe I promised you only that I would answer a few questions."

Amy's head was still spinning from his acidic monologue, when she grasped that he was seriously going to get up and leave her, and 40 million viewers hanging. Ignoring the TelePrompTer message—'Thank you, Baruch. It was kind of you to join us'— Amy jumped up, put down her notebook, and, holding Baruch's shoulder, pleaded.

"This is your chance to tell our viewers—*your* viewers —your side of the story. "

The reporter waited anxiously as the producer flagged her to end the interview.

Baruch draped his famous black linen sport jacket over his arm and said nothing.

"Would you like to at least make a final statement?" she asked, agitated.

Baruch laughed, almost embarrassed, like a minister who had just heard a dirty joke. Still chuckling, he asked rhetorically, "A final statement? No, I stand by what I have said, Ms. Laurance. As you would say in the corporate world, 'read my book'."

Baruch motioned gratefully, bowing his head subserviently to the camera and the audience. Smiling gently, he walked away. Those words had been the last spoken by Baruch before he disappeared a week ago, August 26, 2013. The show had a rating of 38: higher than the Super Bowl.

Sitting at her desk, Maggie Helbling's head jerked back as she clicked the 'file close' icon from the video file 'Baruch Interview' which she had just viewed for the third time. The savvy senior reporter ridiculed Amy Laurance with the voice of a bratty teen.

"Anything else you would like to share with our viewers?"

She threw her hands towards the heavens and said out loud, "What a stupid question! What a bimbo! Barbara Walters wasn't beautiful, but she had a brain."

Maggie grabbed the video and exited the AZI-Group's multimedia center, slamming the door behind her. Moving down the long, posh hallway, she dialed 'Store #2' on her phone and came to a halt at the elevator. The door opened and the phone's display read 'connecting: Charley Hardeway'.

CHAPTER 3

GREG LANCY, WHOSE SHAGGY BROWN HAIR AND BOYISH BUILD DEFIED his fifty-two years of age, wore a blue blazer, white open-collar shirt and black jeans on the first evening in September 2013. Perfumed women in ornate gowns accompanied by men in tuxedos surrounded the lonely WNN reporter in Munich's glamorous downtown theater. The elegant guests matched the beauty of the eighteenth century surroundings and the glorious sounds of Johann Strauss's operetta, *Wiener Blut*.

The playful operetta takes place in Vienna in 1814 amongst a relieved European continent following the fall of Napoleon's army. The music of the orchestra and the joy expressed by the actors conveyed the essence of the operetta, whose German libretto written in Austrian dialect made it difficult for any foreigner, and even some Germans, to understand.

Greg, who had only decided to attend the gala thanks to a last-minute tip from his cabdriver, was amused by the theme: a series of misunderstandings which—abetted mostly by a flirtatious Graf—leads the entire cast to become jealous of one another. There is no foundation to the jealousies and, in the end, they all meet in a Heurigen wine garden to find out that their common fears were common nonsense. Greg left directly after the performance, not waiting for the encore.

With the operatic melodies filling his head, Greg noticed how strange it was sitting in the front seat of the Mercedes taxicab that headed toward the Isar River. Sitting in the *front* seat of a *spotless* taxicab. Yeah, that might happen in New York, he thought to himself. Greg had forgotten many of Germany's special characteristics, like clean taxicabs. Excluding a brief vacation with his wife Jenny and son Jeff last year, Greg's last trip had taken place twenty-six years ago, in 1987, on assignment to interview then foreign secretary Lentz. 1987, 2012, 2013. To Greg's eye, not that much had changed on the streets of Munich, or, for that matter, Chicago. Not even a globalization that had guided most industries into oligopolies and encouraged the growth of virtual corporations seemed capable of changing the threads of certain societal fabrics, the most notable German thread being its formal mannerisms. "The Germans even look uptight when they try to relax," his wife, Jenny, had observed.

Although he had just arrived today, the energetic senior reporter was only now feeling the jet lag. Greg's good spirits were courtesy of his neighbor, Freddie Parks. Freddie was an executive for Berlay/Cybric, an international pharmaceutical company that was owned by WNN's biggest competitor, Bates/McMillan. He had given Greg a psychotropic—a clear gel tablet that changed the circadian rhythm. Greg, not much for technical lingo, referred to these drugs as 'Valium without the side effects'.

Freddie had handed Greg the half dozen pills in a white envelope, meaning Greg didn't even know the name of this cocktail-in-a-capsule. Greg laughed, flashing back to his overnight flight where, having toasted one of Freddie's pills to 'a good night's sleep' with a glass of sparkling wine, he had asked himself, "Freddie did put the right pills in that envelope, didn't he?" Greg continued chuckling at this thought as the cabdriver stopped in front of the Hotel Admiral. He suddenly understood why the cabdriver appeared irritated: the hotel was only a couple blocks from the theatre.

"I didn't know we were that close!" Greg said innocently.

"If you would have asked, I would have told you," the elderly cabby said with a sympathetic smile.

"*Aufwiederschauen.*" Greg bid the driver farewell with a Bavarian touch and entered the hotel. The pleasant woman at the narrow reception desk handed him his key and wished him a good rest. Greg hurried to his room, took a steamy shower, popped one of Freddie's magic pills, and went to bed.

◆ ◆ ◆ ◆ ◆

The morning of September 2 was serene and dark. The Hotel Admiral hid quietly from the busy streets of downtown Munich. Greg's room, like so many European hotel rooms, was understated. The white walls appeared coarse because of the textured wallpaper that had been painted. An antique wooden headboard framed a bed no bigger than the Superman bed of Greg's nine-year-old son, Jeff. Besides the television and phone, only the modern bathroom, with its ivory ceramic tile and cultured marble tub, reminded the guests that they were thirteen years into the twenty-first century.

Greg sprang out of bed at 5:00 AM, exhilarated to be back in Europe. As he pulled back the heavy, brown drapes, he could see the tall, glass structure across the street—the German Patent Office. He turned on the TV while dressing and was greeted by D-WBG, the German satellite connection of WBG, Greg's biggest competitor. Lacing up his brown hiking shoes, Greg watched the German-speaking anchor and read the English subtitles.

"In Baku, the capital city of Azerbaijan on the Caspian Sea, the environmental terrorist group Human Race held a rally on a dozen trimarans surrounding a dated oil rig of Oiltron Industries. Timing their demonstration to coincide with the annual meeting of Oiltron's virtual parent, the AZI-Group, the demonstrators called for 'dangerous and obsolete' oil platforms to be shut down. Separately, the socialist party in Baku, SPA, lodged a formal complaint with the United Nations concerning what they consider to be the AZI-Group's overwhelming political influence in Azerbaijan. SPA has asked for a UN audit of the Parliament."

Greg barked at 'the screen', the generic name Mike McMillan had given to the thin, flat device that merged TV, computer, and satellite technology onto a surface that could be as large as a living room wall, or smaller than a pocket-size notebook.

"That's my stock plan you're messing with! Go picket Total or Shell!"

"Oiltron's President and former mayor of Baku, Mr. Haig Abku, noted that all Oiltron facilities are in total compliance with guidelines set down by the international community. Responding to the UN complaint, Mr. Abku declined to comment." The silver-haired anchor continued his summation of the lead stories. " On the economic front, German unemployment remained stable at 10.5 percent with unemployment in the east *Länder* down slightly at 13.8 percent."

Greg pulled a gray sweater over his University of Chicago T-shirt and added, "Are those the same 10.5 percent who weren't working thirty years ago? Unemployment is a damn industry over here!"

He moved to push the 'off' button when the image of Baruch flashed on to the screen.

"The spiritual leader Baruch, missing since his August 26 appearance on WNN, is feared to be in danger. The man who has awakened Germany's dormant spirituality made his last appearance in Europe on October 24 in Munich's English Garden."

The report switched to the stoic, handsome Austrian speaking in his rich, song-like native language to a huge gathering.

"My friends, the power of the media lies in its ability to control the message. We must wage war with actions. Have you not noticed that the more we talk about God, the less we believe? Let the media fight with its empty words. Let New Age gods twist their 'religion' into industry. But we shall create a new path. We shall lift greatness to authority!"

The crowd roared as the anchor faded back on screen.

Greg clicked 'off'. "Wow, Baruch. You've got some serious followers over here!"

He grabbed his pocket-size notebook and a pen to go for a walk.

◆ ◆ ◆ ◆ ◆

In his Chicago neighborhood, Greg caught strange looks when he stopped on the sidewalk to make a note in his tattered 3 x 5 notebook. Active Chicagoans who ventured beyond their home gyms generally opted for more strenuous activities— leisurely walks were for those who weren't 'busy'. Greg dismissed that 'I've gotta pretend I'm busy' charade. He had told his neighbor Freddie, "It's when you've got to pretend you're busy that you're not!"

Being one of WNN's rare journalistic supertalents, Greg could afford to be unconventional within certain bounds and he had always had a knack for knowing the limits, like the many occasions during his high school days when he turned his vacationing parents' house into party central. However outrageous the bash, he always cleared everyone out by 2:00 AM to avoid the imminent visit by the cops. Stealing a line from an old Clint Eastwood film, Greg often joked, "A man's got to know his limitations."

Besides being the only leisurely walker on his block, the fitness buffs were armed with microdisc players, not paper and pen. Greg had picked up this notebook-carrying habit from two separate experiences. A year living in Europe had taught him that walking was much more agreeable to the soul and less stressful on the joints. His pen-and-paper routine came from his early studies, which had included reading the philosophical materialist, Thomas Hobbes. The British philosopher had observed that men read too much and think too little.

"If I read as much as other men, I suppose I would know only the same," said Hobbes.

In this vein, Greg walked daily with pen and paper recording any thoughts he felt relevant. At 5:30 AM in the English Garden he was alone with his thoughts.

◆ ◆ ◆ ◆ ◆

Munich's English Garden is a winding park that has an atmosphere as contrasting as the seasons. In winter, the park is peaceful and empty. Its paths are wide and well-kept. The trees are naked and traffic is limited to commuters on bicycles. This being fall, gone was the energy of summer that filled the Garden; gone were the groups of teenagers skating in bliss; gone were the topless sunbathers that Greg had admired years ago. He was close to that long, tree-lined fairway, where he had once adored the exposed, tan breasts of college-aged sun worshipers. But now his mind could see only the tens of thousands of Germans listening intently to every word Baruch spoke.

Greg's assignment—Baruch—had been the bulk of his work the past six months.

He had seen Baruch ascend from a haughty intellectual leader of the enlightened to full-fledged folk hero. As he took a seat at a concrete park bench, he reflected on what he had seen only minutes ago on TV: How does one guy stir up such a commotion? Do people really believe he's a prophet or do they see him as a symbol—their great hope?

Greg opened his notebook and mumbled as he turned the pages. Occasionally, he paused, stared up at the sky, and spoke as if someone else were taking notes. "Born in Austria. Raised in a foster home. Intelligent. Wise. Common sense and the humility of a farmer. Only wrote one public work, *Apocrypha Truth*. That book's dedication rang in Greg's head like a tuning fork: "*Certain truths are so clear, they become demons in an untrue world.*"

Greg wondered if chance had brought him to the operetta last evening, that folly of untruths and fantasy. He scribbled in his notebook, "Certain truths are so clear.... What did he mean?"

CHAPTER 4

TIRED FROM THE TWELVE-HOUR FLIGHT FROM BAKU TO CHICAGO, Scott McNally fought to keep his composure, as he paced around the oblong table of the tenth floor executive conference room of the WNN Tower. But his caged anger was obvious to those who knew him. He was sweating bullets.

"Where the hell is he?" he pleaded, gesturing with his hands. "In today's world, you can't just vanish! We find screws that fall off satellites. How can our friend Baruch just disappear?" Scott looked around the room like a coach whose football team was down 30-0 at halftime.

He had called in his 'Red Team', which consisted of the most important staff members. There was the powerful chief editor, Walter Butwin, whose lack of skin pigment, short portly figure and dated fashion made him, at thirty-five years of age, look like he could be Greg Lancy's dad. Sharon Tucker, VP of Operations, carried with her an air of confidence and intensity normally reserved for athletic competition or war. Her ebony glow made up for the deathly whiteness of Walter Butwin, who she referred to as 'pale face' when alone with her friend and fellow Red Team member, Maggie Helbling.

Maggie, WNN senior reporter, possessed a middle-age beauty, that elusive combination of mind and body. She appeared harmless, almost defenseless. In the tough world of business, this could be a distinct advantage. Surveying the conference table, she smiled warmly at Walter and Sharon. Before Scott could continue his tirade, the newest member of the Red Team opened the walnut doors of the conference room.

"Sorry I'm late," Amy Laurance said timidly.

Scott shook his head, "Listen, Amy. This is the *Red* Team. *Red* means important. Don't be late."

Recently, to the dismay of many senior reporters and staff, the young Amy Laurance had been added to the Red Team, or what Maggie had dubbed 'Scott's Wailing Wall'. Walter, the youngest member of this small group, brought to the table a strong industry track record and the solid backing of Jim Anderson. Sharon, along with Scott, represented WNN at all major negotiations. Greg and Maggie had both spent three decades working into the ranks of senior reporter. So why was Amy Laurance here and, more importantly, who made it possible? Greg, absent due to his European trip, had convinced Maggie that Amy was being used as a corporate lever to pry the hold that Greg, Maggie, and WNN world anchor Charles Waters held on the prime-time news.

"It's planned human obsolescence," Maggie told Greg. "We teach her everything we know, then our stock falls and hers goes up."

"Well," Greg added, "one thing we don't have to teach her is how to knife."

Scott continued to rant, "Is he dead? Did he go to visit fuckin' Jim Morrison in Africa? He's a folk hero—no, make that a religious icon—and I'm standing here holding my dick!"

Sharon tried not to smile at the thought of Scott, the robust Irishman, holding his dick. "First of all, Scott, we don't know where he is, nor do we know if he's even alive."

She spoke staccato. This was supposed to show her

understanding of the earnestness of the situation or perhaps her fear of Scott McNally's famous temper.

She continued, "There is no reason to believe he's dead. We have every domestic reporter on the case. Plus, we've sent all of our top foreign correspondents on the road. If he's out there, we'll find him. Greg will find him."

Scott looked unimpressed.

"Two days ago, I'm moderating the question and answer session of the shareholder meeting in Baku. Would anyone like to guess what the first question was?"

As Scott surveyed the room, he could find no volunteers.

"They could have asked about any one of the AZI's thousands of companies. But some bean-counting, four-eyed, banker-type stands up and says in an *annoying* nasal tone: 'With all due respect, Mr. McNally, the appearance is that WBG is moving dangerously close to us in the ratings. What's the game plan?'"

Scott paced back and forth.

"Luckily, I wasn't on the panel with the ten executive *gods*, so I deferred to Jim Anderson. Then..."

"Well, how did Jim answer?" a curious Maggie interrupted.

"Oh, the usual bullshit. Told 'em we were aware of the challenge by WBG and that I was 'on top of it'. But that's just shareholder bullshit, Maggie—I can deal with that. The second question, though, blew my mind. Guess what that that Bloomfield guy from the BNG Bank's advisory board asks me."

"About the Baruch interview?" Amy asked, hoping her answer was wrong.

"Bingo. With the ratings we got last week, he wants to know why we don't interview Baruch every evening, instead of trying to paint the guy as a dangerous cult figure."

"He is persuasive," Walter suggested.

Exposing a twisted smile, Scott responded, "I'll tell you how persuasive he is. Baruch could make you watch your helpless grandmother being beat to death and then convince you that she needed it."

"Is that what ol' Jimbo said?" Maggie asked, taunting her boss.

"Get this. Jim tells them that Baruch is our enemy. He compares our spiritual friend to the Athenians with their gods and says, 'We're the Spartans; we're the warriors'." Scott shook his head and lifted his eyes to the ceiling. "We're the fucking Spartans!" Then he laughed, "You know Jim and his high-flying bullshit. The big boys like that metaphorical crap."

"But the Spartans eventually lost to Thebes," Sharon said with conviction.

"Yeah, and Athenian culture lived on. But Jim never lets a fact get in the way of a good metaphor!" Scott replied, chuckling.

Walter Butwin jumped in, "And that was it?"

"Well, no. Jim went on for about five minutes explaining how Baruch was probably funded by some crazy group looking to ruin the corporations—one of those groups that chain themselves to the McDonald's drive-ins. He even speculated that the government could be behind Baruch."

Scott had another flash. Laughing at his thought he said, "You should have seen the goddamm protesters in front of the building, you guys; burning giant pictures of Jim; screaming 'AZI-NAZI'. I think the shareholders were scared to death!"

"Baruch's followers were doing all that?" Maggie asked in disbelief.

"Probably not. There were three or four groups protesting," Sharon responded.

"Guilt by association!" Scott added.

Slowly, he turned to his chief editor. "Well, Walter, what's your read on Baruch?"

"This is a sticky situation, Scott. First, the guy is more than a spiritual guru. I'd call him a philosopher slash historian slash social commentator. One thing for sure: he makes every other corporation, and us, look like a horse's ass. Then there's the question of whether we want to find him. I mean, the guy has a huge following. If you want my opinion, sending out a posse will only manifest the entire deal. I say leave it be and hope he does join some tribe in Africa. Anyway, I think he and Jim Morrison may get along just swell."

Walter waited in vain for a response, then continued, "Seriously though. We've all seen the big stories come and go. There'll be another war, a head-of-state will die, or some nut will shoot up a post office and—voila—he's old news."

Scott relit his long, thick cigar and gazed toward the white-paneled ceiling. He had seen a lot in his fifty-eight years. One thing he understood: Baruch was more than a fall fashion to be replaced by the spring collection. He was dealing with a modern day prophet, a spiritual revolutionary, who had exposed the New Age gurus for what they were and captured the imagination of millions.

Scott spoke in an even-tempered voice, "Jim Anderson was on the phone with me this morning from headquarters in Baku."

Just mentioning a simple call from Jim Anderson, the CEO of a group that had revenues higher than the GNP of all but three nations, created tension in the room.

"The energy division has been getting hammered politically by regulators. Haig Abku has assured us that those problems are over with the deal our virtual struck with the Azerbaijanis."

"They're called Azeris now," Sharon noted.

"Whatever, Sharon. The important point is that he has the institutional investors all over him about our division's performance. The market says WBG is going to waste us—make us number two in the market."

Scott paced nervously.

"Good news is that even though our margins are thin, I got him to approve the spending for the regional ad campaigns. And he's going to work on a decentralization plan so that we can react more quickly, like our friends at WBG."

"OOOHH," Maggie and Sharon hummed in unison.

"You mean Jim's going to actually let us do the reporting?" Maggie threw in, ignoring the presence of Jim Anderson's pawn, Walter Butwin.

Scott dismissed her barb.

"More importantly, he wants Baruch exposed."

Maggie put her elbows on the table. "We all know that revenues are down, but if it was all because of Baruch, wouldn't WBG be down as well?"

WBG, under the guidance of virtual parent Bates/McMillan, had posted profits four consecutive quarters during an economic down cycle. Their owners, financier Jerry Bates and Hi-Tech King of the multiverse Mike McMillan, had gone from a tiny wannabe ten years ago to a major player in insurance, banking, electronics, metals, and agribusiness. The only area where the AZI-Group maintained a dominant position was in the energy division.

"Maggie, that's a valid point. But our friend Mike McMillan has been buying up companies quicker than I pop antacids. In other words, I doubt if his comp revenues are up."

Sharon pulled out a colorful chart. "Bates/McMillan has added twenty-two global affiliates this year but their revenues are only up 5 percent."

"What exactly do you mean by 'exposing' Baruch?" the young Amy Laurance asked Scott.

"What I mean is, let's dig in and find out what Baruch is all about. *Here's an idea*: quit worshipping him.... Investigate him! He has enough fans already."

Scott smirked, relaxed his shoulders, and declared, "OK, everyone, Baruch is top priority. Use anyone and anything you can to get to him. But..." Scott raised his arm like a second-rate actor delivering a line and looked at Walter Butwin, "for the time being, every report we air about Baruch will show compassion. Officially, we empathize with our prophet-child. Understood? "

As Sharon, Walter, Maggie, and Amy filed out of the conference room, Scott spoke to the ceiling: "Baruch, my friend, you're fucking with the wrong guy!"

CHAPTER 5

IF THERE WERE EVER A TEAM THAT CLICKED BETTER THAN MAGGIE Helbling and Greg Lancy, it would have to have been the Marx Brothers. After attending graduate school together at the University of Chicago, the mighty duo landed jobs at the *Detroit Free Press*—Greg as a reporter, Maggie as an assistant to the communications director. Greg found the city depressing and the paper too biased in its reporting. After only one year, he took an offer from *The Express*, an upstart new daily paper in Chicago. Two months later Maggie followed. That was the beginning of a tandem journey that had persisted to date.

Shortly after leaving Detroit for *The Express*, World News Network devoured the puny Chicago paper. For WNN, buying up specialty publications was nothing new. The virtual corporations had taken their strategy straight out of the late-twentieth-century business books: look for an entrepreneur to develop a niche market, see if the business is viable and, if the competitor starts racking up market share, try to hijack their concept and ruin him in the process. If that failed, the virtual would bring them under its wing.

The young *Express*, strapped for cash, afforded WNN and the AZI-Group an ideal takeover scenario. They offered *Express* founder Scott McNally an insignificant amount of cash and the job as CEO. Jim Anderson made Scott's options all too clear.

"Here's how it works, Scott. You take the offer; you get a fat salary. You're a happy camper, I'm a happy camper. Turn it down and I'll have to ruin you."

The ability of the AZI-Group to carry out a corporate death threat could make any firm, big or small, run for cover. Oiltron was a case in point. After the Azerbaijani oil consortium blocked the AZI's bid at $95.00 per share, Jim Anderson set into motion what for him was standard operating procedure. First, he triggered a sell-off of commercial paper through BNG Bank, a powerful member of the Federal Reserve. As foreign currencies plummeted, Moody's was *persuaded* to lower the Azerbaijani government bond rating. While the market scrambled to figure out what was up, BNG Bank bought vast reserves of devalued currencies. Then Jim would wait, like a poker player waiting for the other player to fold. Three weeks after Jim began his hunt, Oiltron's paper value had dropped $10 billion in one day and Jim devoured them whole at $80.00 a share.

"Eighty bucks a share? No way. With the currency pick-up, we paid sixty-five max!" Jim had said in an interview with *The Express* before the takeover. The reporter who interviewed Jim was Scott's lead reporter, Greg Lancy.

"Scott, once you sell, you're a salaried employee. Worse yet, Jim Anderson will own us—in more than one way. But if we turn this thing around on our own and hit budget next year, you'll be worth $300 million. What are they offering you, five million bucks?" Greg argued, trying to keep *The Express* and himself independent.

"Listen, Greg. You know better than anyone how they work. They'll squeeze the advertisers, most of which they own. Then they'll start legal battles at every corner to make my life hell. Nope, Greg, I'll take the $5 million in the bank."

The market valuation of *The Express* in the second quarter of

2013 hit $1.3 billion. Greg was right, but Scott was wealthy. Both of them were transferred to WNN three weeks later.

♦ ♦ ♦ ♦ ♦

Greg reported in a penetrating and factual style. Never one to mince words, he laid a story out in plain English, crediting the reader with enough intelligence to form his own opinion. His style was highly unorthodox in this era of newsmercials—news stories shaped by corporate PR bits.

"If you want a story on retired lesbians with toe warts, just search the satellite data bank and you'll find a report. If you want to find out who sells chemical weapons to China, we just don't know."

That was Greg's take on modern 'reporting'.

Greg's favorite example of corporate news shaping society was the skin care industry. The producers of ego-in-a-bottle had generated five-minute 'reports' on how the ozone layer would destroy society's collective epidermis if you didn't protect yourself. Like an actor being fed a line, the tanning industry responded the following season with reports on why the sun was indeed healthy for the body. This corporate volleying had been going back and forth since the 1980s. Only the level of hyperbole had increased throughout the years. Greg once joked with Maggie:

"It's like the AZI-Group. They own Oiltron, which pollutes. Then they have Environmental Resource to clean it up. My bet is that the same person owns both the tanning and skin care industries! What did Baruch say? ... 'Life is a progression of conspiracies'."

Maggie was the consummate professional. However, unlike Greg, she would sometimes bend a story to fit a particular spot. Just the week before, South Africa had celebrated the nineteenth anniversary commemorating the end of apartheid. Maggie remembered an essay she had written in college in which she predicted that the end of apartheid would lead to anarchy and revolution. To the contrary, not much had changed: there was still apartheid, it just wasn't official any more.

That's what Maggie believed in her heart, but the truth didn't always make good copy. The report ran showing black entrepreneurs who had successfully developed a trading company that specialized in importing used clothing from wealthy Western nations. These clothes were then distributed throughout the African continent. Greg had teased Maggie about her report.

" Quite a step forward, Maggie. Used clothes. That's what I call progress!"

"At least I didn't suck up to McNally," Maggie retorted.

"You're talking about my fine documentary?"

"You should have been ashamed of yourself, Greg, extolling the virtues of the Nazi's charity program..."

Greg, Maggie, and Sharon had created their own internal vocabulary. 'Nazi' meant the AZI-Group. Insiders like Walter Butwin were SS officers. Takeovers were coined 'The 1000 Year Reich'. Jim Anderson, known as der Fuhrer, did not find these references amusing, especially since the group Human Race had made AZI-NAZI their standard protest chant.

"Oh, come on, Maggie! You're telling me that I didn't get a great shot in at the end of that documentary?"

Maggie laughed as she remembered how Greg had closed the show documenting the entire $5 billion of charity outlays the AZI-Group had donated.

"When asked if the charitable spirit of the virtuals contradicted his five pillars theory of the evil corporations, Baruch replied, 'Slavery wears many disguises. Plantation owners gave their forced labor food and shelter, yet the workers were no less enslaved. Charity in this form is another attempt by virtual corporations to take the throne from religion and show they, too, are worthy of praise. This diversion of the truth should fool no one.'"

Greg and Maggie were willing, at least in theory if not in practice, to bite the hand that fed them.

♦ ♦ ♦ ♦ ♦

"Ich möchte Herrn Lancy sprechen."

Maggie turned on her college German to ask for Greg at the Hotel Admiral reception.

"His line is busy. Can you wait one moment?" the receptionist asked in beautiful English.

"Yes, no problem," Maggie answered sheepishly.

It always amazed Maggie that Europeans switched languages on and off as easily as using the TV remote. She had studied four years of college German, yet still found it difficult to conjugate the most basic verbs. Her only consolation was the assurance that she wasn't working as a hotel receptionist, she thought. Maggie quickly reprimanded herself for having such a condescending flash.

"Hello," Greg answered in a peppy tone.

"Hi, Greg. It's Mag. How are things in the fatherland?"

Greg slid into his southern drawl. "So far so good. I got me some culture last night here in good ol' Münich. Dadburn—they sure as hell pour a big brew, my little southern belle."

Even though he still sounded like a Chicagoan, Maggie loved when Greg did his southern thing. She especially noticed how energetic his voice was, but it was eight in the morning European time. In Chicago it was one in the morning and she was bushed.

"I'm happy to hear that, cowboy!" she joked back. "I found

some real interesting news on Baruch. It should be in your e-mail file."

"Sounds good. By the way, you sound tired."

"Greg, it's 1:00 AM. Of course I'm tired."

"Well, get some sleep. I'll call you tonight."

"Stay out of trouble," Maggie remarked, only half-joking.

"Roger, out." Greg was off to the races.

Maggie sat naked before the mirror of her Chicago town-house scrutinizing her figure. Her breasts were firm. They no longer lifted upward as in her younger days, but she was still a solid 38C. Around her dark nipples remained the soft, almost transparent skin that showed several veins, a distant blue that wanted to be seen. Even when she was in high school, she was, as her mother had said, a "full-figured gal". If only gravity would give me a reprieve, Maggie thought.

Moving on with the self-inspection that she would only undertake with the bathroom door shut even when alone, she pinched her triceps, tucked in her belly, shook her thighs, and, as the final test, turned to check her derriere.

"Yeah, just like you said, Mom—a full-figured gal."

In general, she was pleased, although she had noticed the fact that a little bit of cellulite had formed on the back of her thighs.

"Not bad for fifty-three," she said to the mirror.

Maggie continued looking at the mirror as her twenty-some-thing body appeared magically before her. Dark brown hair falling over her tanned shoulders; tight skin showing every lean curve of her body; and those beautiful rounded breasts that levi-tated outward. Suddenly and uninvited, Amy Laurance's image, a twenty-five-year-old hardbody, overtook the wonderful recol-lection, jolting Maggie back to reality. As if speaking to Amy, Maggie said tersely, "At least I didn't fuck my boss." The mirror wasn't responsive to her allegation, so she put on her T-shirt and jumped into bed.

As she lay spread out across the mattress, she wondered why Baruch had so captured her. She had seen all the self-proclaimed healers, New Age philosophers, and TV con men throughout the years. In college she had even written a paper on "Religion and Human Behavior". It seemed so strange. She opened her diary and wrote:

"September 2, 2013. In an era where songs stay on the charts for one week, TV series die before they're born and people are hit with millions of images a day, it's hard to imagine that anyone could capture the world's attention without even trying. If my own senses hadn't heard his wisdom, saw his strength, or felt his power, I wouldn't believe Baruch could exist. But there must be something behind his fame. Maybe he's the creation of some PR guru. Could he be a marketing genius who saw a void in the media? Is he another niche product? I don't know, perhaps he's just in the right place at the right time. Or...he's really a prophet!"

Maggie set down her pen and massaged her eyes with her soft fingers.

"My God. What if he's really a prophet?"

She grabbed her pen.

"Whatever the case, Scott has given us the green light to find out, whatever the cost. It's funny. McNally and the Nazis won't even open their pockets for Christmas gifts, yet for this guy he gives us a blank check. Signing off, Maggie."

Maggie set her alarm for 7:00 AM and turned out the lights.

CHAPTER 6

SCOTT MCNALLY SAT WITH SHARON TUCKER IN THE SILENCE OF THE executive conference room on the secure tenth floor of the WNN Tower. Private meetings were held here—not even Scott's secretary was privy to discussions that took place between these four wood- paneled walls.

"Tell me, Sharon," he leaned back to a reclined position, "what does this guy have that motivates so many of *my* viewers to turn off *my* station?"

"Well, like you said this morning, Baruch is convincing. Anyone that could convince you Grandma needs a beating..."

Scott laughed. "OK, perhaps I exaggerated a bit."

Sharon, a regular at Westside Baptist Church, had just yesterday told Maggie that Baruch was a 'light in the darkness'. Contemplating Scott's viewership question she moved uneasily, looking to formulate a response that balanced what Scott wanted to hear with what she believed.

Stuttering slightly, she said, "Well, I don't have the answer. Some say he's the Dale Carnegie of philosophy. Or, you know, in the 1960s there were beatniks. The Christian Coalition was strong in the 1990s. It's 2013. We're in a period that *projects* self-control, prosperity, and morality, but leaves a lot of people empty inside. Two centuries of New Age thought opened people up to accept everything: now they believe in nothing. Baruch cuts beneath the surface—he digs at your soul."

"Yeah, you've got a point. But Baruch's message is pretty vague. He almost reminds me of the populist in the late nineteenth century."

"He does have that appeal, but I'd say he's more of a pantheist. You know, god is above everything, yet god is in everything. Baruch Spinoza was a pantheist." Sharon kept her eyes focused on the desk in front of her. "Did you know that the Baruch in the Old Testament was the closest friend and secretary of Jeremiah? That the biblical Baruch supposedly wrote the book of Jeremiah?"

"Is this fucking vacation bible school? What's the point?" Scott asked, rolling his eyes flippantly.

"Well, Jeremiah was known as the prophet who preached that individuals need to be responsible for themselves. He also told *his* Baruch to avoid the temptations of ambition." Sharon spread her arms and opened her hands. "When I read that, I saw a lot of similarities. Just a thought."

Scott stared. Still reclining in his chair, he began to run both his hands through his red, curly hair. Scott had heard the stuff about the 'Baruch of old', but never paid much attention to it.

"Avoid ambition? Come on, Sharon. The only similarity I see is that our friend Baruch preys on human weakness. Until science eliminates death, humans will believe in gods and people like Baruch will be around."

"You're getting cynical in your...middle years, Scott. Maybe God wants us to die so we can't do too much damage. I don't think it's a coincidence that human cloning is more difficult than we thought. And don't we play on human weaknesses, too?"

Scott's shirt was stretched to the point of tearing and he grunted, throwing in an occasional 'hum'. Sharon knew that 'hum'. It signaled his desire to be asked what his opinion was.

"What are you thinking?"

Flying off on a tangent, he asked, "Did you get that e-mail from Charley Hardeway?"

"No. I've haven't heard from him for years, since he quit."

Reaching in his briefcase, Scott pulled out a file and said, "Well, he's got that newsletter called *From the Heart*."

"Oh, yeah, I read that," Sharon acknowledged.

"Well, last week he featured Jim Anderson in a cartoon with Baruch."

Scott set the printout down in front of Sharon.

"He put me in the text!"

Sharon looked at the bald, gnarled-faced cartoon of Jim Anderson screaming at a secretary who looked curiously similar to the curvy Amy Laurance. The bubble read: "So Baruch says the people aren't free? Well, call Scott McNally and he'll *tell* the people they're free, damn it!"

The next frame showed Baruch sitting in a lotus position in his black linen sport jacket, thinking as he hovered over Jim and his secretary: "When people have to tell you you're free, that's not a very good sign."

Sharon laughed. "That Charley *is* a treat!"

"He's an asshole, Sharon. A little attention-seeking weasel."

Scott tried to impersonate Charley's staunch New York accent, "Question: Why am I publishing a newsletter that no one reads. Answer: Because I'm a little, self-centered weasel."

Scott, with his question/answer bit was referring to a technique Charley used when he was on to something. Charley would fire his questions and answers at lightning speed and with comedic precision. Sharon refrained from mentioning how much she loved Charley's question/answer thing.

"OK, so forget Charley, the weasel. Let's get back to Baruch."

"Oh yeah—about your Jeremiah theory: I don't believe in

prophets. What I do believe is that Baruch is really smart—and no doubt very convincing as well. I mean, did you see him lay into Amy Laurance the other night? Heck, Sharon, I was ready to send a donation myself! But, of course, he doesn't take donations. Which leads me to the million-dollar question—how did he get so far without help?"

"It seems to me he played us pretty well," Sharon said, offering her opinion.

"No, that theory's a bunch of garbage. My business professor at grad school always told me to follow the money. Well, who's got money, Sharon? We do. The government does. And so do the churches. Basically, everyone he attacks controls the purse. Baruch, on the other hand, has no money. Maybe Jim is right; maybe there's some big group behind him."

"Senator Ortega of Arizona says it's the Chinese. According to him, Baruch is one of their tools to break American hegemony."

"Bullshit. It's someone in the West. Let me give you a little clue, Sharon. The Chinese aren't that fucking smart." Scott slapped both hands on the desk and threw in, "What would your prophet Jeremiah say about that?"

CHAPTER 7

THE SIGN AT THE ENTRANCE OF THE ORDERLY, LARGE OFFICE IN THE Bavarian capital of Munich read:

"It is thus plain from what has been said, that in no case do we strive for, wish for, long for or desire anything because we deem it good, but on the other hand we deem a thing good because we strive for it, wish for it, long for it, or desire it" Benedict Spinoza, *The Ethics of Spinoza.*

"Good morning Mr. Lancy. Please excuse me for making you wait."

"No problem. I was just reading this quote. It's..." Greg was taken aback by Frank Schleier. The professor was much more dignified than Greg's sloppy, bearded philosophy teacher in school. Frank Schleier's blue German eyes seemed misplaced against the dark, almost Arabic complexion. A full, thick head of black hair groomed to the left bordered a face full of warmth and kindness.

"It's very philosophical," Greg stated briefly—attempting to regain his composure.

"Whenever something is true or hits the essence of life, we most often choose to call it philosophical," Frank Schleier remarked in a casual manner. "When something becomes philosophical, we can easily reconcile ourselves to ignore it due to the fact that it's just, well, philosophy."

He made little quotations with his fingers each time he said "philosophy" and "philosophical" to clarify his place as narrator.

"Come in and have a seat, Mr. Lancy."

Frank Schleier's flawless English and light Scottish accent struck Greg. His speech rhythm was conspicuously like that of Baruch's. The difference was that Baruch had mastered American slang, as had most of the Western world, and had no accent at all. The only peculiarity in Baruch's English was that he would rarely use contractions. He would say 'I will' rather than 'I'll'. This gave a scholarly ring to his delivery; however, no one knew if he did this intentionally.

"Where did you learn such marvelous English, Mr. Schleier?"

"The same place as everyone—World News Network."

Frank paused a moment and laughed. Greg, after realizing this half-truth was a Bavarian joke, followed suit.

"Actually, I studied and taught at Edinburgh, the home of David Hume and Adam Smith. Did you know, Mr. Lancy, that the great thinkers of the early centuries—David Hume, for example—were often teachers who were paid directly by their students? Granted, many students of that day had well-to-do parents. Nonetheless, the family chose freely which courses their child would take. That meant the professor had no guarantee that he would be paid until class registration was over."

Frank seemed amused by his remarks and, like a professor lecturing his class, continued.

"This led to the conclusion that only the most intelligent, motivated teachers filled the classrooms—the rest became farmers, craftsmen, or traders. Teaching, however, was an honor. Well, it should be. Remarkably capitalistic, wouldn't you say?"

Greg, trying to play along with the dialogue, looked so as to make sure his interviewee was finished.

"You're promoting the old argument that our education system should be based more on merit, Mr. Schleier?"

"Oh no, I go much further than that. We *indoctrinate* our children; we certainly don't *educate* them. And I'm not talking about those silly tests that say only 12 percent of college freshmen can find India on a map. Imprinting this or that ideology on the brain merely fills up space. *Education* is the contemplation and analysis of theories and opinions. Today, we limit education by the very way we define it."

"Could you expand on that?" Greg asked in a reporter-like manner.

"In the Middle Ages, Mr. Lancy, there was 'education'. But the way it was defined—as a distant, mystical analysis—affected the outcome. For Greeks, education was very theoretical. The Romans defined education in a utilitarian sense—they made things. The common denominator is that every time a civilization gets away from the fundamentals, they fail." Frank paused. "Did you ever study Edmund Burke or John Locke, Mr. Lancy?"

"Yeah, but a long time ago."

"They went to battle over the very nature of the world around us, the forces that motivate humans; they wrote thousands of pages to develop their thoughts about the world around them; they debated democratic vs. aristocratic systems. Nothing was beyond question. Under twenty-first century democracy... " The thin professor puffed his pipe and continued, "We have lost our inquisitiveness."

Greg removed the tape from the Dictaphone and inserted a new one. The professor waited patiently and continued.

"I was in Rome last week and my colleague asked me if I saw the smog. I told him no. 'Then you must be in it,' he said. We are blind, Mr. Lancy."

The phone rang and the professor spoke what sounded like German into the intercom in a soft voice. Greg took the time to sip his coffee and read his notes. Terminating the call after only a few seconds, the professor raised his index finger towards the plaster ceiling and asked, "Where were we?"

"If you can't see the smog, you're in it," Greg said with an agreeable smile.

"Oh yes, and then there is our historical amnesia. We forget that the great thinkers never *expected* to find truth. It was the *pursuit* of absolute truth that brought them nearer. Our 'educated' elite of the twenty-first century begins with the assumption that there is no absolute truth and works from there. Do you think there is an absolute truth, Mr. Lancy?"

Greg paused. "I believe Einstein proved that most things are relative."

Frank Schleier shook his head. "Is it not ironic that Einstein's search for the truth led to the theory of relativity—the very theory which we use today to explain that there can be no truth? Mr. Einstein never said that because things are relative to one another that we should give up on seeking truth. We are a confused world, Mr. Lancy. Today's world wants a 150-page double-spaced book written by a doctor to tell us about our lives—a list of ten things we need to do to be successful. We are more interested in disproving truth than finding it."

Frank grabbed the silence as a sign to move on.

"Baruch gave me some sage advice in college: 'Don't fool yourself into thinking that there is no truth. That is exactly what the people who control us hope that we will believe.'"

"Who does control us, Mr. Schleier?"

"I believe only Baruch knows that, Mr. Lancy. That's why he is so feared."

Greg again sat patiently, waiting to be sure the professor was finished. Looking to get into more familiar territory he shifted gears.

"Speaking of Baruch, did you receive my message?"

"Certainly," Frank acknowledged.

"Then you're aware that I came to discuss Baruch, I assume?"

"Yes." The professor sat calmly in his wooden chair and began repacking his carved wooden pipe.

CHAPTER 8

CHIEF EDITOR WALTER BUTWIN, WHO LOOKED MORE LIKE A FIFTY-YEAR-old accountant than a thirty-five-year-old hotshot, had migrated to the AZI-Group with Jim Anderson from British MediaCom. Simple, direct, and well past his years, he was referred to inside the WNN Tower as the 'goalkeeper', because if any story was to get full distribution it had to go through him. Reporters were paid a bonus for reports that played on all of WNN's 218 newspapers, TV outlets, radio stations, and on-line networks. Baruch had reprimanded the media more than once for this 'full distribution' incentive.

"Not only does this policy encourage reporters to pursue only mainstream reports, it lifts average thought to a position of power."

Walter had just last week refused to play an excerpt from one of Baruch's speeches in New York:

One axiom of democracy is freedom of the press. In theory, and certainly in the eighteenth century, this proposition was valid. But I'm reminded of the king who, finding several mice in his bedchamber, told the servants they would receive one stone for each mouse they killed. After several weeks, the king's treasurer informed his majesty that he had paid over 1000 stones for mice carcasses. The king investigated and found that the servants were breeding the mice. The king's idea—much like freedom of the press—was good in theory. The results, however, understate the devious side of human nature when provided with a too lucrative incentive. The media wants us to believe that it insures our freedom via its ability to speak freely. And what is it the media speaks so freely about? It reports the same murders, the same basketball games, and the same business reports. Its sole creativity seems to lie in the way they can perpetuate a story and find ways to distribute the same mouse-trap across its various news outlets. Today's media doesn't care about freedom in the spirit of the constitution. Today's media wants to constitute what freedom is. Today's media has made certain that it has abundant freedom and the people have none.

Business magazines, however, never wrote about people like Walter. He was one man in a maze of senior employees at WNN and his title didn't truly distinguish his position or power. In order to get around media regulations on content control, Walter needed to be a persona non grata.

Jim Anderson looked at his media outlets as a 'product' that he was trying to 'brand'. To do this, he needed consistency throughout the AZI-Group's vast media holdings. But this 'consistency' could appear to be controlling editorial content. Jim's answer was Walter Butwin.

Like an artist, Walter would paste, cut, and edit every story that came across the main computer and onto his screen. Only the secretive operations room, known as MIS, had access to what came through Walter's office, and they were instructed not to interact with normal employees.

However powerful Walter was, his power was granted to him like a knight who is ordained to serve his master. A student of the Napoleonic 'divide and rule' strategy, Jim Anderson needed Walter not only to control the WNN media message, but, more importantly, to offset the influence that Scott McNally exerted as president.

Maggie once made the mistake of asking Charley, "Why Walter?"

"Because, Maggie, Jim needs someone who is smart and, more importantly, someone he owns. If it weren't for government regulations, hell, Jim would write the stories himself! Jim wants Walter to be his Goering. And McNally? Jim only wants him to run WNN—not decide *how* it's run."

For his loyalty, Walter was paid well and protected by Jim if, for example, a story went bust: Like in 2008 when Jim tried to strong-arm a few congressmen into filing a formal investigation against the president a month before the elections. Getting wind of the plan, a congressman from Ohio, a friend of the president, implicated Jim and Walter in an environmental scandal at Oiltron. But Jim had deftly left a paper trail that led to someone who was 'replaceable'—Oiltron CEO Dennis Howland. With Howland, a banker and former BNG Bank executive, forced to resign, Jim Anderson found a convenient opportunity to appoint his friend, Haig Abku, to run Oiltron Industries. Walter and Jim walked away from the Oiltron investigation free and clear.

Walter savored his sheltered world where, like the king's knight, he enjoyed the king's might yet was accountable to only the king himself. But Walter's true gift was that he didn't see himself as a powerful person. He was merely 'the goalkeeper'.

◆ ◆ ◆ ◆ ◆

Entering the conference room, Walter saw Scott and Sharon huddled around the oblong, chrome table as the reporters gathered for their daily 3:00 o'clock meeting. Six writers and the Red Team occupied half of the massive table - the balance of the herd had been shaved thin due to a shakeout at WNN's print division, some hot financial news, and, of course, Baruch. The small audience seemed to disturb Scott McNally.

"Is this it?"

"Yep, boss. The rest of the team is out and about."

"So, what's up?"

Walter shuffled the papers on the conference table as he began his summation.

"The local editor, Hicks, is sick. So, seeing as I did it, I'll give you the local wrap first."

Walter, pale and portly, adjusted his suit, put his finger against his ear, and hopelessly tried to impersonate the suave, handsome, jet-black WNN anchor, Charles Waters.

"Tonight, on action news at 11:00, we have the beat on a fire on the north side. The mayor answers questions about an alleged affair, and our sports reporter offers the Cubs, 'a season in review'. In fact, the wrap-up is much better than the season itself!"

While everyone chuckled, the spaceship-shaped conference phone on the middle of the table rang. Scott stretched his mass of flesh to reach the small receiver. He livened up a bit and grunted, "McNally. What ya got?"

"Put her on the conference line."

"Good afternoon everyone!" Maggie said playfully.

Scott let a boyish grin slip. Maggie was his favorite. Her charm was simply irresistible.

"Well, Greg and I have got some exciting stuff on Baruch. First, each of you has a video-mail of an interview he did in New York in 2010. He indicates in this interview that he has a 'council' of sorts. It's short but very, very sweet. Second, besides this Professor Schleier who Greg met today in Munich, I found an old buddy of his who lives in Vienna. Greg's on his way there now. One last interesting point: I talked to the publisher of his book and no one can find the original manuscript or the file..."

Maggie hummed the tune from *The Twilight Zone*. "That's it!"

Walter leaned toward the speakerphone. "Have you found

out anything on his financials? Where does he get his money? Does he have a car? How does he pay his rent?"

"We got his tax details through our bureau in Austria. He receives a check for seven thousand dollars a month from a numbered account in Liechtenstein. Because he pays his taxes and doesn't work, he's in good standing with the Austrian tax folks."

"But where does the money come from?" Scott asked loudly.

"Charley Hardeway's newsletter claimed it's a family trust. But there are no facts, nada. Even if you find the numbered account, the legal guys are certain it's hidden in a trust fund. Unless you get the CIA involved, you'll never find it."

"OK, Mag, thanks for the update. Keep up the good work." Scott pressed the off button without waiting for a reply.

His secretary stuck her head in the door. "Mr. McNally, you have an overseas call."

"Let's get back to work everyone. We're wasting time." He hurried to his office to take the call.

CHAPTER 9

GREG ARRIVED IN VIENNA AT 9:30 IN THE EVENING.

"City Hotel, please."

The cab pulled away from the noise of a jet landing.

"I usually take the underground, but it's late," Greg noted, trying to stir up a conversation with the stocky, bearded cabdriver, who wore the expression of a bulldog.

"Vienna has not an underground," the cabdriver replied.

His accent and deep-set eyes tipped Greg that he was from the Czech Republic or maybe Hungary. Vienna was littered with Hungarians and Czechs who were looking for the good life and ended up as taxi drivers. Greg sat back in his seat and remained silent, rather than face a laborious conversation in Pidgin English.

Looking at the map of Vienna and its circumfluent, spider-web-like streets, he spotted his hotel: two blocks from the Danube canal, a critical waterway that links the Black Sea to the North Sea ports. During a weekend trip in Vienna back in his college days, Greg had water-skied on one of the smaller canals; it had a lift some thirty feet high which pulled the skier around a rectangle-shaped course. It was like riding behind a boat that drove at perfect right angles. Greg remembered having both arms almost pulled out of their sockets as he was slung around that first ninety-degree turn like a human projectile. And when he had fallen on the side opposite the pier, the swim to the grassy shore and subsequent walk over the bridge had taken a good ten minutes.

His memory of the canal where he had skied over three decades ago crystallized. He could see a slender, innocent-looking sixteen-year-old Austrian girl in her bikini standing on the pier, his skis hissing as he whipped around the corner. She later asked him to meet her at the Prada, Vienna's amusement park and adolescent hangout. They spent the night playing carnival games and going on rides that tested Greg's digestive resolve. Later they took the streetcar to the first district in Vienna's center and visited a pub.

Greg could never forget the entertainer at that small, dark pub. The handsome, broad-shouldered kid had had the crowd in tears with his magic and comedy, speaking a dialect that Greg couldn't understand. It was the way he had about him that made the audience laugh. Doris, a flowered skirt draped over her thin hips, a tight black T-shirt showing her youthful breasts, and a nose bright red from the day at the canal, smiled as the entertainer smoothly delivered his lines.

"He has what we call the 'Viennese Schmäh'. It's something you can't translate," Doris said.

Greg looked it up later and found out that Doris was right: the English word—patter—literally meant something peculiar to a language or culture that an outsider couldn't understand. However, Greg did understand. He reflected on some of the people who had 'patter'—Jack Paar, Jimmy Durante. Greg strained his memory bank to come up with anyone in his age group who possessed 'Schmäh'.

"Why was Jack Paar, the original *Tonight Show* host, heads and tails above today's TV personalities?" Greg had frequently debated with his former boss at WNN, Charley Hardeway.

"Am I being nostalgic about an era that I experienced only through reruns, or are the types of Jack Paar, like the great nineteenth century orators who went from village to village telling stories, a lost breed?"

The small but feisty Charley had replied, "The fundamental difference between Jack Paar and later hosts was that he wasn't raised in the TV era—he wasn't part of the machine. Jack Paar talked to real people about real issues. The guests were scientists, writers, and politicians. And he traveled around the world and shot shows from Europe, Japan, Africa. He had more than movie stars who appear today only to promote a new movie or book."

Yep, you're right, Charley, Greg thought, as the cab, having exited the highway, sped through the narrow, empty streets of Vienna's east side.

Baruch has something like 'Schmäh', but that 'something' is far more compelling than just fan appeal, Greg thought.

Greg's mind wandered as he caught glimpses of downtown Vienna's majestically lighted center and towering phallic domes at the openings provided by major intersections.

Doris, her long black hair and glowing nose, reentered his mind suddenly and unexpectedly. Like watching an old silent movie, he saw Doris and himself. They began kissing in front of the Opera House. They must have kissed for hours that evening—Greg could taste her lips. His hands could feel her tiny frame under the soft, flowered skirt as his hand ran up the curve of her backside. She trembled as he explored her body.

"My God," Greg mumbled out loud, "what I'd give to freeze that moment in my mind as my single moment in time."

"This is your hotel, sir."

Greg jumped from his fantasy back into Vienna, 2013, only to see the old, tired eyes of the cabdriver in the rearview mirror.

"That was just getting good," Greg said, taking a deep breath.

"Sorry, I not understand you, sir," the driver said politely.

"Oh nothing, I was talking to myself."

Handing the driver the colorful currency, Greg added, "I need a receipt."

♦ ♦ ♦ ♦ ♦

As happened so often, having now been ushered to his hotel room, Greg was wired. This was no wonder, considering the three cups of mud—his definition of the strong European coffee—he had downed before landing. As this was his only evening in Vienna, Greg decided to leave the grim hotel room that someone seemed to have magically transported from Munich. He opened his leather bag, grabbed the digital recorder, clipped it on his shirt sleeve, hit 'track 1', and headed for downtown Vienna.

Moving along the canal high above the calm water, he observed a nineteenth or early twentieth-century building that played host to a high-tech electronics showroom. The display in the store wasn't any nicer than Wallace Electronics in Chicago, but the granite block building gave a grandiose, museum-like feeling.

Greg's thoughts were displaced by his own voice moving through the headset. In the lighted bay window, a sharply-dressed male mannequin held a tiny sattelite phone. The plastic "happy customer" dawned an exaggerated smile that overshadowed his blank eyes. 'Think smart. Think Austriacom' were the words on the banner hanging over Greg's head. Greg, taken by the scene, recalled Baruch's statemen: "Today's consumer has that glazed look of someone effectively mind-programmed by a $20 million ad campaign."

"Tell me how you first met Baruch, Professor Schleier."

"We grew up in neighboring villages outside of Graz. There

weren't many schools in the area so we ended up attending the same schoolhouse. Have you ever been to Graz, Mr. Lancy?"

"No. But I plan to be there tomorrow."

"That's wonderful. Graz is truly where East meets West. The buildings that line the Mur River could be mistaken for any city in Europe, until you raise your head towards the heavens and spot the Ottoman-influenced Gothic towers, which top the buildings. And the people.... so many have the beauty of Turk-inspired deep skin and gentle brown eyes, mixed with the sharp lines of the Germanic peoples."

Greg recalled Frank Schleier tapping himself on the cheek, rather effeminately. "I'm sorry, Mr. Lancy, I believe this is your interview, not my walk down nostalgia lane."

"No, don't be sorry. It's fascinating."

Greg pushed the 'stop' button and looked down the long pedestrian zone that marked the beginning of Vienna's town center.

Why did this interview seem weird, he asked himself. He then realized that he had somehow lost control of the interview before it had begun. Or was it that he knew the interview was going nowhere? Still walking slowly, he broke out of his mental trance and realized he was square in front of a towering temple of stone, an architectural monument of late-Roman, Gothic, and Renaissance styles—the Stephansdom.

Quickly he uncurled the rolled-up map in order to get his bearings. He clicked the 'on' button and headed toward the Hofburg.

"Was Baruch an unusual child, Mr. Schleier?"

"I myself was a child. He didn't seem peculiar to me."

"I'm curious. That quote at your entrance is by Benedict Spinoza. According to a report I read from the Ecumenical Society, Benedict is a name Spinoza took after being expelled from the Jewish faith I mean, wasn't his name *Baruch* Spinoza?"

"The Ecumenical Society, Mr. Lancy? I have to wonder how 'ecumenical' this group is? Since Baruch entered the picture, church attendance is up over 5 percent. Then they have the gumption to attack him. And as far as the seventeenth century Baruch—Baruch Spinoza—is concerned, my friend would consider Benedict Spinoza *the* greatest thinker on the subject of morals and ethics."

"Greater than Jesus?"

"Well, both were great thinkers. Spinoza was a philosopher, not a..." Frank hesitated, "religious figure."

"Any other similarities?"

"As far as the two 'Baruchs' are concerned, I'd say they both were, or are, feared because they don't say 'go to this particular church'. Have you ever heard of Philiponus, Mr. Lancy?"

"No, I can't say I have."

"He was a sixth century scientist in Alexandria who first proposed that motion is constant, over a thousand years before Newton. But the Church branded him a heretic and burnt his books."

"Where books burn, people shall soon follow," Greg blurted out Heinrich Heine's quote that he had read when leaving the Holocaust Museum in Israel.

"Yes, that is true, Mr. Lancy. One must remember that religious institutions are novices in the art of freethinking. Just consider the irony that religion flourished in the Dark Ages."

"Are you saying that the Church will try to destroy Baruch?"

"No, simply stated: anything that *appears* to transcend the need for a formal church is beyond the grasp of most theologians."

Frank glanced at a book on his desk. "Do you know who else studied Spinoza?"

"No, I'm sorry I don't."

"David Hume. And who was a good friend of David Hume?"

Greg shrugged his shoulders, wondering if this was one of Charley Hardeway's question/answer sessions.

"Adam Smith. Yes, Mr. Lancy, Spinoza talks about free trade, Hume reads Spinoza, and Smith is influenced by Hume. Life does have a thread."

Greg jumped in, "And is there a thread that leads to our Baruch?"

"You see, Mr. Lancy, had you read *Apocrypha Truth*, you would know everything about him—even why my friend chose the name 'Baruch'."

Frank Schleier reached in the drawer of his enormous oak desk and took out a copy of Baruch's book. "Here, let me read for you."

The professor put on his thin-framed spectacles and, opening the worn book, said, "The chapter is titled ' Everyone is Baruch'." He repositioned his body to a more vertical line and articulated his words like a true professor:

My parents were killed before I was at an age to understand what a parent is. They certainly loved me more than life itself. But for a child, a parent executes the only true law of nature—the struggle to insure his survival. That they loved me enough to fight this fight is remarkable enough. I was raised by a kind, gentle family against whom I could never find reason to say one unkind word. For those who say my background is 'dysfunctional', your insufficient judgment of my loving family brings discord - I ask you not to cheapen my family's love, for this is the way my life was to have passed. As I child, I was fascinated by the thought that religion appeared to breathe life into an otherwise suffocating history. By religion, it must be said, I refer to a people's beliefs, for we in the West are guilty of calling our beliefs 'religions' and those of others 'philosophies'.

Frank Schleier chuckled as he read this passage. He continued:

For example, Christians often refer to the four-hundred-year void between the Old Testament and the Time of Jesus as a time of spiritual silence. To the contrary, this was a time of mankind's social and spiritual experimentation. We should not be so bold as to believe we are capable of getting God right the first time. Are we not still experimenting today? While reading the Bible as a child, I recall being in my father's study and running across a leather bound book entitled "Apocrypha", I asked my father what that word meant. "It's books that aren't accepted as doctrinal by the Church," he explained. After he clarified the word "doctrinal", he went on to explain the politics behind the book. "You see, Stefan, there were two groups of people—the Protestants and the Catholics—who didn't agree on the contents of the Bible." This statement set off a thousand questions. I thought the Bible was from God, so I asked what is there to agree upon. My father, a patient man, explained the Council of Trent in 1563 and how the different churches chose the books that constituted 'their' bible. As it turned out, the Catholic Church wished to include all the books of the Apocrypha; however, the Protestants had already included the two Esdras in their official bible. Thus, the Catholic Church excluded the two books that the Protestants had taken, and integrated the remaining books into their bible. I remember telling my father that this seemed like the Romans dividing Jesus' lot. I read the Apocrypha intensely. It disturbed me, in particular, that Baruch had been relegated to a few pages in a non-doctrinal book. After all, Baruch was Jeremiah's secretary and many believe that Baruch actually wrote the book of Jeremiah. I would later discover that Baruch was responsible for some, or much, of the content of Jeremiah's work. This alone made me feel as though Baruch had been slighted. When I read the verse where Jeremiah warns Baruch not to succumb to the temptations of ambition, my heart dropped. I thought what a great man Baruch must have been to toil at the height of intellectual ability, yet remain in the deepest anonymity. The history of our world is that the greatest men go unnoticed. These men of greatness succumb to men of mere and mortal power. And when a great mind, capable of changing our very world, does try to rise we, like the hunter eyeing the flock of geese, always shoot the bird that flies highest. In honor of these men, not as a heretic, I began calling myself Baruch.

He set the book down and pointed at Greg with an irritated expression.

"Mr. Lancy, it amazes me that I have never heard anyone from your company or any media make reference to that passage. You refer to Baruch as 'mysterious'. To me," he pointed at the book, "this is very clear. Does WNN just run with an opinion and then go in search of the truth?"

Greg tried to clear his dry throat and recover from the body shot delivered by the slightly-built scholar. "I *have* heard of this passage. It's just that I have no way to document anything in that book."

"Have you *documented* the purchase of Oiltron by your virtual parent, Mr. Lancy? Have you documented BNG Bank's relationship with the Kirov drug ring? Or were you afraid of losing your job—like Mr. Hardeway?"

Greg, sideswiped and speechless, sat haplessly by as the professor continued his lesson in oration.

"Baruch has often told me that most worthwhile things cannot be documented. Did you ever wonder why that big drug scandal in Baku—oh, about five years ago—was buried? Is it not ironic that the mayor of Baku, Haig Abku, became President of Oiltron only weeks later? And is it not coincidental that Mr. Abku orchestrated the sweet deal for the AZI-Group's new headquarters in Baku? My sources say that Jim Anderson himself set up Dennis Howland's fall, just like he set up the fall of Oiltron before he purchased it."

This interview had jumped right past the normal niceties Greg had experienced in previous interviews with Europeans.

Frank Schleier was obviously more a fan of Baruch than the AZI-Group or WNN.

Greg wetted his lips and spoke. "Well, seeing we're being so direct, let me first say that I wasn't involved in the case concerning the Baku drug connection. But let me ask you this: Some people claim that Baruch is either a nihilist or a cult leader. What's your..."

Frank Schleier's roaring laughter cut off Greg. "My, my, you are reaching. If he's a nihilist, then Jesus was agnostic! And a cult leader? You dare compare Baruch with the Moonies or New Age figureheads..." The Austrian professor searched for a precise word in English. "...Or those silly millenarian cults back at the turn of the century? That's a good one, Mr. Lancy."

The small professor gathered his composure as if on command and continued, "Oh yes, Baruch most certainly leads. He leads a blind mass of people to be able to see past their media screens. He leads by example. And he asks nothing in return. Is this what he's guilty of?"

Even though Greg knew Frank Schleier was probably right, it was time to don his corporate tough-guy persona. Being a hot shot at the AZI-Group included taking a bullet now and then and, sometimes, having to cause some collateral damage. Greg shot back.

"Baruch may not be as pure as you think."

"Nor as evil as you wish," the professor said in an utterly disgusted tone of voice.

Touché, Greg thought as he took a reprieve from Frank Schleier and stopped before the tall, elaborate gates outside Vienna's expansive Imperial Palace. His ears only now captured the buzzing sound of cars speeding over the cobblestone streets and groups of well-dressed Austrians who had most likely been at the theatre. What a magnificent building, he thought.

The endless rows of white stone were the preferred residence of Elisabeth, despite the fact that the Schönbrunn Palace—all 1440 rooms—lay just outside Vienna at her disposal. What an elegant period in time, Greg thought as he removed his headset for a moment, feeling frustrated because he couldn't place the events of the nineteenth century Hapsburgs in the correct time sequence. There was Maria-Teresa, Sophie, and Elisabeth—that much he knew. But when were they in power and what exactly were they famous for? He did know that it was only one hundred years ago that the last emperor, Franz Joseph, ruled Austria. And it was Franz Joseph's representative and heir apparent, Archduke Ferdinand, who, thanks to one of histories many wrong motorcade turns, was assassinated, thus providing a reason to start the Great War.

Greg continued to search his memory for the names of all the Austrian rulers.

Why do so many Europeans have the same damn names? Didn't they ever get tired of Josef and Mary? Greg asked himself, only half-joking. With that thought, he turned his back on the palace and, veering back towards his hotel, continued listening to the interview.

All he heard, though, was Frank Schleier's ridiculing voice.

"Mr. Lancy, you really do not expect me to answer that, do you? Mr. Lancy, I went to school and studied with him. He wasn't my lover!"

Greg's internal screening device seemed very apt at picking out the most biting responses Frank Schleier had to serve up. As he entered the lobby of the City Hotel, he heard his own closing plea.

"Mr. Schleier, my employer will offer you a large sum of money—seven digits—for an exclusive interview about Baruch. But we have to have some details."

Greg visualized Frank swinging his chair to the left in order to stand up. Walking around the large wooden desk and moving unusually close to the taller reporter, he looked Greg dead in the eyes. "Mr. Lancy, when I was fifteen, a young girl, a classmate, became pregnant. Terrified that her parents would find out, she climbed the grain silo at my father's farm and prepared to jump. Baruch and I saw her nearing the top and yelled at her to stop. Baruch ran to the silo and climbed up to within a few ladder rungs. They were up there for maybe two minutes, and then they both came down. She embraced Baruch and said she had seen God. Today, she and her beautiful daughter still live in Semriach near my family's farm."

"What did he tell her to make her come down?" Greg asked more out of personal curiosity than journalistic instinct.

"He told her that God had given her the gift of life in that child and God was counting on her to be a good mother. He told her that she would be a fine mother. Then he told her, 'Even if your parents hate you, I will always love you.'

Fighting tears, Greg's glassy eyes looked back in silence. Baruch's friend continued: "That woman now teaches high school math and has three beautiful children, Mr. Lancy. That should make a fine report for your media empire. And it's free. I'll expect to see that on the evening news."

Greg fought back tears.

"Mr. Schleier, I'm just doing my job. Thank you for your time."

CHAPTER 10

SHARON TUCKER SAT IN THE STUDY OF HER POSTMODERN SUBURBAN home on Chicago's west side, propped against the curve of the burgundy recamier. The beige Berber carpet extended into the spacious living room, whose vaulted ceilings provided ample room for her collection of Lichtenstein, Warhol, and Robert Indiana prints, most of which she had received as gifts during her 'previous life' as CEO of WQRT.

The house, although it seemed cold to conventional tastes, was her reward for escaping the desperate streets of an area in downtown Atlanta referred to simply as 'Zone 3'. Lounging on her ornate recamier provided a welcome reprieve from the symphony of ringing phones and irritating keyboard clatter at the WNN Tower downtown. Sharon's mind strayed from work only occasionally, like when she had a date. Maggie, who frequently went to movies with Sharon, had commented earlier in the day during the Red Team meeting, "Sharon, you find Mr. Right. Then you dig like a reporter until you find his mountainous weakness and you dump him."

James, her last boyfriend, had been madly in love.

"Honey," she told Maggie, "That James just sticks like glue."

As VP of Operations, Sharon was captured in an actuarial maze where next month's operating statement was her only reality. Especially now, not having the distraction of a boyfriend, she had spiraled further into a world of numbers, cost control, and bottom-line profit. Her latest self-appointed task was figuring out new ways to chart viewer numbers in order to respond more quickly to 'negative consumer response', i.e. viewers who were turning off WNN.

She had performed a series of marketing studies concerning the 'Baruch effect'. What was clear from all the reports was that when Baruch was in the media, numbers went up, at least short-term. Then, to use the phrase Sharon had coined, the viewers become 'Baruched', which meant they abandoned mainstream media. Market research showed this normally happened after reading his book or having multiple encounters with his message. To be sure, whether Baruch was being exposed or ignored presented Sharon and WNN with a major challenge.

Spending a weekend alone with her portable screen, that paper-thin image projector that stored an even thinner digital keyboard, seemed surprisingly normal to her—everyone in her circle had the same ritual. While doing fine financially, Sharon felt insignificant in her role at WNN. It was only four years ago in 2009, that—as one of the first African-American women to run a major television station—she was on top of the world. As CEO she had made all the calls and had taken all the responsibility. She did such a good job that the AZI-Group bought her station, WQRT. The major shareholder received $40.00 a share for a company he had bought at $28.00 two years earlier. Sharon still fumed she had never had the opportunity to put together a management buyout. Instead she had to decide what to do next.

With most of the media under the control of WNN, WBG, and WRX there wasn't a big choice if she wanted to maintain her upscale lifestyle. WRX, a relic with a dim future, interested her only as a last act of desperation. On the other hand, Sharon liked the quirky, intelligent Mike McMillan who owned and ran WBG.

He had rocked Jim Anderson's world when, out of the blue, he befriended and joined forces with Jerry Bates, perhaps the most powerful money lord on the planet. Jerry Bates, known as the Great Black Hope for the power he possessed, was rumored to have been the driving force behind President Johnson's successful campaign to become the first African-American leader in 2008. Bates and McMillan exhilarated Sharon; however, they could only offer her a management job.

WNN, still the reigning heavyweight champion of the media world five years ago, had her friend Charles Waters—another successful black American from Atlanta—who had gained celebrity status around the globe as 'that guy who does the news for WNN'. Sharon liked the power Jim Anderson wielded and she respected WNN for having the guts to put a black man in its number one anchor spot. So when she was offered a V-P position under Scott McNally, she accepted.

Scott and Sharon mirrored twenty-first century American diversity. Coming from a lily white, middle-class subdivision in upstate New York, Scott's past couldn't have been more removed from Sharon's poor black community in Atlanta. What they had in common was that they had both worked their way up to run major news operations. It was also a sign of the times that both their companies had been gobbled up by a virtual corporation, like an insect being snapped up by a frog.

While she had found a good friend in Maggie, enjoyed being around Charles Waters and found Scott entertaining, Sharon longed for the excitement of being on the front line. Instead, she sat in a fancy office where she was supposed to be involved in strategic planning. But it wasn't like the old days when the stockholders and the consumer ran corporations; when the CEO was always struggling to balance the wishes of these two groups. The virtual corporations had changed the rules of the game. With institutional investors consolidating industry by industry, individual investors could go along for the ride, but they couldn't effect any decisions. Management, too, was increasingly squeezed out of the process. They became low-ranking officers, expected to execute the orders of the Joint Chiefs of Staff.

"Remember when they said information and decisions would be made on a broader level instead of top-down?" she had asked Scott over coffee at the local hangout of the WNN news staff, the West Egg Diner.

"Yeah," Scott had said, "and Lenin told the Soviet people he'd give them democracy; Lyndon Johnson said he'd give us the Great Society; and my mom told me there was Santa Claus. Smart people never tell you their real intentions, Sharon!"

Repositioning herself on the recamier, she glanced at an article she had cut out:

"Business has become a poker game. The investors sit around a table playing with entire industries as cards. The cards may get shuffled and redistributed. They let the small investor look on and feel important. But at the end of the game, the same people hold the same fifty-two cards."

In Sharon's mind, the banks both fueled and drove the vehicle known as 'the business community'. They supplied the poker chips to the table and then sat back and let the players fight over who could build the biggest stack. "The banker's industry is control and their product is money," Sharon had argued on more than one occasion. She was happy to see Jerry Bates, a black man who grew up in the same poverty as she, playing the banker's game so well.

Sharon suddenly dove to the left and caught her screen before it hit the ground. During this moment of contemplation she had fallen into a trancelike state and forgotten the almost-weightless screen balancing on her leg. She set her electronic friend on the carpet and pulled out Baruch's *Apocrypha Truth* from under a stack of newspapers.

"Can anyone *famous* summarize their life's thoughts in seventy-five pathetic pages?" Scott asked the Red Team that morning, ridiculing Baruch while waving the book in the air. "This—what you see in my hand—contains the work of a fucking genius!"

Maggie answered Scott by reminding him that Thoreau had written *Civil Disobedience* in less than thirty pages. "*Civil Disobedience* was the book that inspired Gandhi," she added matter-of-factly. "And don't forget that Baruch's only thirty-nine years old," Maggie boasted.

Sharon's dark skin glowed, recalling Scott's surprised expression following Maggie's comment. Anyone else probably would have gotten negative karma for such "insubordination". Somehow, Maggie could say the most biting things and yet sound so harmless. Sharon pulled a folded piece of paper, now a temporary bookmark, from Baruch's tattered book.

Baruch: Excerpt from Central Park Speech: 'One World':

There can be only one world. A world is either spiritual or not spiritual, just as an individual either believes in a spiritual being or doesn't. Secularism attempts to remove from humans the coherent spiritual power that allows us to ascend to a higher human level. Can a person murder by day and be a loving parent by night? We have seen that soldiers can only switch their souls from a killing spirit to that of a loving parent with a term we call 'debriefing'. Many soldiers will tell you that they never again feel human at all. They lose the 'oneness' they felt before war.

The war of our modern world differs only slightly. We who are spiritual souls are surrounded daily by a secular war. We can try to buffer ourselves, to hide, from the noise and distractions around us. Yet we are, by day, expected to make corporate decisions based upon a secular, unemotional world. Why should we, the citizens of this planet, be forced to hide from our own world? Are not they—the virtual corporations, the power mongers—the ones who should be hiding?

Abraham Lincoln, paraphrasing Jesus in the Bible, said that we could not live in a house divided. We who aspire to live in a spiritual world cannot live in a soul divided.

Sharon folded the page, inserted it between the open pages of the book, and, steadying it on her thigh, extended her arm to pluck the new Bible from the end table. Although she had a collection of Bibles upstairs in her study, not one included the Apocrypha, the name that Baruch has borrowed for the title of his unrelated book, *Apocrypha Truth*.

Having finally overcome the vacuum-sealed plastic that clung stubbornly to the Bible's soft black cover, she cocked her head back slightly and balanced her reading glasses precariously on the arch of her nose. Studious eyes followed the movement of her finger, as it moved from verse to verse across the pages and words written by Jeremiah's secretary, Baruch.

She let out an "Amen," underlining verses twelve and thirteen chapter three:

You have forsaken the fountain of wisdom. If you had walked in the way of God, you would be dwelling in peace forever.

Her eyes bulged, moving to verse seventeen:

Those who have sport with the birds of the air, and who hoard up silver and gold, in which men we trust, and there is no end to their getting; those who scheme to get silver, and are anxious, whose labors are beyond measure? They have vanished and gone to Hades, and others have risen in their place.

Two weeks earlier, after she had expressed to Scott the people's sincere trust of Baruch, Scott had responded, "I'll tell the people what they should like and who they can trust. We're dealing with a destructive, manipulating pseudo-god. Somewhere along the way, this guy made mistakes. I'll find it if I have to do cavity searches personally. We *will* find that one chink in his armor. I'll marginalize the hell out of him!"

Sharon sat calmly, rereading the short biblical book of Baruch. Smiling and letting her head swing from shoulder to shoulder, she whispered, "My, Baruch, you are a wise man—both of you."

CHAPTER 11

AMSTERDAM IS THE COSMOPOLITAN HUB OF THE NETHERLANDS, THE country still known in the twenty-first century as 'Holland,' a term that infuriates the Dutch citizens who live in other provinces of the Occident's most densely populated country. On this typical autumn day, wind-aided rain and the 45-degree temperature did nothing to deter umbrella-armed bicyclists, or 'fijters', who nonchalantly passed businessmen protected by trench coats and wool caps. One of the best hospices in such weather is a "brown room", a Dutch cafe where coffee, beer, and spirits are served in a cavernous den of stained wood. What seems dark to the outside world brightens up the days of the Dutch folk.

De Plank cafe was particularly local in flavor. Long and narrow, certainly no wider than twenty feet, the cafe was host to a bar occupying the right wall and protruding no more than an arm span, witnessed by the fact that the bartender could pour coffee and hand it to the patron at the bar without moving. About a dozen small wood tables covered with the traditional woven oriental carpets enveloped the remaining space. The combination of the wood floor impregnated by centuries of spilled beer, old table rugs, and the heavy cigarette smoke of the patrons smelled normal to the guest of De Plank.

Besides the slumping, union-uniformed Dutchman at the bar,

only two tables were occupied at three-thirty on this particular afternoon. Three men sat at one table playing cards and smoking a Dutch staple of hand-rolled cigarettes.

"The problem is that we pay to support all the provinces. I say let them collect their own taxes and pay for their own roads," one of the rough manual laborers chided, pausing to enjoy his cigarette. "And I read today that the southern province of Limburg has its own lobby group at the European Parliament. Shouldn't we be looking out for our national interest?"

The apparent leader of the small workingman's think tank received approving looks from his two colleagues.

Out of the hidden corner of the bar resonated a powerful articulate voice. "Nationalism. The story of Europe..." The male voice continued in a highly sarcastic, almost mocking tone, "A continent fragmented into small provinces and regions throughout history; a history altered with the stroke of a pen to prove some national bond; politicians clinging to the concept as their last great hope. Nationalism: a collective unfounded fear, gentlemen."

The three uniformed men turned to the lone youngster in the corner who had the physical appearance of a high-flying financier. Smiling warmly at the three workers, he spread the German language *Wirtschaft und Welt* newspaper over the patterned table-rug. The silence only increased the distance between the three rugged workers and the young man with the golden tongue.

"Nationalism saved us from the *Prussians*," the group leader insisted, pointing at the German newspaper and stressing the word "Prussian", the Dutch way of showing distaste for Germans.

"Whatever," the young man said, rolling a cigarette with the same brand of tobacco as the labor triumvirate—possibly the only link joining the two views of the world.

"Coffee?" the robust owner-bartender asked, arriving just in time to gracefully end the awkward discussion.

"Yeah, sure. And bring me a ham Stookbrood" the young man said as his cellular phone rang, prompting the three laborers to snap their heads around in search of the beeping noise. Satellite technology remained twenty-first century witchcraft to a city worker who repaired cobblestone streets.

"Van Wels," the young slickster stated confidently.

"Mr. Van Wels, it's Scott McNally's secretary Monique. I just spoke with Mr. McNally and he said to tell you that he would call at 5:00 PM central European time."

"Fine. I'll be back in my office at four-thirty. Anything else?"

The young voice answered hastily, "No, Mr. van Wels. Just make sure you're on the secure line. Talk to you soon."

Marco Van Wels possessed a melange of talents and interests. On the social side, he liked chilled beer as well as tall Dutch women, neither of which were difficult to find in Amsterdam. At the age of thirty-eight, he could easily be mistaken for a twenty-eight-year-old athlete, and he was, in fact, a master instructor of Hapkido, the Korean martial art form that he had practiced since his youth. Much of his time was spent in cafes, often referred to as his second office, where he would sit for hours sipping rich coffee, smoking, and reading a litany of journals in a number of languages. Being near his apartment, the cafe also offered the convenience of meeting one of his several "friends" for an afternoon "appointment", as he preferred to call it. Today, he had no such meetings planned; he knew a call from the U.S. was expected.

Professionally Marco held people at a distance with his complexity. The son of a well-to-do family, he had studied law at a German university in Berlin. Law he found monotonous—he quit the practice at age thirty-three and began working for the Dutch secret police as an advisor. After only one year, the international intelligence agency Interpol, located in The Hag, recruited Marco. His first assignment hooked him up with the GSC—the Global Software Commission—that had been mandated by the UN to track down software pirates. The GSC was the result of years of lobbying by the largest software suppliers, who were no longer in the business of giving away products and free downloads. That was a twentieth-century initiative. The big boys now had sufficient clout and market dominance to line their coffers with royalty money.

Marco, no fan of the companies he was protecting, explained the strategy of the software business: "First they get the camel in the tent. Then they shit all over."

While the GSC was much more interesting than pure legal research, he still found himself spending most of his time in a legal morass of documents and case studies. The European government had created a level of bureaucratic nonsense that he felt surpassed the combined incompetence of individual European states. The Interpol gig, however, provided one positive result for Marco: it would propel him on a new life path, the world of corporate investigation.

It was thanks to a recommendation by Haig Abku that Marco got his start in the corporate world under contract of the AZI-Group's BNG Bank, which was looking to acquire the insurance arm of Bates/McMillan. In his days at Interpol, Marco had worked closely with Haig Abku, then the mayor of Baku, on the Kirov drug cartel case. In fact, Marco had been actively investigating BNG Bank, which was suspected of laundering money for the Kirov family as early as 2008.

That investigation was closed and five years had passed. BNG Bank needed the now independent Marco to investigate a more discrete issue: They felt that Bates/McMillan had cooked the books in order to prevent BNG's acquisition. Marco was charged with the task of penetrating the deepest financial circles of Bates/McMillan; however, his three-month investigation turned up only minor discrepancies. The final report concluded:

"After attaining extensive documentation concerning the accounting methods of Bates/McMillan, I can find nothing to lead me to any conclusion except that they have accurately stated the position of their insurance company, BMC."

Through contacts with the AZI-Group, Marco received contracts ranging from legal advice concerning takeovers to corporate 'black ops', i.e. investigations that never officially happened. Marco got a rush from his new identity, always walking the line of legal issues, trying to gather information without breaking the law, and working to satisfy his client without getting caught in the act by his target. He enjoyed playing the game.

At 4:45 PM central european time he arrived at his office overlooking the Casino. As he sat reading his favorite newspaper—the *Dagblatt*—he tugged on his suspenders and ran his left hand repeatedly through his slicked-back hair. His perpetually cool look masked whether these were acts of expectation or mere fidgeting.

At precisely 5:00 o'clock central European time, the secured phone line rang.

CHAPTER 12

JENNY LANCY, GREG'S COLLEGE SWEETHEART WHO HE HAD MARRIED exactly one year after graduation, sat on the edge of her son Jeff's bed, her short brunette hair pulled back in a ponytail, reading *The Little Prince*.

"Once when I was six years old I saw a magnificent picture in a book, called 'True stories from Nature,' about the primeval forest. It was a picture of a boa constrictor in the act of swallowing an animal..."

Jenny, Maggie's college roommate, had found this first edition print at an estate sale in the Chicago suburb of Crystal Lake. Maggie's ex-husband, a financial planner from Switzerland who still managed Greg and Jenny's modest portfolio, had mentioned that the library of a recently deceased client, Professor Williner, was being sold to help finance his wife's retirement. The professor's basement library had been created for the local children "in the spirit of America's forefathers", referring to the many private libraries in colonial America.

"That book was one of his favorites," the dignified widow had told Jenny.

"How many books are here?" Jenny had asked, amazed by the mounds stacked over six feet high around the perimeter of the two-car garage.

"Over four thousand, ma'am. But *The Little Prince* was his

favorite. He told me that everything we adults need to know is in this children's book."

Jenny's beautiful bedroom eyes looked past the book's color pictorial of the boa constrictor eating the animal and, fixating on the wall-size Tiger mural that she had painted before Jeff's birth over nine years ago, she wondered about the poor professor's widow. Mrs. Williner had spent over fifty years with a profoundly educated man whose favorite life metaphor was a children's book. A faded, handwritten note on the inside cover read:

Dear William,
Be true to yourself. Make each day your masterpiece. Help others. Drink deeply from great books. Make friendship a fine art. Build a shelter against a rainy day. Pray for guidance and give thanks for your blessings every day.
Best of luck in high school!
Professor Williner

"In the early twentieth century, it was tradition that a young boy would receive this creed at the age of twelve," the widow had informed Jenny. "I don't know who William was, except that he was one of my husband's students when he taught elementary school back in the 1950s."

Professor Williner must have been something very special, Jenny thought.

Jeff pulled on Jenny's white robe snapping her out of a trance. "Are you going to keep reading, Mom?" he asked, whining.

Jenny obliged her son and read on about the little boy who drew the picture of a boa constrictor digesting an animal. When he showed his masterpiece to adults, they would say it looked like a hat, even when the little boy explained it was something quite different. The boy in the story continued: "Then I would never talk to that person about a boa constrictor, or primeval forests, or stars. I would bring myself down to his level. I would talk to him about bridge, and golf, and politics, and neckties. And the grown-up would be greatly pleased to have met such a sensible man."

Jeff, an overachieving and inquisitive fourth grader, jumped in as she finished the first chapter. "Why do adults only talk about bridges and golf and other stuff like that, Mom?"

"It's bridge, honey—a card game, like go fish," Jenny laughed.

"Well, why do they only talk about cards and stuff, then?"

Jenny thought to herself it was because some adults are superficial and just blurt out idle words.

Jeff's ears heard the official parent explanation: "Well, honey, adults have to behave differently than children. They have to be more responsible. We'll talk about that more tomorrow."

"Why did the person think the picture's a hat?"

Jeff was wide-awake now.

"Because it sort of looks like a hat, Pumpkin—if you glance at it quickly."

"It doesn't look like a hat to me!" retorted Jeff.

"Well, let's read more tomorrow night and maybe we'll understand better, honey."

Jenny ran her fingers through Jeff's fine hair until he fell asleep. She kissed him on the forehead and went downstairs to her office.

Before Jeff was part of her life, Jenny had run a computer programming operation out of this very office, occupied by a U-shaped desk supporting four screens and a simple Swedish posture chair. She called her company Hot Coffee, referring to the fact that she specialized in Java programming. That was ten years ago. Now, armed with an MBA and shouldering the responsibility of a child, she preferred teaching others how to program through a correspondence course she had developed.

She sat down at her screen and checked the message box. There was Greg's voice mail from last evening, but the daily pop-up file showed only new mail from students—and she didn't have the stomach tonight for work. She shut the French doors behind her, moved onto the comfortable sofa, and flipped on WNN.

Charles Waters—the handsome forty-something anchor—read his script with authority. It was clear that the anchor was reading one of Maggie's scripts. Jenny had developed an ear for reports that originated from Greg and Maggie, even after they had been edited. The eloquent anchor turned his attention to the adjacent desk.

"Joining us in our studio from the global consulting firm Tower & Associates is James Towers, CEO.

"Mr. Towers, we have recently heard the term '*intranational trade wars*', referring to the regions within the forty-eight continental states that are battling one another for foreign investment. Is this a growing trend?"

"Most certainly. The shift from nationalism to federalism to regionalism is in full force. The city of New York doesn't care about the U.S. trade balance or any other state. They have narrowed their interest to New York, period."

"And how has this affected the business community?"

"Imagine if you wanted to build a home, but let's pretend that land was limitless. You could negotiate a great deal. Well, the desire of cities to attract investment seems infinite in market terms. This allows foreign companies to be very divisive."

"Explain to our viewers what happened with the Christopher Day affair."

"He's a lawyer out of LA who specialized in finding lucrative deals for foreign investors. On behalf of ChipTech, an Indonesian chip manufacturer, he put together a deal on a light industrial park outside Los Angeles. The problem was that he extracted concessions all the way from the city council down to the unions. On top of that he greased the palm of the Indonesian trade negotiators to the tune of $25 million for subsidies. If that wasn't bad enough, it turns out he owns twenty percent of ChipTech's shares. That's $100 million."

"Sounds like business as usual," Jenny, who had the utmost contempt for financial Realpolitik, snapped back at the TV.

Charles Waters thanked the expert and concluded the report.

"The businessman, Mr. Christopher Day, has been arrested without bond. The SEC and International Monetary Fund are pushing for international laws that would require that all international negotiators be licensed."

Then, much like the exaggerated pause in a piece of Baroque music, Charles Waters dropped his head and glanced at his notes to signal that a new story was coming. His dark, dead-serious eyes caught the camera as he began to speak:

"Baruch, the popular young spiritual leader, has now been missing for over one week. According to reports, his own friends are unaware of his whereabouts. Greg Lancy reports from Vienna on the story's latest developments."

Greg had set up the shooting in front of the tall iron gates of the Hofburg, where the viewers could see stretch limos shuttling in heads of state for a European summit. Jenny's face lit up as she saw her college sweetheart, wearing a dark coat and wool cap, on the big screen.

"Thank you, Charles. As you noted, no new information concerning what may have happened to Baruch has surfaced. Yesterday, I had the opportunity to interview two close childhood friends of Baruch. These people have not seen him since his rise to popularity. However, a university professor in Munich, a confidant of Baruch, assured me that we will hear the rest of Baruch's story and that Baruch is safe."

Charles Waters, the weatherman who had worked his way up to anchor in the course of a twenty-year career, asked: "Greg, is there any talk about the rumors that Baruch has been kidnapped?"

"No, Charles. None at all. Most of the reports we've heard confirm that those closest to Baruch expressed confidence that he *is* OK."

The camera cut back to Chicago..

"We'll keep you up-to-date as this story develops," Charles Waters assured his listeners.

♦ ♦ ♦ ♦ ♦

In a pristine, white stucco mansion nestled among tall oak trees in a northern Chicago suburb, Scott McNally, comfortably reclined on his sofa, grabbed the remote control with his powerful hand and erased Charles Waters from the screen. In the silence of the dark living room, all that could be heard was Scott's heavy breathing and the musical tones of the telephone dialing.

Clenching the receiver firmly, he listened to the message on the other end spit out some guttural foreign gibberish. After the beep, he spoke in an irritated voice that began sentences in tenorlike range and descended nearly an octave, oscillating like a lawn sprinkler.

"Mr. Van Wels, we need to talk again. Call me at six in the morning at my private number. Oh yeah, six o'clock *my time.*"

He placed down the receiver, interlocked his fingers, and cracked an orchestra of knuckles.

CHAPTER 13

THE TRAIN SWAYED FROM SIDE TO SIDE AND BOUNCED WITH THE cadence of the railroad ties, winding its way through the blazing leaves of autumn in Austria's eastern-most countryside. Greg stuck his head out the open window of the train car. To the west he saw the dark green foothills of the Alps, to the east the pastoral flatlands that ran off into Hungary. He was glad he had ditched the commuter plane in Vienna and taken the train.

The pale, yellow cab scurried over a small concrete bridge and sped toward the white stucco buildings of downtown Graz, the idyllic capital of the Austrian province of Staiermark. Greg rummaged through his briefcase in search of Dr. Horstmann's file.

The taxi driver looked back at Greg.

"That is the Mur River."

The slight accent reminded Greg of the Germanic actors in the old James Bond movies.

"On this side of the river you will find all the museums and shops. There's also a very nice open-air market on Tuesday and Thursday. And right here on Sackstrasse you can visit our famous department store, Kastner Öhler."

Beautifully decorated displays of winter coats and ski apparel flashed past Greg's eyes. "You have a lot of ski products here," Greg observed.

"In Austria, skiing is religion," the cabdriver said with open pride.

"And how is Baruch looked upon in Graz?" Greg asked, looking for a grass-roots perspective.

"He is very respected here, but he's not as popular as skiing." The driver let out a good-natured laugh and continued, "In Europe, we have many churches—many *empty* churches."

"Well what do *you* think he is?"

"He's an honest, thoughtful young man. The world can never have too many good people. But his style is not so unusual in Austria."

The humble, understated nature of the Austrian people had impressed Greg as far back as his college days. The cabdriver's insight—that Baruch was pretty typical for an Austrian—had been lost in all the media hype. That angle might make a good feature report, Greg thought.

"You speak better English than our cabbies in New York," Greg said, noticing that the cabdriver had veered into a short narrow street, or what the Austrians call a 'Gasse'.

"Well, not many people speak German—especially *our* kind of German."

Pulling up on the curb, another European thing Greg liked, the driver pointed at a row of apartments. "It's the dark brown door."

Greg paid, thanked the driver for the quick tour of Graz, and jumped out of the dated Mercedes. Wearing his All-American beige trench coat, Greg walked conspicuously on the uneven sidewalk and finally noticed that all the doors in this concrete quarter were brown. Fortunately, Greg found a brass plate marked 'D. Horstmann' and pushed the button.

"Sind Sie der Herr aus den Staaten?"

Befuddled, Greg took a stab at answering what sounded like a question.

"Greg Lancy."

Switching to English, the voice—slow and methodical—said politely, "Please, come up to the second floor, Mr. Lancy."

Greg ascended the two flights of stairs and, at the top, saw Dr. Dietmar Horstmann waiting.

"Pleasure to meet you, Dr. Horstmann."

"Oh, the pleasure is mine. Please come in Mr. Lancy."

The pleasant academic, a tall, full man, wore a woven wool vest and smoked an expensive-looking cigar.

"Can I offer you a coffee, Mr. Lancy?"

Greg had decided to quit asking why it was that everyone in Europe spoke English better than New York cabdrivers or why every European asked him if he wanted a cup of coffee.

"Thank you. That would be nice."

The retired doctor of philosophy moved slowly with the two small cups, one in either hand.

"How was Baruch as a child, Dr. Horstmann?"

"Stefan was, and remains, brilliant. But he was always very understated."

Yesterday in Munich, Frank Schleier had referred to Baruch once as Stefan. This was now the second time Baruch had been addressed by his given name—Stefan Mostl.

"When did Stefan become involved in philosophy?"

The lively old Austrian laughed, "I'm afraid I corrupted him at an early age. By the time he was in Gymnasium—your high school—he was teaching me."

"Exactly how did he do that?" Greg asked.

"Oh, let's see if I can give you an example, Mr. Lancy." Packing his pipe, he reflected. "Yes, here's a good example. In his ninth school year on the very first day, the history teacher asked rhetorically what had made Alexander the Great so great. Stefan replied, 'His teacher, Aristotle'."

Greg knew he was getting a look into Baruch's—Stefan's — mind that few had seen.

"And what happened then?"

"Stefan got into a debate with the teacher about primary cause. He told the teacher, who was, by the way, not a big fan of Aristotle, that Aristotle so exceeded his time that he had to rebuke his own theories. The teacher called me that evening and told me that Stefan was disturbing the class."

"And what was the final verdict?" Greg pushed on.

"Stefan's teacher got a free lesson in Aristotelian logic. That was the final verdict, Mr. Lancy," Dr. Horstmann giggled as he recalled this incident.

"And I thought Stefan was understated," Greg added.

"Indeed. But you must not underestimate him. Stefan finds unconventional ways to accomplish things."

"Like...?" Greg probed.

"Our old home was in the country near Semriach. The house settled from time to time and none of the doors would shut. So I began to take the doors off one by one and to plane the bottoms. Before I could finish one door, Stefan had fixed every door in the house, by simply using a hammer and a piece of wood to flatten the metal moldings under the doors. He was twelve years old!"

"Very inventive! I'm fifty-two and I can't change the oil in my car," Greg stated.

The two men laughed, while Dr. Horstmann poured another cup of coffee that had the viscosity of heavyweight motor oil.

"In the letter you sent me, Mr. Lancy, you inquired about any writings Stefan may have left behind." Dr. Horstmann grabbed a small notebook. "This is all I could find—Stefan wasn't much for idle writing. Socrates believed that the minute you write something, it loses its meaning, like a painting loses its life after the artist makes his last stroke. 'The paper is patient' was one of Stefan's favorite sayings."

"The paper is patient?" Greg repeated.

"It's an old Russian expression. In English one would say that blank paper waits for anything to be written on it—paper's not very particular, in other words."

"Isn't that the truth!" Greg declared, pulling a copy of WNN's newspaper from his attache case.

Greg spent nearly two hours with the foster parent and mentor of Baruch. They talked about Baruch's studies, his inner struggles, and his brash departure from school. At 11:45, Greg jumped back in a cab to head back to the airport. He pulled out his portable screen and wrote:

Graz, Austria. September 3, 2013

Headline: Baruch raised by philosophy teacher.

In an interview today at the home of Dr. Dietmar Horstmann, WNN learned that Stefan Mostl, known as Baruch, was orphaned in 1985 at age 11 when both of his parents died in a car accident in Budapest, Hungary. He has no surviving family members. Dr. Horstmann and his wife legally adopted him in 1986. "I heard of his parents' tragedy through one of my colleagues. My wife had lost two children...they were stillborn. She so wanted children. When we first laid eyes on him, we knew he was a special young boy," recounted Dr. Horstmann. He added that Baruch was a "young lad with extraordinary learning capabilities" who possessed a "human sensitivity he had never seen in a youngster."

Dr. Horstmann lost his wife in 1999, the last time he claims to have had contact with Baruch. "He always struggled with himself and embraced others," continued Horstmann. Asked why they had such little contact, Horstmann stated that Baruch "asked permission" to go out into the world alone and discover its wonder unbiased. He apparently explained to Horstmann that he might never return, saying he "had certain things to be accomplished."

Baruch did call his foster family frequently and Dr. Horstmann *wept when faced with the thought of Baruch being gone forever. "God has angels. Baruch is one of them," he said. Horstmann, sixty-six years of age, serves as an honorary member of the Graz University philosophy department. To date, no missing persons report has been issued for Baruch.*

Looking uncomfortable and tired, Greg sat in one of the hard, plastic chairs at departure gate four of the drab Graz airport terminal. His eyes scanned the words that filled his screen, while his mind replayed the Horstmann interview in stereo sound. Dr. Horstmann's voice echoed in his head. "Stefan finds unconventional ways...The paper is patient... You must not underestimate him."

Closing his eyes and stretching his neck to one side, he typed *Certain truths are so clear, they become demons in an untrue world.* He quickly deleted the words and e-mailed Maggie and Scott his report before boarding the plane.

♦ ♦ ♦ ♦ ♦

Jim Anderson followed Haig Abku, the leader of Jim's precious Oiltron Industries, into the auditorium-like conference room of AZI-Group headquarters in Baku. The hundreds of luxurious, high-backed seats that had been filled by the most influential people in the world, those invisible faces that mystically steer the lives of ordinary citizens, were empty. The shareholders had moved on to their next meeting.

Haig and Jim stood alone in the corner where, last week, the chubby BNG executive had looked down at the rowdy protesters gathered outside this retro-concrete building. But through the darkness of night from the eighth floor, Jim and Haig only caught a glimpse of a single street peddler selling newspapers. It was quiet.

Moving his hands like an artist framing a vase, Jim looked north towards the glimmering, starlike lights of oil rigs ringing in the distance. "Just think. That's what makes the world go around. The Middle East. Norway. Texas. Here. Without oil, this planet would crumble."

"Come on, Jim. If it wasn't oil, we'd just build our business around some other energy source," Haig replied with certainty.

"But oil requires only that you land on it. Look at an energy source based, for instance, on magnetic force. It could be produced anywhere. Oil is the civilized world's way of subsidizing countries that would otherwise be nothing more than twenty-first century hunters and gatherers."

"And for our oil, you give us dollars. We give you fuel and you give us dirty paper," Haig said, laughing.

"You're right. But don't you find it interesting that oil defines the entire geopolitical structure of our world? The Azeris want us here to build infrastrucure. The U.S. government wants us here to develop a beachhead for capitalism. How? Why? It's all about oil. Take away the oil from this city and you'd hear nothing but a giant sucking vacuum. It's fucking incredible."

"We, the Azerbaijani people, would still be here," Haig said tersely.

Before Jim could respond, a thunderous noise vibrated through the conference room, physically shaking the ground below and sending the street peddler running for cover. An orange fireball spread high over the Caspian Sea, glowing like molten lava. Boom! Boom! A series of short explosions followed.

Haig braced himself on Jim Anderson's shoulder and dropped his head. "That's our rig."

CHAPTER 14

SCOTT MCNALLY CLICKED THE WORLDNET ICON ON HIS OFFICE screen. It was 8:00 AM in Chicago and, as was the custom, he accessed his personal report first thing. He loved the novelty of the Instant-Call satellite program that allowed him to select relevant world issues and have them downloaded to his screen. WorldNet even provided real-time translations of foreign reports. The fact that Mike McMillan's satellite division had perfected this technology didn't seem to bother Scott.

The fire at the Oiltron facility in Baku dominated the news. A barrage of channels flashed across the screen. Reports from Moscow, Kobe, São Paulo, and a dozen other main markets piped an orchestrated reportage, showing the blaze, an interview with Jim Anderson, and then a background on the importance of Oiltron to the AZI-Group.

"I'd say that masterpiece could only be the work of Jim," Sharon noted. "He's a real pro."

"Yeah, Jimbo knows how to weave a story."

"Scott, you may want to wash your hands before you ruin your white shirt," Sharon suggested, noticing his blackened fingertips that had plainly been through the morning papers.

Inspecting the deep black stains, he chuckled. "It must be the lack of sleep. Jim called me at least a dozen times last night."

Scott moved to the wet bar and, rinsing his hands, asked, "Didn't the old print stick to the paper, not your damn hands? And weren't we supposed to be a paperless society by now anyway?" he joked, grabbing a paper towel.

He dried each finger one by one. "Sure—a paperless society, electric cars—I've heard enough bullshit in my life to fertilize the state of Iowa!"

Sharon smiled and picked up Scott's thought.

"When my grandfather was in school, they told him we'd be totally metric by the 1980s. Thirty years later and I bet you can't tell me how many centimeters that 40-inch screen is."

"Yeah, you're right," Scott admitted.

Sharon looked down at the newspaper on her lap.

"OK, Scott. Quiz: How many households have broadbrand technology?"

He looked at the four white walls as if to ask 'Why ask *me* this question?'

"I have no clue!" Ignoring her question and clinging to his previous thought, Scott snapped his fingers. "Here's the greatest lie, Sharon. Think about the poor schmuck working as a mechanic for the airlines. He, his father, maybe even his grandfather—they were all told how this information age would make them more powerful. What a fucking joke! They sit in their homes with their family, watch TV every night, and have no clue who controls the information age. It's really pathetic."

Scott was all worked up. "It's like there's this ill-prepared, disinterested mass of people. We sit up here in our virtual castle with all the information and look down on the peasants tilling the fields. The gap will always be there, Sharon."

Scott seemed proud of this intellectual endeavor.

In her Atlanta, inner-city dialect reserved for special

moments, Sharon sang like a Baptist preacher, "Boy, I think you need a girlfriend!"

Scott couldn't help but grin. "No, I'm serious!" he insisted and went on. "There is no information age. Don't you get it? It's a false messiah; a wolf dressed up as a sheep. That's why the economy's been sagging since 2010! The promises have worn thin. The airline mechanic says 'Great, we have all this technology and information' then he goes home, cracks a beer, and watches a modern version of *I Love Lucy*."

Scott was on a roll and Sharon knew the signs; namely, when he paced back and forth while waving his hands, occasionally putting them behind his head as if he were being shaken down by the police.

"Technology. Information. As if we were the first generation affected by a new technology."

"We may be the first era to bathe so deeply in our progress," Sharon proposed.

"So who really controls the power of the information age?" Scott asked, and without allowing Sharon to conjecture, he hurried to his conclusion: "The government, the virtual corporations, and us. We're the power bases. But we've been promising a better life for twenty years. The public doesn't see a better life, Sharon. They see more work, more pressure, more..." he paused, "bullshit!"

Leaving her home dialect and moving back to her corporate-speak, Sharon persisted, "Which explains Baruch's popularity, Scott. You just summed up in your vernacular what he's been saying for years."

"Yeah, yeah, Sharon, I know. But a lot of people have been saying what he says!"

"The people believe Baruch. That's the difference."

Scott either ignored or didn't grasp the double meaning of

Sharon's last remark. He sat down in his chair and spoke at the ceiling: "Yes, now we have Baruch. Isn't that just swell."

He turned back towards Sharon.

"I mean, the peasants were hard at work tilling the field until this schmuck convinced 'em that they were being duped. In the old days, the king would've just killed the bastard."

A tingle ran through Sharon's body as she digested that metaphor.

Scott continued, "Baruch tells the peasants that we're the ones driving the shaft! What about the government? Or, even worse, the goddammed banks?"

"You know, Scott, it's not only the 'peasants' that are listening to Baruch. So are intellectuals, white-collar business folk—you name it. The government? People are too distracted trying to make ends meet. And come on—the bank conspiracy was valid last century. Heck Scott, now we own the banks!"

"So, Ms. Know-It-All, if they're so distracted, why do they listen to Baruch?"

"In our poor community in Atlanta, the feds always had a social program du jour. We would hear about these programs—programs that never made it to our school. The ones that did get past the school board's sticky fingers never worked. Then one day when I was twelve years old, Latricia Williams, the famous jazz singer, came to our school and talked to us about hope. Man, you've never seen so many young girls walking on air. You see, Scott, the government never understood that we need money much less than we need hope. And Baruch gives people hope. You can *see and experience* what he talks about. He talks to our common sense."

"You're exactly right, Sharon. But this guy isn't a *jazz* singer. He gets people to do drastic things—like turn off our fucking network. He's more dangerous than you think!"

"I bet if you sat down and had dinner with Baruch, you'd think he's a nice guy."

"Good idea. Tell me where I can send the fucking invitation."

Sharon laughed at her undone boss, and said, "I've got a meeting with a polling company. Here's something Greg got from that Schleier guy in Germany. Baruch wrote it for a UN speech he gave in 2010. I thought you might find it interesting."

Heading for the door Sharon added, "Oh yeah, Greg called and was asking a lot of questions about that Kirov drug deal back in 2008. Do you remember that case?"

"Sure do," Scott responded tersely.

"Greg said there's some new information—that some of the AZI's..."

Scott stepped on Sharon's words: "Listen real good. That's over. Finito. Tell Greg to find Baruch and keep his big nose out of Baku. Maggie's on Baku!"

"Don't get your blood pressure up, Scott. I'm just relaying a conversation." Sharon flipped her hand and whispered, "You're a treat today."

Scott ignored Sharon as he studied the pages she had left on his desk. He skipped to the highlighted paragraph of Baruch's speech:

In Uncle Tom's cabin we no longer find only the repressed black man, spiritless and beaten down to the point of believing that his white master symbolizes his greatest hope. To the contrary, oppression has now seduced all of mankind into believing that the greatest hope lies in their own Uncle Tom—the virtual corporation.

Shaking his head in disgust, Scott caught the silent, life-size picture of Amy Laurance on the wall screen with Baruch's photo superimposed in the upper right-hand corner.

"Uncle Tom! No wonder Sharon likes this guy," Scott said, throwing the papers into the garbage can next to his desk.

CHAPTER 15

THE WALL-SIZED SCREEN OF WNN'S CONFERENCE ROOM WAS OFF. Maggie couldn't remember the last time she didn't see news images flashing against the blue backdrop. As a rule, Scott liked large groups and lots of distractions, like having something on that screen.

Being around Scott and having silence is not an encouraging sign, she thought to herself. She recalled the time before his third divorce two years ago. His wife had proposed marriage counseling and the counselor had suggested some 'quiet time' together. So off they had flown to St. Thomas—no satellite phone, no computer, no files. After three days, Scott called off the vacation and their marriage.

Maggie thought the government should make everyone take a test *before* marriage. "You've got to take a test to get a drivers license and shoot a gun!" was her credo.

"A dollar for your thoughts?" Greg asked boyishly, sitting down next to his college classmate.

"You're back!" Maggie said, pleasantly surprised.

"Yep, just got off the plane—I'm feeling pretty special." Greg ran a hand through his flattened hair and then shoved a stick of gum in his mouth.

"Maggie, one day I'm going to find that little man hiding in the airplanes—the one who shits in your mouth."

Maggie grimaced. "That's really gross, Greg!"

"Not half as gross as my mouth tastes. So anyway, changing topics—what were you smiling about when I interrupted?"

"Reminiscing about Scott and Cindy. About their 'quiet time' in St. Thomas."

They both laughed, catching the attention of the rest of the table.

"Just an inside joke," Maggie said.

Walter Butwin raised his eyebrows as if to ask ' Please, do tell!' And Maggie was prepared to do just that when Scott and Sharon entered the conference room, bringing with them a stern silence.

Scott studied the group with a serious gaze. "It's game time. So, what's the scoop, Walter?" he asked.

"In business, the World Stock Index hit 24,000 for the first time since June, 2011. Utilities are up. Oil prices are up. Tech stocks are still flat. AZI-Group slipped three," Walter responded in a rehearsed manner.

Hearing the date June 2011 sent Scott's thoughts drifting to a recent feature article by Walter Butwin. Although the article never mentioned it, the stock prices could, using Sharon's method, be directly charted alongside the Baruch craze. When Baruch's story—"The Prophet and His New Vision"— hit back in 2011, WNN's viewer ratings and stock prices soared. But as Baruch's fame increased and people began reading his book, virtuals came under increasing scrutiny and viewer ratings fell. While Sharon reminded Scott that her own method could be a result of retroactive logic, Scott was convinced otherwise.

In his book, Baruch had noted that power was not a bad thing, but it was finite. The base of power, he insisted, was in the "compounded spiritual strength of the populace." He believed that the virtuals were systematically secularizing the world in order to fragment spirituality, thus fragmenting the universal balance of power in their favor. Further, Baruch detailed in his writing how the virtuals had "used the global economy and global competition to disguise their master plan—the spiritual neutering of the populace."

Scott perceived Baruch's attacks as a systematic attempt to fragment the AZI-Group's empire. Scott noted in particular Baruch's comment about the media profession:

"The media understands quite well the idea of freedom. They simply wish to keep it all to themselves."

Scott contemplated this 'Baruchism', looking at his stumpy editor, Walter, whose article had ignored Baruch's influence and failed to mention that the recent attacks on Baruch by the media had only increased Baruch's following. Omitted as well was the copy of the article Sharon had passed around the office comparing virtual corporations to poker players who held all the chips.

Scott had received unambiguous orders from the top: "Kill all Baruch stories."

"When are they sending the memo that says 'Kill Baruch!'? " he pondered.

Walter continued his summation of the day's events: "European stocks are still in the dumpster. Hong Kong suspended trading for the second time this week. I guess the Chinese are having another bad century!"

Scott loosened his iron jaw and burst into laughter.

"The Chinese are having another bad century!" he chuckled. "That's funny!"

Scott threw in a topper, "Hell, the Dark Ages only lasted five hundred years. China should be back on track by... oh... the twenty-fifth century."

"And our pension fund invested billions over there," Greg added.

"That's because we're stupid, Greg," Scott said. "We blew it the minute we let those gooks think that we needed their billion farmers to buy our hamburgers. Did you guys ever hear what happened when we tried that billboard campaign for WNN?"

Sharon had heard this story at least a dozen times.

"They ripped them down and used them to build houses," she said, rolling her eyes.

Scott was laughing in disgust. "They're building shacks with billboards! And you're going to tell me we need them? I'm sorry, Walter, go ahead with the *real* news."

"The big story is the Palestinian bombing in Jerusalem. I mean, the Israelis give them a third of the city and now they're bombing two years later. Terrorism used to be just a sport. Hell, now they're actually getting serious about it."

This didn't get a laugh.

"Boy, tough crowd." He continued, "Oh yeah, we picked up the ceremony of Turkey becoming the twentieth full member of the EU."

Walter reviewed his notes, looked up and concluded: "Besides the reruns, that's it, boss. What do you have?"

Scott looked as though he knew what he wanted to say but not how to say it.

"As you all know the Baku oil facility is in flames. The inside scoop is that it looks like sabotage. Anyway, Maggie, I need you there tomorrow. Monique's arranging your trip as we speak. I'll brief you separately."

He stood up, walked over to the empty blue wall and pointed.

"We know nothing of substance about Baruch."

He wandered toward the end of the table.

"Greg, is that all you could turn up in Austria? I mean, it's nice stuff for a high school yearbook, but it doesn't help us find this guy."

Greg smiled sweetly. "How did you know I wrote for the high school yearbook, Scott? Seriously though, we did make some progress. My plane just got in an hour ago. Give me until noon and I'll have a report on your desk. Deal?"

Scott nodded at his star reporter. "Let's get back to work."

Everyone filed out except Maggie.

CHAPTER 16

"I HAVE TO LEAVE FOR A FEW MINUTES. I'VE GOT A PHONE CONFERENCE at 11:30."

Scott clicked the icons on the multimedia unit several times before the screen displayed *Oiltron Industries: Baku broadband video site. Click here to begin.*

"OK, Maggie. Watch this video for a little background. I'll be back in ten."

Maggie looked perplexed. Oiltron in Baku had a crisis and she was a senior reporter. But why send her to Azerbaijan? She hadn't been on assignment in the area known as the European Balkans since the oil rich countries of Uzbekistan, Turkmenistan, and Azerbaijan had declared total independence several years ago. Her report had focused on the titanic struggle between Iran, Turkey, and Russia to dominate the flow of oil in the region. While most political tacticians decided who would influence whom, Oiltron moved in on the black gold.

For the past five years, Said Aman, an émigré from Egypt, had been the expert on 'STAN', the internal code for this region where almost everything ended in 'stan'. Scott liked to poke fun at 'Iranstan', 'Armeniastan', 'Jim Anderstan' and the likes.

Maggie clicked 'Begin here', an icon of a deep-sea oil rig.

"Nice touch," she said out loud.

"Welcome to Baku, Azerbaijan, the headquarters of Oiltron

Industries, the world's largest refiner of crude oil. Please sit back and relax while we inform you about the latest developments of Oiltron, part of the world's premier Virtual Company, The Azi Group."

The moderator was a handsome man in his mid-forties. He looked Indian, but his impeccable Oxford English told Maggie that he had definitely been educated in England.

The video showed a gigantic Oiltron trade show booth featuring a twenty-foot model of an oil rig that looked exactly like a champagne cork, an excellent symbol for the explosive nature of what lay beneath. Maggie remembered as a child hearing about Oiltron Chemicals. Like so many companies at the dawn of the politically correct movement, the word 'industries' was substituted for 'chemicals'. The same damn pollutants, rendered harmless by a nondescript noun, Maggie thought in disgust.

The video jumped to oil platforms cast off the golden coast of Baku in the Caspian Sea.

The video moderator continued:

"In the past ten years, Baku has produced more oil than North America and the North Sea combined. The Baku/Turkish pipeline and the Caspian region supply over thirty percent of America's oil and account for eighteen percent of the world's production."

The refined presenter went on to describe the movement of the pipeline in 2005 following the peace accord between Turkey, Armenia, and Azerbaijan, stressing the importance of Baku as a banking center in the Transcaucasian region.

A cultural expose then featured the architectural jewels of Baku. Maggie looked with cautious admiration at the Synykh-Kala, Azerbaijan's oldest and largest minaret, as a 'crier' shouted Islamic prayers from the haughty tower of the stone fortress. The AZI-Group headquarters could be seen as the camera panned the commercial landscape of the downtown district, whose white buildings towered over a pitifully poor populace. She remembered a quote from Baruch: "As intelligence and wealth become more prolific, so do poverty and ignorance."

Omitted from the story of Baku was the interesting fact that this capital city served as a temporary home for a twice-exiled Josef Stalin; that Baku was the base for the Bolsheviks' covert operations leading up to the October Revolution; and that the most feared man of the post-Lenin era—secret police chief Lavrenty Beria—used Baku as his base. In one of histories many evil twists, the freedom that Baku offered Stalin, Beria, and the Reds, would be taken away by those very same people.

Today's battle, however, continued to be fought over the flow of oil out of the Caspian Sea. America's pious behavior the century before—boycotting any business deals remotely connected with Iran—had allowed the French and Middle Easterners to dominate the Caspian oil jackpot. President Johnson, now in his second term, could thank Jim Anderson for asserting American dominance in the region via the purchase of Oiltron Industries. The independent commentator Charley Hardeway first posed the question: Is Jim Anderson the leader of the New World Order?

◆ ◆ ◆ ◆ ◆

Waiting for Scott, Maggie reached into her briefcase and continued reading a collection of Baruch's speeches that she had received from Charley over a coffee at the West Egg Diner.

The Planet's Newest Species: University of Graz, September 2011.

All species have gone through a long series of changes, adaptations, and, in some cases, failures. Certain species have become so prolific that they incapacitate another competing group. We have seen our own species expedite the extinction of certain birds, mammals, and the like—species which may, or may not have continued to flourish without human encroachment.

But I would like to infer a much different point. Nature has one universal law: the law of self-preservation. All species fight to the last molecule of life to defend this law. However, humans have created a species whose goal is to compete with itself—a very strange voluntary action. Why would we create machines that destroy the ability of average humans to work? Do the new positions created by technology bear out any higher nobility than, say, farming? Is there anything self-evident about technological efficiency? Where does one draw the line between efficiency and self-annihilation?

Maggie browsed to one of Charley's handwritten notes: "Do we all buy the premise that humans must necessarily be displaced by technology? Is technological progress an irrefutable law of nature?"

Before Maggie could pursue Charley's questions, Scott, carrying a cup of steamy, freshly-brewed coffee in each hand, burst into the room: "OK, Maggie, here's what's going on in Baku."

CHAPTER 17

THE TITLE *APOCRYPHA TRUTH* SEEMED TO INVITE PERSECUTION.

Although everyday churchgoers didn't give much weight to the fourteen writings and 250 pages that constituted an extension of the bible known as the Apocrypha, most clergy felt that the title *Apocrypha Truth* mocked the Church, a quasi act of war. The Catholic Church had taken exactly this position. They claimed Baruch knew his writings constituted heresy and that he chose to throw gas on the fire by adding the word 'Truth'.

Baruch responded by saying he meant that the truth lay outside of what was generally accepted to be true. Therefore, he reasoned, this could not be heresy.

The war against Baruch had many fronts. The pope publicly chided Baruch for using the media as an artificial enemy, a way to rally the masses. The Ecumenical Society issued an edict to refer to Baruch as *Stefan Mostl* in all its official commentaries. They didn't want to create any association between the ancient Baruch—secretary of Jeremiah and descendant of Hilkiah—and the modern-day 'impostor'.

This tactic backfired because no one outside of the Church elite knew who Stefan Mostl was. They resolved this touchy issue by adding 'the man who calls himself Baruch' alongside all Stefan Mostl references.

Despite this current crisis, the religious institutions of the

Western world, the seemingly unstoppable organizations that had defined spirituality for over two thousand years, had survived the secular onslaught of irreverent twentieth century pop culture. This spiritual Darwinism came at no small cost. Churches, unable to hold the line of traditional values because the congregations no longer valued those traditions, began creating nondenominational material. This made religion more catholic with a small 'c'—what Baruch called 'the first last step':

Diluting religion to a non-confrontational amoebic structure failed. We can never beat the media in its battle. They choose the when, the where, and the how. And it wins every time, without exception. And do we learn? Do we take the battle to the deepest part of the human soul? No. We merge together into behemoth structures. We mimic the massive corporations we denounce. Like a dancer with the teacher, religion follows every step that the virtuals make, going so far as to make entertainment the focus and God peripheral.

The Church's response wasn't unique. Educational systems dealt with media competition by reasoning 'if we can't get kids' attention, we'll change the way we teach them'. Baruch compared this reasoning with giving a child chocolate for breakfast, because it won't eat bread.

"Small truths consist of replicas of larger truths and vice versa."

Baruch based this saying on the geometric principle of fractals—any object contains infinitesimal replicas of that image. In other words, Baruch argued:

"If the smaller truth is feeding a child bread, the larger truth is to feed that same child a sound education and healthy spirituality."

Baruch's direct attacks on the media and virtuals made very clear why he was big business' worst nightmare. The government, while not being fond of Baruch, saw him more as a blessing in disguise—a dagger in the side of the seemingly unrelenting growth of the virtual corporations. But something much different threatened the staggering establishment called religion.

The monumental dilemma for the Church was that Baruch was himself a scholarly Christian, albeit a bit unorthodox. His mastery of reason and strength of conviction paralyzed attempts to wish him away. But his selfless sense of cause, an intangible windfall once known as character, made the sage Austrian unassailable. At the UN Conference on Spirituality two years ago, Bishop DuPree of Paris had thrown some difficult questions at Baruch.

"You have written that Christianity causes blindness, yet you wish to be considered a Christian."

"Bishop Dupree, let us not mistake Christianity for Christ. What is taught today does indeed cause blindness. Is there a difference between what certain churches teach today and what drove our Western world into five hundred years of intellectual bankruptcy? Christ taught enlightenment, not censorship. My God removes your blinders and lets the horses run onto freer pastures. Your Christianity dictates a path. Christ's enlightenment opened endless paths."

The bishop kept trying to pin Baruch into bashing his particular church, any church. But Baruch never fell for this trap. He spoke affectionately when asked about different faiths: Catholic, Protestant, Jewish, or any other.

"Your Honorable Bishop, the faithful know that I aim to redirect a stray institution, not ruin an excellent one."

However, when it came to other subjects, Baruch was less kind.

"Are you a New Age Christian?" the bishop asked.

"New Age philosophers are spiritual piranhas who feed off the ills of society without the common courtesy of chewing them to the bone. They offer topical solutions that don't work, will never work."

The bishop closed with this onslaught:

"In the introduction to your book you state: 'I find it disturbing that the churches have turned against me. I only challenge those forces that have neutered religion and made the media, the government, and corporations the almighty. Is this my great sin?' You state clearly that religion has been neutered! What kind of enlightened words are those? Is this your revelation?"

Slightly irritated, Baruch had shot back:

"Bishop DuPree, I stand by what I say. And about your question, yes, religion has been neutered. And, yes, my book is a twenty-first century revelation—it's the truth."

With more and more Generation Xers and post-Xers gravitating towards Baruch, one thing was certain: the ecumenical fight against Baruch, whatever it was they were fighting for, was most important. Baruch's 'sin', the best-selling philosophical gem *Apocrypha Truth*, had caused more media hysteria than anything current generations had seen.

The president of the Ecumenical Society duly noted the biggest problem: "We must decide whether he constitutes our worst enemy or greatest hope."

♦ ♦ ♦ ♦ ♦

"Let's see: the church, big business, and the media. You've pissed most everyone off, my friend. The press calls you the king of chaos." The male voice rang from the dark foyer through the large, open room that had the rustic decor of a mountain lodge. The unfinished wood floors and high ceiling gave the words an ominous ring.

Baruch sat in a wide leather recliner near a stacked-stone

fireplace. His thick, short black hair, dark skin and deep brown eyes glowed, the crackling fire casting dancing shadows on his handsome face. His eyes were magnificent, a marble-textured rich brown surrounded by a white more pure than untouched snow. He appeared to have been deep in thought when his visitor arrived.

"How are you?" Baruch asked in a kind tone. "You should know that I like a little chaos now and then..."

CHAPTER 18

MAGGIE'S LOFT APARTMENT ON CHICAGO'S EXCLUSIVE NORTH SIDE used to be the warehouse for Byron Meat Packing in the 1980s. After laying waste for two decades, a commercial builder had converted the brick warehouse to one hundred and five luxurious one-room condos. The building owner, fed up with collecting rent, took advantage of a loophole in the city's eviction laws and forced the tenants out by 'altering the function of the residence.' This age-old tactic did offer the renters a disingenuous olive branch: pay a half-a-million dollars or leave! Maggie, feeling attached to the quite North Side neighborhood, accessed the trust left by her parents and bought. For the handful of tenants who could afford to buy, it ended up being a good investment.

The building was brick inside and out, which, in Maggie's case, contrasted nicely with her modern furniture. She was snuggled up in the corner of the couch with her legs and body twisted in an almost yoga like position. Her right arm hung lazily along her angled body, her left elbow perched on her knee, with her hand forming a cup in which her chin could rest.

She reached for her glass teacup, studying Charley Hardeway's newsletter *From the Heart*. Her eyes warmed at the curly black hair, thick-framed glasses and cynical smile of her former boss who had quit World News Network because articles critical of the Oiltron organization had not been printed.

She heard Charley's heavy New York accent as she read:

Looking for the twenty-second century, by Charles Hardeway.

And with the second stroke of a clock in Times Square, God created Utopia. Well, I wished I'd studied Greek in school, then I would have known that Sir Thomas More's "Utopia" in English means "not a place". But no one told me that on December 31st, 1999 at 11:59 PM. Oh, how I waited for that glory of a new time—a time without war and poverty. Drinking chilled Moet Champagne with my college buddies, we made our prognoses: this century would be different than all the rest. Our generation would, we knew, not fall prey to the combined human weaknesses of our ancestors.

Sue me if I'm wrong, but isn't the twenty-first century supposed to be the age of knowledge and progress—where access to information cures poverty and technology heals the sick? Governments are supposed to get along. People travel without passports from Kiev to Gibraltar; from Santiago to Seattle. Employers care for, and about, their employees, those very employees who work in clean, automated work environments. To quote an old rock 'n roll band, we're supposed to be a bunch of 'shiny, happy people'.

Give me an optical exam if I'm seeing poorly, but has anyone else noticed that not many people are shiny and happy? Like the soldier ants laboring for the queen, thousands of employees toil for their virtual corporations every day, building little anthills for that greater goal. When will we stop and ask, "Hey, Ms. Queen Ant, why in the hell are we building this hill?"

The last thirteen years have convinced me of one thing: we humans were much smarter without technology. Take my ninety-year-old grandfather. Never used a computer, doesn't have a college degree, and doesn't have much money. He wasn't sent to a private school as a 'gifted' child and programmed to make other students look stupid, like a boxer trained to decimate his opponent. No, he wasn't a young, sassy, prodigy.

His only claim to fame is that he makes the most beautiful wooden furniture on the face of this planet. Last week he took a block a wood, spun it on his lathe and cut out a pineapple that looked good enough to eat. Throughout the years 'experts' told him that his little business wouldn't survive the 'wave of technology.' But he didn't listen to gurus and futurists telling him to re-engineer or 'right-size' or, as we say today, 'go virtual'.

My grandfather thinks for himself. He doesn't go to the store and buy 'future in a box'. He sticks to his guns and makes things of beauty because he has pride. He doesn't understand our modern language that spits out nonsense like 'value proposition' and 'consumer efficiency gauge'. My grandfather never had to be told to 'add value' to anything he ever did.

"Offer me a quick nickel or a slow dime—I'll take the dime every time," is what he always told me.

The great irony of our modern era lies in our regression. Take art, for example. My grandfather teaches kids at a local high school how to work with their hands. "Those kids can do wonders on that software program—they just can't make the real thing," he observes.

Grandpa doesn't understand that the 'real thing' isn't a modern concept. He comes from an era that doesn't comprehend how youth could be driven to computers, because they have no diversions outside of movies, shopping malls and fast food—what he calls weapons of mass distraction. He and I were watching the news the other night when he asked me, "Charley, how can kids be so depressed about the only life that God has given them?"

I started to say that things have changed when he stopped me short. "I've never met a thing," he said. "Remember that people change, not things."

Which brings me to Baruch. If I were he, I'd look for another century, one where technology doesn't serve people, but where people serve people. When I saw Baruch speak in Chicago, his words reminded me of my grandfather:

"Think about the world around us. Think about the towns and cities we grew up in. Does it look that much different to you? Have things changed? Ask me and I say we have changed. I think that sometimes we forget."

Signing off,
Charley

Maggie grinned and shook her head. She finally understood the root of Charley's relentless pride—his grandfather. He was such a good editor and his trademark 'signing off' had left a legacy in the editorial world. To think that he got fired for writing a feature report titled "Descartes' Ghost". In it, he outlined how the top investors were calling the shots behind the scenes of the world's seven largest virtual corporations, hinting that these men were the 'ghosts' in the machine. The article went on to report the influence of Jerry Bates and Jim Anderson on the financial markets. Then came a hard-hitting attack on the BNG Bank scandal in Baku, accusing BNG of facilitating the Kirov drug cartel.

In the end, the AZI-Group 'persuaded' WNN that Charley's news could provoke a war with the media group of Bates/McMillan, the World Broadcasting Group. Scott McNally towed the party line and refused to run the story.

"There's no room for heroes in my organization," were Scott's words.

"As editor, I have the authority to decide what runs and what doesn't," Charley had argued.

"Charley, you're obviously confusing authority with accountability. We use the concept of authority in order to extract accountability from people less smart than you. If anyone should know the difference, it should be you and your endless sarcasm."

Charley walked. Getting a parting shot by posting his resignation on WNN's web site, he noted that from now on he would take his authority from a much higher source. Charley set up shop in his home and went to war against the virtual corporations. When Maggie spoke to Charley in August at a creative writing seminar in LA, he told her: "I thought I was a lone warrior. Then Baruch arrived."

CHAPTER 19

THE FLIGHT THROUGH MOSCOW HAD GONE SANS INCIDENT. THE sharply-dressed Dutchman arrived at 4:30 local time on September 5, toting a designer garment bag. He stepped onto the white, poured terrazzo floor in the lobby and was stopped by an Oiltron security guard.

"Who are you here to see?" the old man asked in the local tongue.

"I have an appointment with Mr. Abku," Marco answered in Russian.

Inside Oiltron's cement palace, an exact replica of the AZI-Group's headquarters only a couple blocks away, vivid images of his days with Interpol scrolled through Marco's mind.

Only one block from this very building, Interpol had busted the Kirov's cocaine clearinghouse five years ago. The Kirov's 'product', an overused term from the twentieth century that gave a nice, generic name to everything, had been destined mainly for the Russian market but, to the dismay of regional drug lords, several shipments were diverted to Western Europe. Controlling distribution was an age-old problem. Famous brands of clothing, perfume, electronics, and sporting goods were frequently moved around the globe via third and fourth tier trading channels to the chagrin of producers. Cocaine dealers, however, couldn't take their beef to a court of law. Instead, there had been gangland justice to the tune of eight murders on one busy Amsterdam evening. Several other murders—including those in New York and Los Angeles—were subsequently linked to this Baku-diversion. The Kirovs had sent a very strong message: diversion would not be tolerated.

Marco had spent weeks working on the financial aspect of the Baku-Amsterdam connection of the case. Both the Baku police and Interpol suspected a gang member had penetrated a banking group in Baku in order to facilitate the transfer of drugs funds. However, nothing came out of Marco's investigation. More successful were the connections he made with several powerful local businessmen and politicians, not to mention the opportunity of meeting Jim Anderson and Mike McMillan.

Marco liked to fly in high social circles and one of his acquaintances who carried a big stick was Haig Abku, the former mayor of Baku and current President of Oiltron Industries, the largest oil refinery in Azerbaijan since the buyout of Conto two years ago.

Foreign investments in the Caspian oil belt, which pre-dated the Great War, were nothing new to the citizens of Baku. Nationalized shortly after the communist victory, the Caspian oil reserves were slowly divested in the 1990s. Working for Jim Anderson, Haig Abku had been instrumental in lobbying the Azerbaijani government to privatize the offshore oil operations in 2008. He upset many locals who would have preferred that a Turkish, Arab or French group control the fields. But Haig, now considered next-in-line to Jim Anderson, sold out his local friends: he understood what it meant to be aligned with the most powerful man in the world.

♦ ♦ ♦ ♦ ♦

Haig Abku's office was old, as was most everything in the commercial district of Baku. The walls were white concrete block. A series of three railroad paintings—most likely bought as a set at a flea market—tried to cover the long wall behind the small writer's desk that rested on sisal mat. Marco sat across from Haig Abku and, despite his chair resting at least six inches lower than that of the Oiltron President, towered over the Azeri.

"How can I help you, Mr. Van Wels?" he asked.

"It's been a long time."

"Yes, it has," Haig concurred.

"I've been hired by WNN to investigate Baruch. I'm working directly for Mr. McNally and I report directly to Mr. McNally. Understood?"

"Yes, Mr. Van Wels. This conversation stays in this room."

Haig had a devious smile as he continued: "I was curious when I heard you may be coming. I asked myself 'Why *did* WNN hire someone of your caliber to investigate this gentleman, this Baruch?'"

"Not to be rude, Mr. Abku, but you know I never ask why. They're paying me to find Baruch. End of story."

Marco clenched his lips together and raised his eyebrows as if to ask 'any questions?' He continued: "I've been studying our friend Baruch *officially* for over six months. But I first noticed him two years ago when he organized the week-long boycott of all the broadcast media. Remember? Over two million of his 'converts' boycotted your parent company's TV, newspaper, and radio for over a month."

"He said they were 'cleansing themselves'," Haig finished the thought in disgust.

Finding something amusing in what he had just said, Haig laughed. "That was impressive. Let's face it, getting an American to turn off the TV is probably tougher than parting the Red Sea."

Haig and Marco both chuckled, releasing a bit of the tension in the room. *Mayor* Haig Abku had welcomed Marco as an Interpol specialist mediating drug wars. As President of Oiltron, he was tolerating Marco's presence.

"Anyway, Mr. Abku, there are some things that simply don't make sense. I was hoping you could help me."

"Of course, Mr. Van Wels."

"Well, there were several memos dating back two, or in some cases three years, that WNN received from Oiltron—some directly from you—which requested that all reports concerning Baruch be handled only by certain people at WNN. Why would an Oil division be telling WNN who should write reports on Baruch?"

Haig Abku's expression remained relaxed. His eyes rolled back, suggesting he was either searching his memory or searching for a good answer.

"Mr. Van Wels, I know you understand the politics inside all corporations. Let's face it, today we deal with more politics than the goddamm United Nations."

"That's why they call the virtual corporations the GN, 'ghost nations'."

"I'm not familiar with that expression, Mr. Van Wels."

"At Interpol we created the term 'ghost nation' to explain the elusive power of global corporations. Your company has the power and authority of a nation, but you can disappear like a ghost—totally escape accountability."

"Authority has many forms, Mr. Van Wels. The authority you just described to me sounds like every government, every religion I've ever run across. We simply innovated."

"Ghost nation, United Nations...it really doesn't matter to me, Mr. Abku... as long as I get paid. Anyway, about the WNN memos."

"If, hypothetically, the AZI-Group in Baku were to send a

directive to WNN in Chicago about how to handle a story, it *could* appear to the outside world that it was controlling the content of news. If, however, another organization were to send that directive, the trail would end, for example, here in my office. One can't forget that I'm expendable."

Marco looked unimpressed. "Makes sense. The classic fall guy." He paused.

"But why would the AZI-Group tell only certain people to handle the Baruch story?"

"It's politics, Mr. Van Wels. Like when you investigated the Kirov drug ring here in Baku in 2008. You told me you had information to bust the BNG Bank. Then, after your meeting with the AZI-Group, you show up and tell me the case is going nowhere. You head back to Amsterdam and the next thing I know you're working for the same company you were investigating. On some fat retainer, no doubt."

Marco sat in silence as Haig continued, "Mr. Van Wels, you may well be young, but I know for a fact you are not naive. I know why you and your Interpol buddies pulled off the BNG case, so please don't play innocent."

"Why did we pull off the case?" Marco asked, calling his bluff.

"Because you found out the Kirovs were part of Interpol. The big guns at Interpol just didn't think you'd ever figure it out! And that's not to mention that Jim Anderson and Bremmer, your former Interpol boss, sit collectively on over sixty boards."

Marco didn't move or change expressions. Haig continued.

"Getting back to WNN and Baruch. He's a phenomenon like we haven't seen in our generation or in centuries for that matter. Think how explosive the situation was with Ghandi... or Dr. King back in the 1960s. One false move by the government and those protests could have turned into war. Baruch has a much wider following than Dr. King ever had. Mr. Van Wels, WNN simply wanted a cohesive reportage from the best reporters to avoid any mistakes. You saw what happened to Ms. Laurance. Baruch said it best: 'You have to control the message.' We're following his advice."

Haig smiled and added, "I assume this is off the record."

"Hell, officially, I don't exist!"

Marco kicked back and puffed the cigarette he had rolled while listening to Haig Abku's explanation. Marco flashed a boyish grin that said 'Even if I told someone, it wouldn't matter.'

"Are you saying that Baruch is as *dangerous* to the establishment as Dr. King was?" Marco asked, sounding like a trial lawyer.

"Certain types never seem to make it to an old age. If Baruch were a stock, my advice would be not to sell it to widows or orphans."

Marco noticed the conviction of the words Haig Abku spoke, but remained calm and changed direction. "You have a point there. So—tell me your analysis of Baruch, Mr. Abku."

Haig sat forward and leaned his elbows on a stack of papers. "Young man, this short fat body has been around for sixty-two years. I've seen a lot of so-called spiritual leaders pass through life's grinder, including all the New Age guys who sold BS in a book. I've seen a Buddhist monk lead a million Christians and an American evangelist hit it big in Korea. But Baruch, he's different. One thing I do know," Haig Abku leaned back in his wooden chair, clipped off the end of a cigar and said slowly, "this guy is either a messiah or a future Academy Award winner."

"For me, he's good business," Marco laughed, breaking the serious tone. He added, "You're right about me backing off BNG. But it's equally curious that you started working for Jim Anderson two weeks after that investigation ended."

"I guess he liked my work, Mr. Van Wels."

Marco grinned. "The problem is that I have copies of a bank transaction, e-cash, that was paid to you *before* the investigation ended."

Haig laughed and put his arm around the young Marco as the two men stood up.

"May I call you Marco?"

"Sure."

"Marco, I think you and I have a lot more in common than you think. Now... you haven't brought up that bank transaction before. Nor have I brought up your about-face at Interpol. How about we pretend that we never had this particular discussion?"

"Haig, you've got yourself a deal. I look forward to working together."

Haig ushered Marco to the door and, pointing out the window at the smoke in the distance, smiled. "Sorry to have to cut this short. I have a fire to put out."

Marco thanked his old acquaintance for his time and took a cab to the airport. Pressing the phone against his ear, Haig spoke: "Jim, you shouldn't hire a pro if you want amateur work. Your friend is taking his job very seriously. You better let him know what's going on."

CHAPTER 20

MAGGIE, TRYING TO WAKE UP AFTER THE LONG OVERNIGHT FLIGHT, SAT in a dated Soviet army transport helicopter turned charter service on a remote landing pad at Baku's new International Airport. The mechanical beat of the helicopter engine combined with the violent noise of a jet flying overhead made it difficult for Maggie to even think. Looking at the untidy, bearded pilot wearing a turban, her first thought was: why am I here?

In fact, she was in Baku to report the oil rig explosion, period. Greg had asked her to take a few minutes to interview Haig Abku about the BNG/Kirov connection, but Scott told her to drop that idea. Charley must have really ruffled some feathers, she thought, partly shutting the side door, trying to reduce the deafening noise. Standing up, she moved from the back of the craft and nestled into the passenger seat next to the pilot.

"What are we waiting for?" she asked.

Before the pilot could answer, he pointed at the Dutchman jogging towards the landing pad. "I think that's the other passenger, miss."

Marco Van Wels ducked through the doorway and jumped on the dirty vinyl seat behind the casually dressed pilot.

The pilot spoke to the control tower and received clearance for takeoff. Fiddling with the dozens of primitive switches and dirty buttons, he said, "I've been flying jets lately, so give me a few minutes to get adjusted."

Maggie laughed loudly, until she realized he was serious.

"Don't worry. I flew over a thousand sorties in the 1980s as part of the Afghan resistance force. I was trained by Americans," he assured.

Marco spoke for the first time. "That was only, let's see, four decades ago."

"But I'm much smarter now," the witty pilot answered, as he slammed the door and secured the latch. He engaged the craft and ascended smoothly towards the black cloud in the distance.

♦ ♦ ♦ ♦ ♦

"Are you a reporter?" Maggie asked.

Writing in his notebook and minding his own business, Marco thought, Typical American. Always has to be talking.

"No, I'm an insurance investigator. Just going out to inspect the rig, if we can get close enough."

The pilot interrupted with his finger pointed down. "That's Nargen Island below. During the October Revolution, you know, 1917, the Bolsheviks took our political leaders, merchants, and bourgeoisie and murdered them."

Marco extended his body between Maggie and the pilot. "Do you know *why* they took them there?"

Maggie shrugged, but the pilot answered, "To kill them, of course."

"But they could have just killed them at a local barn," Marco insisted.

"They were worried about diseases from the corpses. So they took them to the Island, lined the prisoners up in front of trenches and shot them." Maggie seemed distraught, as Marco continued,

"After using the prisoners for target practice, they'd throw lime on top of them and shoot the next row of prisoners."

"My God!" were the only words Maggie could muster.

"Yeah, those Russians killed all our best people and then jailed us all for fifty years. You people in the West ask where our leaders are?" The pilot turned, looked at Maggie, and, emphatically, pointed straight down.

"There they are. In the soil below us."

"Biological destruction. Some people just don't quite make it," Marco said softly to the window.

Still picturing rows of men being gunned into trenches, Maggie pulled out her mini-camcorder and began to take photos. She looked at Nargen Island, but couldn't bring herself to film that which, in the last minute, had transmuted from a distant island to a vast killing field. Instead, she scanned the barren northern shore of the Caspian Sea and the tundra that lay in the distance. The lens progressed north of Baku, making its way to the rigs. She turned her attention from the right side of the helicopter, which provided a southeasterly view, and aimed the camera behind the head of the pilot to film more towards the north.

Suddenly, she saw nothing. Marco's hand blocked the lens.

"I'm a bit camera shy," he said politely with a big grin.

Maggie pointed the camera away. "Oops! Sorry about that!"

"No problem," Marco answered in a very soft voice, his eyes fixed on Maggie's burgundy leather carrying-bag. The tag, complete with four-color graphics and a corporate logo, a wing-spread eagle perched atop a pyramid, was meant to assist in speeding reporters through foreign security checks.

Marco read: *Maggie Helbling, WNN foreign correspondent.*

Chapter 21

After finishing the report for Scott shortly after lunch, Greg left the WNN Tower to head home. Going directly from the airport to the office this morning hadn't been his idea of fun, and he rejoiced at the thought of a relaxing afternoon. Walking across the street to the parking garage, he realized how good it felt to have his feet on the ground, his body upright, and blood circulating through his stiff muscles. The text of the report he had completed only minutes before simmered in his head:

Internal Memo

To: Scott McNally

Besides the eternal hell of spending twelve hours breathing recirculated air while sitting in a dollhouse-size airplane seat, I consider the meetings with the two academics, Professor Schleier and Dr. Horstmann, a success. While not realizing the ultimate goal of actually finding Baruch, I was able to establish much background information. I feel our reporting will be more personalized based on the attached interviews. I look forward to your comments.

Greg steered on to Ontario Street and, entering the Kennedy Expressway, headed west. Finally, no clatter, he thought. As he enjoyed the solitude of his car, his mind swelled to that almost scary moment called insight. His car felt more luxurious, the roads seemed wider, and the city appeared so rich with diversity. He noticed the warm eyes of the young Hispanic woman in the battered Buick next to him. Even the unmistakable red of the Coca-Cola billboard on the horizon caught his attention. It was all so clear. Why was it that you had to leave a place to understand it, he asked himself, knowing that tomorrow everything would again be stale.

Europe had offered Greg a needed break, a mental shift, from his office-ridden days. It was nice in small doses, he thought. But living in Germany in 1987 had led him to the conclusion that Chicago was a better place to live.

"For most Americans, Europe's like Disneyland. The tourists show up; they go from town to town as if going on rides; they walk the old passageways on quaint and excessively tidy cobblestone streets and then they go home. That's Europe!"

Greg used this analogy for his friends who couldn't understand why he preferred America to Europe. The fact that Disneyland was modeled after Europe didn't seem to bother Greg.

He parked his car in front of the garage and opened the trunk to grab his baggage. Through the window he saw Jenny sitting at her desk, typing. He felt excited about getting back to his routine—playing with Jeff early in the morning, working until seven or so, eating at the kitchen table, and then chit-chatting with Jenny on the couch in the great room.

"Hey, honey. You made it!" Jenny threw her arms around Greg as he pushed the door open and set his bags on the floor.

"Barely. This globe-trotting wears out even youngsters like me," Greg joked.

He threw his wrinkled sport coat on the couch and continued, "I've got an idea. After this Baruch story blows over, let's get your mom over here to watch Jeff, and you and I can go use McNally's bungalow for a week."

Scott's beautiful second home in Laguna Beach was perched high atop Arch Beach Heights. The view, on one of those rare smog-free days, spanned from Long Beach to Catalina Island.

Jenny's eyes, strained from too many hours staring at the screen, changed from a tired gaze to cheerful excitement. She could picture herself on Scott's expansive, wood deck in a chaise lounge, reading the morning paper and drinking a mug of steamy coffee. She loved the midmorning, ocean-induced fog that hung directly over the house, slowly thinning as the sun fought its way through, finally exposing a blue tapestry.

"You got yourself a deal," Jenny said as if putting her signature on a big contract. "Just one question.... You said when this 'Baruch story blows over.' Will that be this decade?"

Greg laughed. "That's a good question."

"So, what's the deal with Baruch, honey?"

"It's weird. His background points to just another smart, likeable kid who happened to have, besides panache, an affinity for philosophy. And you know how most New Age gurus are basically pitchmen for big religious groups? Well, Baruch's a kind of loner. Then he writes this book and, next thing you know, he's all over the media."

"The book is powerful," Jenny interrupted. She reached for a piece of paper next to the lamp on the coffee table. "I printed this off the web library"

Greg, pulling the edges of the paper, snapped the page and read with journalistic authority:

Plain Speak

Please indulge me with a bit of ancient wisdom.

In the Greece of old, over four hundred years before Christ, a philosopher known as Zeno of Elea hit the stage. He believed the world to be one undifferentiated 'being' and that our senses deceived us into believing something else. To discredit other philosophers—most notably Aristotle—he developed problems for them, or what we call Zeno's paradoxes. One goes like this:

A tortoise and Achilles decide to have a race. In order for the tortoise to have a chance against the fastest man in the world, it is given a head start. The tortoise proceeds to point A and keeps moving forward. Achilles begins his pursuit and arrives at point A. But by now the tortoise has moved on to another point, say point B. But when Achilles arrives at point B, the tortoise is already gone. According to Zeno, it is a philosophical and mathematical certainty that Achilles will never catch the tortoise.

This paradox brings up two fascinating dilemmas we face in the 21st Century.

Let us begin with word. The God of most faiths claims that man was given 'word' as a gift—the greatest gift. Zeno proves how this gift can be used to manipulate. The gift of word can be the most dangerous authority of all, because it appears harmless: paper is patient. Think for a moment that we express our very thoughts through word. Whether at work, play, or with the family, words are the only truth we have.

The Orwellian idea that 2+2=5 scared many, because, like Zeno, it challenged that which we know with certainty. The language of the late 20th Century, what was called political correctness, surpassed even Orwell's greatest fear by attempting to mold the way we act by the way we speak. We were juvenile enough to think that calling someone 'African-American' instead of 'black' would change the way people acted towards one another. This revolution took place through intimidation, without one shot being fired.

The above change manifested itself in corporate-speak, a language that takes simple thoughts and makes them complex. Instead of asking what someone needed, we asked what was the 'value proposition'. While we should remember that it is normal for one generation to try and divorce their language from the previous generation, corporate-speak, a creation of virtual corporations and business professors who use the workplace as their laboratory, created a word game that deceives, however subtly

Greg skipped down the page.

The second dilemma that Zeno brings up I call the truth/certainty paradox; that is, the more certainty of thought we acquire, the less we believe that there is a truth. Through the science of motion, Zeno convinces us, at least on paper, that Achilles will never catch the tortoise. Through words, he stakes his claim with certainty. Yet in truth, we know he is wrong.

Today, we are in the third generation of linguistic mind control, empty-speak, which combines the abuse of words, an assumption of certainty, and a conviction of no finite truth. The script has been written. When we repeat their words and accept their premise of certainty, we empower them.

I ask you to consider the proposition that the language expressed most clearly is best. We need not try to impress our fellow humans with parrotlike recitations of the latest buzzword or sound bite. Words should be used as a precious gift to express sincere, truthful thoughts. Life is too robust to be filled with empty words. Learn to speak your own thoughts in your own way.

"Pretty basic stuff," Greg commented.

Jenny slid behind Greg on the couch and wrapped her legs around his waist, removing his already-loose tie and slowly unbuttoning his wrinkled white shirt.

"Well, honey, it may be basic, but it's exactly the reason I don't work for the AZI-Group," Jenny snapped back in a seductive voice.

"Ouch!" Greg yelled, grabbing his side as if being struck by a bullet. Rolling on his imaginary wound and pulling his playful wife with him, he turned his head to look at Jenny.

"Are we really that bad?"

"When you're in a group, you guys are *unbearable*," she said, kissing Greg on the neck. "Oh yeah, Charley called."

"*The* Charley?"

"Yes, *the* Charley."

"What did he say?"

"He needs to talk with you and Maggie."

Greg began to reach for the phone, but Jenny grabbed his hand and placed it under her breast: "Charley said he'd call back."

♦ ♦ ♦ ♦ ♦

The house was deadly quiet. Jenny slept soundly, making up for the restless nights she had experienced while Greg was overseas. Jeff was safely tucked in bed and had slept through Mom and Dad's sexual reunion thanks to a minor miracle. Jeff's soccer coach had disproved the law of perpetual motion: He had tired out a nine-year-old.

Open on the nightstand sat *The Little Prince*. Greg had escaped all the 'whys' tonight: Why do businessmen only care about numbers? Why do people think they can own the stars just because they can count them? Greg gave his sleeping son a delicate kiss and picked up *The Little Prince*, reading the last line: "Perhaps I am a little like the grown-ups. I have had to grow old."

"They always tell us we're brainwashed as children. I'm starting to question that premise," he said to the room, as he combed Jeff's soft hair with his fingers.

He headed down the stairs and entered Jenny's office wondering if he was still able to think his own thoughts or if he, too, had grown up. He sat in the swivel chair for the better part of an hour pondering his world, his job, his very existence.

"Is it really 2013? It seems to have gone so fast. When have I really had time to *think*?" No matter how far he strayed, an invisible chord kept bringing him back to Baruch. Who is he, he asked over and over?

He thought of L. Ron Hubbard and Scientology. Hubbard's breed of rational 'religion' had made a splash in the 1980s and '90s. But it was really neuro-linguistic programming disguised as rationalism. Further, it had to be sold. How was it that Baruch, without massive organizational support, was able to cast this spell over so many across the globe?

Greg couldn't help but wonder if the virtual corporations had created their own monster. Was it not, he asked, this very consolidation of power that had allowed Baruch to become an unpaid spiritual infomercial? How had WNN and WBG allowed this guy to rise? "But then again, if it was only about exposure, I could be Baruch," Greg said flippantly.

Greg contemplated his spiritual renewal since the Baruch rage turned the world on its head. He somehow felt violated that one man had so changed the way he viewed not only his own employer, but the world around him as well.

"Life was much more simple before Baruch," he thought.

He also knew that before Baruch, life was much less exciting.

CHAPTER 22

MARCO VAN WELS POSSESSED MORE ENERGY THAN A NUCLEAR PLANT.
September 2 he was at work in Amsterdam. September 3 and 4
were spent in Baku. Now, he was peeping from the airplane window at the skyscrapers of downtown Chicago, as the plane veered
west on its final approach to O'Hare Airport on this lovely fall
day.

His convertible rental car pulled out of the airport parking lot
with the radio blasting. The song, with its distinctive 'ska' sound,
could be best described as a group consisting of Elvis Costello, Alice
Cooper, and Bob Marley on amphetamines. Marco sang along:

*"Have you ever been close to tragedy or been close to folks who
have/ Have you ever felt a pain so powerful/ So heavy you collapse"*

Using the steering wheel as a drum and trying to mimic the
vocals of the screaming lead singer, he broke into the refrain:

*"I've never had to knock on wood/ But I know someone who has/
Which makes me wonder if I could/ It makes me wonder if I've never had
to knock on wood/ And I'm glad I haven't yet/Because I'm sure it isn't
good/ That's the impression that I get"*

Marco was twenty-two years old when that song hit the
charts. As he pounded the dashboard and steering wheel on
alternate beats, adrenaline rushed through his veins. Magically
transported back in time, his face regained a youthful innocence,
and he smiled so hard, he thought his skin was going to tear.

"That was the Mighty Mighty Bosstones with their 1997 hit 'The Impression that I Get' here on Chicago's best Rock,WXRT," the disc jockey vocalized with her raspy radio larynx.

Marco cranked the radio louder and louder during the short drive, singing along with every song. Approaching two white gates guarding the entrance to Scott McNally's castle on the hill, he turned off the sound and heard only the gentle breeze.

Scott's maid, Maddie, ushered Marco over the Barolla marble floor, the beauty of which kept the eyes from capturing the stunning detail of carved moldings circling the round, vaulted ceiling. The exquisite foyer, the Louis XIV-style furniture in the grandiose living room and Colonial woodwork framing the study, owed their beauty to Scott's ex-wife. She had designed each room to replicate a distinctive era and, at the same time, keep a certain 'flow' through the house.

"Nice place, Mr. McNally," Marco noted.

"See that painting," Scott pointed at a surrealistic interpretation of a vase.

"The style looks like Renoir," Marco said moving closer.

"You have a good eye. That money was supposed to be for a putting green in the backyard."

Scott became more animated. "That French wallpaper was my vintage 1967 Corvette Sting Ray. Oh, and that vase. Yes, the vase. The sixteenth century Ottoman fuckin' vase. My ex paid $75,000 at an auction in Istanbul, not to mention her first-class ticket, two-week 'layover' in Paris...Shit, I'll bet I paid $125,000 all said and done!"

Waiting to escort the men into Scott's office, Maddie simply gave Scott a motherly smile, recalling the millions her boss had thrown out flying his private jet all over the world, sometimes going to Florida or Seattle for a day to see one of his flings.

Moving through the long hall, past the French country

kitchen and into the traditional, oak-paneled office, Marco asked, "And I take it your wife is no longer here?"

"On earth? Yeah, unfortunately. But not in my house."

Marco grinned. "Some things just don't quite make it. And marriage is one of those things."

"You got that right. Here, have a seat Marco," Scott instructed. "What news do you have, my friend?"

"Well, Mr. McNally, I have a lot more news than your news station does!" Marco said in a harmless, almost humorous tone of voice.

"OK, I can take a hint."

Scott reached inside his coat pocket and pulled out a thick envelope.

"Here you go. 50K—cash. Do you know how difficult it is to get fifty big ones nowadays? The gal at the bank asked me at least five times 'Are you sure you don't want to use e-cash?'"

"If the governments and banks had it their way, they'd be able to monitor every penny," Marco said. Rubbing his thumb and index finger together he added, "Me, I prefer cash."

Scott sat back in the fine, cloth chair and continued: "OK, you've got your cash—a deal's a deal. Now, make me hero, Marco."

Marco pulled out his notes and began reciting six months of investigations in a concise, factual manner:

"Stefan Mostl, born in 1974. Dad's a psychology teacher at Budapest's state school and a member of the party. Mother is a housewife. She had a college education—went to school with her husband-to-be."

Scott interrupted him. "How the fuck did you get that information?"

All the news agencies had been stymied while investigating Baruch's life before his foster home parents. There were more than five conflicting versions of his childhood.

Marco grinned. "If I told you how I get my information, you wouldn't even believe me, Mr. McNally."

Scott had been told by several frustrated journalists that 'Datenschutz', or data protection, was engraved deeply in Europe's post-World War II psyche and made data collection extremely difficult.

"Try me," Scott said.

"Let me put it this way, Mr. McNally. In America, your network controls all the information, because you choose what to tell the people. Where I come from, we realize that a much more powerful source controls information. What I find humorous is that Americans actually *think* they have access to all information. Your reporters are out there trying to peel through layers of garbage to find the real story. Do you want to find the real story, Mr. McNally? You just have to know who wrote the script."

Scott looked at Marco and grinned. "So who wrote the script?"

"We'll all know soon enough."

Marco continued to recite Baruch's rather normal schooling at the University of Graz, a high school exchange program in the USA, and so on. Scott, on several occasions, gave dumbfounded looks as if to say to himself, "This Marco guy is fuckin' good!"

When Marco's narrative reached the year 2008, Scott's interest heightened.

"In 2008, his local province is facing a problem with farming regulations. They have this special wine called Schilcher, made from grapes of the same vines that once passed the lips of Julius Caesar, or so they claim. The locals wanted to protect the name of the region and the purity of this vine, kind of like the French and Champagne. Anyway, they ask Baruch, a smart, educated local guy from a farming community, to take their case to the European Union. This is his first real, well, significant public appearance."

"And what happened with the..." Scott's futile attempt to pronounce the word 'Schilcher' was entertaining for Marco.

"What happened with the *wine* case?" Scott continued.

"He won. Whatever this guy touches turns to gold. He writes a book and it's a hit. He gives a speech and makes world news. He's consistently good—or lucky. That's the one common denominator."

Marco explained that Baruch supposedly wrote the work *Apocrypha Truth* as early as 2003, in conjunction with a small school he opened outside of Graz—a small concrete block structure modeled after Plato's Academy. Up until this point, Marco had played the role of a disinterested moderator. He lifted his left hand and pointed at Scott, who was savoring every word that rolled off Marco's lips.

"Now it gets interesting. This school, a one-room brick building, had, according to my source, only six 'visitors'. They were called the six spirits, because they supposedly had a certain air about them. They met maybe twice a week. Here's what kills me... no one knows who these six men are."

Scott sat silently. He shook his head in total amazement.

Marco grabbed the report and handed it to Scott.

"Mr. McNally, there's one other thing you should know." Marco had a concerned look as his face tightened.

"Go ahead, I'm listening," Scott said.

"I've been to the AZI headquarters and to your friends at Oiltron. They're covering something up. They know something and are burying it."

"How do you know that?" Scott asked, his face suddenly pale.

Marco bit his lower lip, shrugged his shoulders and said, "Mr. McNally, I just know."

CHAPTER 23

THE SOOTHING MELODY OF GREIG'S *MORNING FEELING* PLAYED IN THE background as Frank Schleier approached his former classmate. They spoke softly to each another in German.

"You look well, Stefan," Frank remarked.

"Thanks for coming. How are things in Munich, Frank?"

"Splendid. Since I was named dean of the philosophy school they've kept me quite busy. Lately, you seem to be keeping many people busy."

"It's funny, isn't it? You would think people would welcome a message of hope. But many people embrace me the way they embrace success: they appear to be happy for you, but inside they burn with envy."

Frank, like his friend, was a composed Austrian with much confidence. Yet amidst this hometown aura he sensed a different Stefan Mostl than he had known as a young man. Although the two had corresponded frequently, it had been almost two years since they had last seen each other face-to-face. Baruch seemed taller. His dark, thick hair showed no sign of thinning and he still had that lean, boyish frame. What had changed were Baruch's eyes. Still deep brown, the cocky gleam of that twenty-something Stefan Mostl had been replaced by a penetrating spiritual wisdom normally reserved for society's elders. Looking into his eyes, Frank saw a wonderful silence.

"I have to admit, Stefan, I don't understand this world. As much as I want to believe we're enlightened, I simply can't find any proof."

Baruch laughed. "Frank, the philosopher. Always looking for the proof."

The two men moved towards the fireplace. Baruch spoke.

"I looked for the proof. Read every important book. Wrote thousands of pages of commentaries. Then one day I found out that trying to prove this or that was exactly what kept me from finding the answers."

"But we have to go through that process to gain the understanding," Frank added.

"The process was designed to keep us from understanding," Baruch said humbly, words flowing effortlessly from his mouth.

That's it, Frank thought. The transformation—it's that he does it with no effort. As a university student, Baruch had been contemplative. In typical Austrian fashion, he would always 'turn his tongue seven times' before he spoke. This contrasted sharply with the sanguine and lucid philosopher the world had seen on TV.

Baruch interrupted Frank's deliberations. "Come and join me. Do you still drink Ceylon tea, Frank?"

"Certainly do." Frank appeared pleased that Stefan had remembered his drink of preference.

The two men moved to the corner of the rustic cottage near the fireplace, where the small, round wooden table was placed.

"Frank, I called you because you're the person I trust more than anyone. Some important affairs need to be taken care of, but I can't get on a plane or walk down the street—at least without..." Baruch dropped his head and left the sentence unfinished.

Frank sat mesmerized, feeling insignificant as he listened to that little boy he used to play soccer with; the little boy who didn't understand history; the little boy who had himself seemed so insignificant. That little boy, who was now the subject of every dinner conversation in Germany and the Occident, for that matter, sat adjacent to him sipping a cup of tea, asking for help.

"Please understand, Frank, that this work is dangerous. The media fears me. The Church calls me a heretic. Governments don't seem to know what to do with me. Ironically, the only fans I have are the people ... and that doesn't count for much today. That was supposed to be a joke, Frank! I guess I've lost my sense of humor lately."

Frank seemed relieved to see Baruch relax. For a moment he saw the Stefan Mostl he knew.

"Stefan, I don't understand why they hate you so much."

"It isn't for you to understand. Remember when you used to tell me that the hardest thing to do is to do nothing? That everything in the world isn't a mechanical object we can fix?"

Frank nodded and quoted the Bhagavad Gita: "The perfect act has no consequences." He added, "But your cause is worth the fight. How can I help you."

Baruch showed his appreciation with a humble grin, and dropped his head.

"Frank, here's what I'm asking you to do."

He handed Frank a white envelope that, upon first touch, felt like disks. "Please deliver these disks to the names on the envelopes. The one for Greg Lancy at WNN you must deliver personally. Also, there's a list of some items I need."

Embarrassed, Baruch went on. "I cannot access my money right now. Can you take an IOU?"

"Stefan, I'll be glad to help you."

Then, with the diplomacy of a statesman, Frank turned the conversation away from Stefan's financial predicament to a more pleasant subject.

"Do you remember the paper you wrote our final year? It was about the eternal bondage of humans."

Baruch nodded.

"Tell me, Stefan, what was that quote you finished with?"

Baruch's face lit up.

"Oh, yes. I remember. It was from Etienne de la Boetie's *Discourse on Voluntary Servitude.*"

Baruch stood up and began reciting, as if he had been over-taken by the student, Stefan Mostl:

"There are always a few who feel the weight of the yoke and cannot restrain themselves from attempting to shake it off. These are the men who never become tamed under subjection; these are the ones who, having good minds of their own, have further trained them by study and learning. Even if liberty had entirely perished from earth, such men would invent it. For them, slavery has no satisfaction, no matter how well disguised."

Baruch moved back towards the table, contemplating the words he had just spoken. "He wrote that in the sixteenth century, supposedly at the age of nineteen."

"That's your battle cry, isn't it? You're trying to free men from a slavery which they cannot even see," Frank suggested.

The student Stefan disappeared behind the curtain after his brief soliloquy and Baruch reemerged, sitting down softly in his chair.

"Frank, my friend, you always could dig in the dirt and find the seed from which the plant germinated. But how do you free people who don't realize they are enslaved? Damn, Frank, I'm not a prophet. I wanted to be a symbol of an intellectual freedom that most people may never experience. I wanted to give them a way to see inside great minds, like yours. But people in the streets don't care, Frank. They can no longer differentiate my message from the late-night talk show host or a 60-second sound bite."

Frank jumped in. "Then why have tens of millions of people followed your message?"

"That's the point, Frank. They are *not* following my message. People are seeking to hide their unbearable reality *in* my message, like the New Age fads that they grab at desperately and the magic pills they ingest. Instead of freeing themselves and their minds, they have now subjugated themselves to me."

Frank swallowed with difficulty as he digested Baruch's words. He said in a soft, reserved tone, "Baruch, you once told me that people will always believe in something. Even you may not see the truth that you so fervently long for. You are winning. Trust me."

"I know I'll control the message. I just hope people will hear it."

Frank wanted to understand what those confidently spoken words meant, but he sat motionless in an autistic-like trance.

"You'll understand soon enough," Baruch replied to Frank's silence.

Frank, the philosopher, sought refuge in a more concrete dialogue.

"Stefan, there's one thing you should know. Remember when you contacted me and told me some people would be coming? Well, they came. The first man who came was a young Dutch gentleman who tried to pass himself off as German. He worries me. He knew more about you than I."

Baruch set his right hand on Frank's shoulder and assured him, "Frank, no one knows me better than you do. If they threaten you, tell them where they can find me."

"I couldn't do that, Stefan."

"You're a very important person, Frank. Trust me."

"Is there anything else I can do for you, Stefan?"

Baruch reflected. "One small favor. Use MED II and pull this information from the Interpol files. There's an access code in this envelope."

Frank tucked the envelope in his shirt pocket and left the room.

CHAPTER 24

JIM ANDERSON DIDN'T NEED TO BE REMINDED THAT HE WAS PRESIDENT and CEO of the AZI-Group. He made it perfectly clear to everyone who ruled the kingdom. When Jim entered a room, tension followed.

"I don't have anxiety. I give it."

That was Jim's life motto.

Jim had finagled his way from one media group to the next, parlaying a quick success into an instant promotion in another group. He enjoyed the luxury of starting fresh at each port-o-call. This was common in the virtual corporations, but it posed a problem in that an executive never stayed at one place long enough to see if his or her success was lasting.

Much like a baseball player, an executive needed only one stellar season—preferably early in his or her career— to create a value image. Executives in Jim's circle had learned a valuable lesson from the virtual corporations themselves: it doesn't matter if you win or lose, as long as it appears that you win. So when Jim left second-rate British Mediacom's print division, and revenues plummeted 20 percent, he released a statement that British Mediacom had decided to 'execute strategies that were counter to my recommendations'.

Jim was smart. In his life philosophy, movie stars and heroes didn't exist. Rather, permanent vacancies needed to be filled in order to give the masses something to shoot for. The more formats the media created, the more stars they needed. He understood that in a society hungry for preconceived icons, his unique position allowed him to manipulate the titan corporations who were not enamored by the thought of having to tear down their figurehead, only to be forced to find another.

"I'm disposable, but my position is predestined," Jim had confided to Haig Abku.

This century's CEOs were held in the same esteem as grand statesmen and Nobel Prize winners. All in all, the virtuals found this arrangement beneficial: they used the CEOs almighty power to diminish the positions of other employees.

"The more important we are, the less the bloody divisional and regional managers can crawl up our shorts. We have to remind them once in a while who's boss."

Those were the words of the late Sir Kenneth Hancock, Jim's mentor and first boss at British Mediacom. He had died only weeks ago of heart failure and Jim, who could see himself through the now deceased Kenneth Hancock, made sure WNN treated his friend's death as one of the century's most important events.

He even called his biggest competitor, Mike McMillan, and asked him to run Sir Kenneth's death on all the prime media.

"You know, Mike, that could be us one of these days."

The loose, unconventional Mike McMillan had replied, "In the old days, wealthy families paid mourners to attend their funerals. I used to think 'How pathetic is that?' Well, now I know. When I die, I won't have to ask people to write about me, Jim!"

Despite his contempt for the idea of being a paid mourner, Mike McMillan played along with Jim's wish and had his top reporter, Todd Zone, run a feature on Sir Kenneth. "A man who lead his company and the stockholders to victory in the war of global competition" was the sentiment expressed by Todd Zone.

In truth, Kenneth Hancock had taken one of the most powerful twentieth-century telecoms and 'grown it' from 12 percent to a paltry 5 percent of the world market. WBG, on the other hand, had rocketed from 2 percent to over 23 percent of the global media market—dangerously close to WNN's 26 percent piece of the pie. When Todd Zone, who was rarely edited by his freewheeling boss, had this information cut from his story, Mike told him:

"Just run it, Todd. When it comes to personalities, people don't want the truth anyway."

♦ ♦ ♦ ♦ ♦

Scott was as surprised as anyone to find Jim Anderson in his office when he arrived at 8:00 AM on Friday, September 6.

"Good morning, Scott. Sorry to barge in on you like this."

Scott had no beefs with Jim Anderson. The fact he didn't trust Jim merely insured that their relationship was mutual. Scott liked Charley Hardeway's assessment of Jim Anderson: 'the most insincere person I've had the pleasure of meeting'.

"What's up, Jim. Is the coffee too strong in Baku?"

"Well, now that you asked!"

"Hey, Jim. Who was that prick at the stockholder meeting who kept bringing up WNN and Baruch?"

"VP of BNG Bank. Has a seat on the Federal Reserve. Thinks he's a hotshot."

"I wanted to kill the SOB!"

Scott flicked his index finger, pulling the trigger on his imaginary gun.

"Bang!"

"Yeah, he's an ass. But the meeting went pretty well."

Jim took a seat across from Scott.

"I have a problem. How many people do you have on the Baruch story?"

"Per your instructions, two: Greg Lancy and Maggie Helbling."

"And the private detective," added Jim Anderson.

"Goddamn, word travels fast in the electronic age!" Scott said with a disbelieving grin. "What, do you have a detective following my detective?"

"No, Scott. The guy was at Oiltron in Baku. He's asking way too many questions. You saw how the stockholders reacted to Baruch. People are scared of this guy. Hell, I'm scared of him."

"Well, I'm just doing my job. Those are my questions he's asking. So, if you have a problem with him, you got a problem with me."

Jim regrouped. Scott's tell-it-like-it-is mannerism was not something the bald, pear-shaped executive was used to dealing with.

"Scott, let me give it to you straight."

"That would be a welcome change," Scott fired back with a half-baked smile.

Jim ignored this slight. "Here's the scoop. Tomorrow afternoon I have an important meeting concerning this whole Baruch issue. But for the time being, I need you to call off the dogs. Tell Mr. Van Wels to sleep for a change, because I don't know who's pissing me off more—him or fuckin' Baruch."

Jim was breathing heavily, his face flushed. Scott seemed impressed that Jim could get that vulgar. "Didn't know he had it in 'im," Scott said to himself.

"So you want me to call off the guy who's getting close to Baruch?" Scott asked. "I don't get it!"

Jim reflected for a moment, then said firmly, "Do both of us a favor, Scott. Tell your friend to sleep for forty-eight hours. Let him know that Jim Anderson, the big boss, wants him off the case."

"Considering I've already paid him, I'm sure he won't have any objection. But I don't get it. First you tell me to attach top priority to Baruch, and now I'm supposed to back off?"

"I'm telling you and Marco to go after Baruch—not Oiltron or any other company I own. Is that clear?"

"OK, Jim. Gotcha," Scott said extending his arms and opening his hands like a mime.

"One last thing, Scott. If any reporter even thinks of opening up that BNG/Kirov investigation, I'll throw them on the Baku oil-pyre personally."

Jim bid Scott farewell, grabbed his jacket and left the building.

Scott breathed heavily through his nose and said, "If he flew all the way here to say that, this is REAL big."

Pushing the intercom button, Scott, trying to be polite, dictated, "Monique, I need to see Greg and Maggie in the conference room at 2:30. And can you please get Mr. van Wels on the line? Immediately."

◆ ◆ ◆ ◆ ◆

Marco listened as the smaller of the two men in dark suits, both hidden by tinted glasses, spoke. The three of them sat in beautiful Victorian chairs in the elegant lobby of Chicago's Drake Hotel, where Marco had checked in the previous evening following his appointment with Scott and a dinner date with a female friend.

"Baruch's got them backed into a corner," the unrecognizable suited gentleman stated softly. "Let it play out and they're going to fall."

"Listen, Martin," Marco said earnestly, "don't underestimate these guys. And *definitely* don't underestimate Baruch."

CHAPTER 25

WITH HALF A ROAST BEEF SANDWICH IN ONE HAND AND A TALL GLASS of Coke in the other, Scott waited for Maggie and Greg to enter the executive conference room.

Scott waiting for us isn't a good sign, Maggie thought as she entered the room.

"Sit down, you two." Scott said. "Mr. Anxiety graced my office this morning and he gave me plenty of it. Let me make this short."

Maggie and Greg both nodded in agreement.

"Up til now, I've given you both free rein concerning our friend Baruch. Yeah, we edited a few stories to save our virtual some embarrassment, but I think I've given you both—especially you, Greg—a fair shot at covering Baruch."

To the contrary, Greg's report on Dr. Horstmann, which aired that day, had been heavily edited. But he was beyond the point of arguing content. He simply gave a quick head movement that signaled more 'yeah, keep going' than agreement.

"The rules have changed. Baruch, as of now, tops our spin list. No news about him unless it's bad news. Got it?"

"There's already plenty of bad press on Baruch. You want us to pile on?" Maggie asked.

"Like a linebacker going after a fumble," Scott said facetiously.

Greg jumped in: "You're not asking us to concoct bad news?"

"You're a fucking reporter. Don't tell me you don't know how to find bad news! Baruch is bad news waiting to happen!"

"OK," Greg acknowledged. "Is that it on Baruch?"

"For some reason, Jim's got a bone to pick with our spiritual wonder. Let's turn the heat up on Baruch," Scott added, rallying the troops.

"But there's something else," Greg said with excitement. "I have a lead that Oiltron and our banking division in Baku are somehow involved in money laundering."

"And where, may I ask, did that information come from?"

"An e-mail—it wasn't traceable."

"An untraceable e-mail. Isn't that convenient?" Scott paced, pondering into the distance and waving his finger like a postulating professor. "Hum. Who would be so shrewd as to try to get us to investigate our own company? It couldn't be Charley Hardeway!"

"I'll take that as a 'no' on the Baku story?"

"Don't even think about it, Greg!"

Greg threw his hands up as if surrendering to a cop.

"Baruch, yes. Baku, no. I think I got it."

Scott picked up his files, moved towards the door and, grabbing the knob, looked over his shoulder at the two senior reporters: "I'm going to go remove Jim's shoe from my ass. Talk to you guys later."

"Boy, they are sure hush-hush on this Baku bank deal," Maggie whispered, as if Scott could still be listening.

Greg leaned close to Maggie's ear. "Charley told me that BNG was a cover for some *really big* deal."

"What deal?"

"He didn't say. He just said it was big."

As Greg and Maggie filed out the door, Amy Laurance approached Greg. "Oh, Greg! I was just looking for you in your office. There's a German guy here to see you from..."

"From Germany?" Greg jumped in.

"Very cute," Amy said. "He's from Munich. He said you know him."

Greg left Maggie and Amy standing in the hall of the WNN Tower's tenth floor executive suite, as he dashed for his office.

"I need to talk to you about the Oiltron story and the Baruch lead!" Amy yelled from the end of the hall.

"Fire's out. Story's dead!" Greg words echoed through the hallway to a confused Amy.

◆ ◆ ◆ ◆ ◆

Greg entered his office gasping for air, greeted by the warm smile of Frank Schleier. "Sorry you had to wait," he apologized, shaking the professor's extended hand.

"I only arrived a few minutes ago. Actually, I'm only here as a delivery boy."

CHAPTER 26

MAGGIE READ WITH DISBELIEF.

Memo: September 7, 2013.
CC: Ms. Helbling

According to Baku law enforcement agencies and an insurance company report, the Oiltron platform fire north of Baku was the work of a terrorist group. An organization known as Human Race is reportedly responsible. We have physical evidence from investigators, as well as a testimony from a member of the group, that corroborate an affiliation between the explosion, Human Race and the spiritual leader, Baruch. See attached information. Contact me if you have questions.
Haig Abku
President, Oiltron Industries

Maggie, still frustrated that she had flown halfway around the globe without stepping foot inside the Oiltron building, studied the attachment documenting the scientific evaluation of the explosion and how 'trace marks' and residues confirmed the presence of an 'explosive trigger device'. There was a lab report full of scientific formulas and chemical analysis.

"That's helpful!" Maggie said sarcastically. Then, staring inquisitively at the printout, she contemplated, "Two groups have been protesting the AZI-Group: Human Race and Baruch's supporters." She remembered the bank in Milan that had been blown up in 1969. As early as 1970, Charley Hardeway, then a university student, had insisted that it was a CIA plot to destabilize the communists in Italy. Thirty years later, he turned out to be right.

"The CIA always covers both sides of an issue," Charley preached.

"Could Baruch be behind both groups?" Maggie asked herself.

She opened the door to her small office and headed off to the editing room, grabbing her talking head, Amy Laurance, on the way. They entered the room referred to as 'Wally's world'.

"Sitting behind that U-shaped board of knobs, buttons, and monitors, Walter could be Captain Kirk commanding the Enterprise... if he was better looking and lost thirty pounds," Amy whispered to Maggie.

"I never thought Captain Kirk was hot to begin with. Terrible wardrobe!" Maggie joked.

Amy's youthful laughter filled the high-tech room, as Walter, oblivious to everything but the screen, hit a direct link voice mail button.

"Jim, re: the interest rate increase by the European Central Bank. Your report says 'the major banks' have indicated they will go along. Give me some names and countries. Is your friend Jerry Bates aware of this? Thanks."

Looking at the same screen, he pushed another button.

"Dinah, re: the Paris fashion show. Are you serious? I've got a fire at Oiltron and a lost spiritual diva and you want me to feature a fashion show? Here's an idea if you want to lead: get Baruch to wear one of

those gowns and have him jump on to the burning oil rig. Otherwise, give it to Sharon. It's RSO."

RSO—regional slot only—designated a story to the regional editor who, in turn, would decide if the story plays.

Walter viewed a video of Hong Kong's recent regional election. Two 'winning' candidates had been disqualified by the Chinese parliament for 'inciting and fomenting rebellious acts against the state'.

He clicked a direct link button.

"Sharon, re: Hong Kong elections. We'll run it on the 9:00 AM today. Hold the web posting until 9:05 —we'll throw the local networks a bone. Tell Mr. Li the footage of the candidate being handcuffed is classic."

Walter, entranced more by the stories unfolding in front of him than two beautiful women, only now noticed Maggie and Amy. Pointing at the still frame on the screen, he commented: "The Chinese. Giving them Hong Kong was as smart as offering a child to a pedophile and hoping the pedophile will be healed by the 'good' in the child!"

"That's an analogy I haven't heard, before," Maggie replied.

"China-bashing sells. What can I say?" Walter said innocently, smiling.

Amy stepped in. "As is Baruch-bashing. Take a look at this."

Walter flipped through the print out and smirked. For a moment, he looked like the young man he was.

"Our buddy Baruch is in deep shit!" he exclaimed.

"If that's all true." Maggie paused. "Doesn't it seem weird that this affiliation with a terrorist group pops up now?"

Without hesitating, Walter confided, "What I find *weird* is that it took this long to strip Baruch down to his true colors: a goddamned terrorist."

"We should probably only run 'sources say' about the terrorist allegation," Maggie proposed.

"I've got a report from a police agency!" Walter insisted.

"Yeah, but it originated from Oiltron," Amy clarified, drawing a caustic look from the chief editor.

"Maggie, why don't you and Alice in Wonderland find some more dirt on Baruch. I'll take care of the story."

CHAPTER 27

BATES/MCMILLAN HAD SCORED SECOND ONLY TO JIM ANDERSON'S AZI-Group in the recent *Global Business* ranking of top virtual corporations. The roots of the two groups, however, couldn't have been more different

The AZI-Group sprouted from American Industrial's unsolicited buyout of Zurich Holding & Investments International—thus the acronym AZI. Jerry Bates and Mike McMillan fused their empires to survive; they forwent the love and chose a shotgun wedding. Known on 'the street' as Ebony and Ivory, Mike McMillan and Jerry Bates contrasted on the surface like competing pieces of a chess game: Jerry Bates, an aristocratic-looking black man, and Mike McMillan, the pale-faced Irishman. But these two men would turn out to be a perfect match.

Jerry Bates, a financial guru and darling of the banks had, through tireless acquisitions, become second in power only to Jim Anderson and the Federal Reserve.

Mike McMillan had singularly brought the world of MIS—or operational software—to its knees. His 'inflation technology', founded upon the inflation theory of creation, utilized a digitalized DNA 'cluster' that self-replicated, creating an adaptable system remarkably close to the human intellect. This technology made it possible for robots to juggle. Asked about inflation technology's impact on humankind, Mike responded,

"Technology will have gone too far the day robots understand avarice."

He had also puzzled the world with an encryption device that made it impossible for anyone, the root server of U.S. government included, to trace the origin of electronic data. This invention crippled the ability of control-freaks to track, for example, e-cash.

From the Heart wrote:

Conspiracy theorists prognoses that e-cash would give governments and banks a Big Brother capacity seemed rational. But the McMillan encryption device, MED II, totally destroyed this theory. I'm reminded of the Middle Age knights who spent vast resources making impenetrable armor to secure their power and livelihood. Then some guy from China showed up with gunpowder. Mike McMillan has brought Jerry Bates' the gunpowder. Will the government and Federal Reserve sit on the sidelines and watch? Will Jim Anderson make a deal with Mike McMillan to share this technology? Be prepared for all-out war.

Signing off, Charley.

Jerry, normally a soft-spoken conservative, made worldwide fame during a controversial interview with *Business of the World* magazine in August of 2012.

"With the presidential elections only three months away, any hints as to who you will vote for?"

Bates shook the New World Order with his answer.

"Voting, what a waste of time. I invest money in issues. Frankly, as long as the issues are resolved, I don't care who executes them. But, if it makes people feel as if they make a difference, let them vote."

When the magazine hit the streets, the cover showed Jerry Bates sporting a crown of cash with the text: 'The King of the World?'

Most intelligent life forms knew the dominating influence virtual corporations exerted over the political system. Until now, no one in as haute a place as Jerry Bates had been bold enough— or, as Jim Anderson said, 'a big enough moron'—to state their own power so bluntly.

♦ ♦ ♦ ♦ ♦

Sitting in the stately office of Mike McMillan, waiting for the thirty-seven-year-old, pony-tailed hotshot to appear, Jim studied a huge portrait of his two rivals and contemplated the determined look in Jerry Bates' eyes—the look of an assassin.

"Good morning, Jim. Sorry I'm a few minutes late. Saturdays are always a bit lazy around here," McMillan's lively Irish accent greeted his competitor, who was dressed in khakis and a busy golf shirt.

It was 8:55 AM and Jim had been waiting only a few minutes.

"Hi, Mike. I was admiring the artwork."

Mike, ignoring the giant portrait, pointed at the framed cover page of his partner wearing the crown of cash.

"Yes, mate. But whenever I start feeling intelligent, I look at this."

The witty Irishman circled behind his desk and took a seat.

"Well, you said this was urgent and asked me to have a screen ready. Here I am—and there's the screen. That's all I know, mate."

"I thought the Australians said 'mate'."

"Oh, just a bad habit that I got as a teenager from spending too many Irish winters in Sydney. The Australian women find it charming—an Irishman saying *mate*," Mike said, grinning.

Jim relaxed his business face and reached in his leather bag.

"If anyone, like Charley Hardeway, gets wind that we met,

I've prepared this paperwork on Little Bits—you know, our commercial software company. The official story is that we're trying to dump Little Bits."

Mike smiled like the devil offering up an apple.

"Goodness, Jim. This must be heavy if you've already created a cover for your visit." Mike shifted in his chair and crossed his legs. Laughing, he said as an afterthought: "Little Bits. How could you ever buy a company with such a ridiculous name?"

"I know you'll never admit that you're eyeing that company with a ridiculous name, but that's not what I'm here to discuss."

"Go ahead, mate. I must admit, I'm intrigued."

"Is this the remote?" Jim asked, picking up a screen remote from Mike McMillan's desk.

"I know you guys at the AZI aren't tech-geeks, but you should know what a remote looks like!" Mike joked.

"And I know you guys aren't diplomats, but you should learn not to divulge trade secrets," Jim jabbed back, pointing at the cash-crowned Jerry Bates.

"Jerry finds humility to be an emotional weakness."

Jim Anderson clicked the satellite control and hit 'WNN'. Mike lit up a cigarette and said as he inhaled, "Come on, Jim. Making me watch WNN? Are you trying to bore me into buying Little Bits?"

Jim chuckled. "I should change the name to Big Losses."

"We've all had our share of losses," Mike said in a conciliatory tone of voice.

Glancing at his stainless steel watch and waiting for the commercial to end, Jim added, "Forget Little Bits. This is about the sovereignty of our companies."

Mike perked up. "Sovereignty? You're not going to ask me to be patriotic, are you?"

"No. I'm talking about Baruch."

"Oh yes, Baruch. A lovely chap. People love him."

Jim stepped on Mike's words: "The guy's a nightmare."

"Oh, I don't know." Mike flipped through some marketing reports. "He certainly attracts a crowd."

"The wrong crowd if you ask me, Mike."

"I have to say that our guy in charge of media operations agrees with you, Jim. Says Baruch makes us look even more devilish than we are. So why do you give him so much play, mate?"

"Watch this."

Jim turned up the volume as Amy Laurance appeared on the screen.

"Can you get me a date with her?" Mike asked.

Jim shook his head in disbelief at the irrepressible Mike McMillan. Whatever Mike did—writing programs, playing piano or turning WBG into a viable threat to WNN—he did with elegance and simple genius. A European post-Xer, he didn't take much seriously when it came to business. He worked hard and loved technology. He read compulsively and preferred an evening playing piano to the wild parties he was often invited to in Malibu. For Mike, business was simply the framework of a much larger game. Jim could never figure out what that game was.

"If you can get me a date with her, I'll make an offer for Little Bits' big losses," Mike persisted.

"I'll get you a date with Amy if you'll just watch this, Mike."

Mike acquiesced, openly enjoying the discussion. "You have my complete attention."

Amy Laurance opened from the studio:

"According to officials in the Azerbaijan capital of Baku, the fire at the Oiltron Baku facility was perpetrated by Human Race, a terrorist group reportedly affiliated with the spiritual leader, Baruch. A member of the group Human Race confirmed today that Baruch masterminded various terrorist acts committed against the Oiltron organization."

The camera footage moved from the dense black smoke hovering over the oil rig on the Caspian Sea to a clipping of the collapsed roof of the recently bombed lobby of Oiltron's Moscow office.

Jim clicked Amy off.

"That's too bad about Baku. But the rigs *were* old anyway. How's our friend Haig, by the way?" Mike asked.

Jim moved uneasily. Charley Hardeway had written an article about the Baku oil rigs claiming that Oiltron had intentionally set them ablaze because the environmental group Human Race was successfully lobbying the International Energy Commission to have rigs from the early twentieth century shut down. Separately, there were stories at the recent executive conference in London that Jim was trying to force Haig Abku out of the AZI-Group.

Biting his upper lip, Jim turned to the young Irishman and said sternly, " Mike, I'll ignore the Baku-Haig Abku innuendo. That's all a bunch of Charley Hardeway bullshit."

"But Charley has been pretty accurate in the past, you must admit. He was the first one who figured out that I developed the MED II chip to protect myself!" Mike threw in.

Jim twitched his tan face and ran his hand over his smooth head, searching for a way to get the negotiations back on track.

"Mike, I know we have our differences. Heck, I tried every dirty trick in the book to beat you and Jerry down. And about five years ago, I thought I had you."

"I bend; I don't break."

Jim became increasingly aggravated: "Let's be honest, Mike. You and I are the only ones who have survived. We sit up here and watch all the dreamers—we watch them fail. The one in a thousand that does make it, the Little Bits of the world, we buy."

"Did you ever think of buying Baruch?" Mike probed.

"I would if I could. He's a loose canon."

"How about Charley? He's all over us, too."

"Charley hates me more than my ex-wife! But he's a drop in the ocean. I mean, you and I are the only ones who know that he is right most the time!"

Mike's eyes squinted, a silent European acknowledgement of Jim's clever comment. Taking a long puff on his hand-rolled cigarette, he leaned back in his chair; curious as to what he was about to hear.

"Baruch's hurting both of us. We have an insider who's penetrated his little clan. Here's the deal, Mike. I'm going to feed you every story on Baruch *before* we go to press."

Jim paused to gauge his adversary's reaction. Mike, poker-faced, said calmly, "Please, continue."

"I need your assurance that you'll run the stories. I can't break Baruch myself. I need your cooperation."

"What makes you think he's so dangerous, Jim?"

"Because I know him. This guy is a piece of work—he's not what he appears to be."

"What is he?"

"He's one of those people who at some point started believing his own bullshit."

"How well do you know him, mate?"

"Mike, I know him. Trust me."

Mike carried with him a reputation as a man of his word, although he never apologized for doing what was best for him.

"You're playing a risky hand, Jim. Betting on my greed?"

"Baruch's our Cuban Missile Crisis. It's time to draw the line."

"So all I do is run some stories? Like the Sir Kenneth Hancock demagoguery?"

"Exactly, Mike—but Hancock was on our side."

Mike spoke, as if there were another person in the room. "So you wanted me to make Ken-the-schmuck Hancock into a hero. Now you're asking me to ruin a prophet?"

He turned back to Jim with fire in his eyes. "My, you and I will most certainly receive a platinum card for opening the gates of hell!"

Jim chuckled under his breath. Mike, calm and straight-faced, pulled out another hand-rolled cigarette and tapped it against his expensive-looking silver cigarette case.

"OK, you have a deal, Jim. But if you feed me one bum story, it's off."

Jim, pleasantly surprised at the quick answer, tried to loosen his stiff body and slide back into his buddy-buddy mode.

"That's great!" He pulled out an envelope and handed it to his new partner in crime.

"You'll find in here the foreign web address we've set up as well as the encryption chip. I'll have to ask you to lift all the reports personally. It's better if we do this ourselves."

Mike ignored Jim and stared at the gold-plated MED II encryption chip he had removed from the envelope.

"Jim, remember when the government tried to regulate this gem?"

"Sure do. The government always tries to regulate things that inhibit its ability to regulate us."

Mike paused and looked up. "A very clever way of putting it. Do you want to know a secret?"

"I love secrets," Jim said enthusiastically.

"In the antitrust settlement, we agreed to provide the encryption software to the U.S. military for national security reasons. The funny thing is that the reverse encoding which allows the sender to destroy the electronic trail isn't even in the software. It's in the chip."

Jim was confused. " So what's the software for?"

"Well, we knew they'd try to regulate us, so we made it appear excessively complex. It's also a nice marketing gimmick—kind of like a shampoo with 40 percent more!"

All Jim could do was internalize a laugh and shake his head in total amazement.

Mike nodded with approval. "Nice stuff. I'm glad you decided to use my chip. Now I know it's safe."

The two men shook hands and Jim headed for the door.

"One last thing," Mike added. "I'm going to make an unsolicited offer for Little Bits at eighteen dollars a share through one of Jerry's holdings—probably MF&M in Zurich. It would be nice if your board accepted."

Without flinching, Jim answered, "You got it," and shut the door behind him.

Mike sat back in his executive chair and tapped his silver cigarette case.

"You were right, pappy—desperate men do desperate things."

CHAPTER 28

THE SMALL PROFESSOR FROM MUNICH WAS EASY TO SPOT AMONG THE Chicagoans eating lunch at the West Egg Diner, one of America's timeless eating establishments that had changed as little as the conversations that took place in the beautifully simplistic booths. Despite futuristic predictions that fashion, food, entertainment, and human thought would converge in a monolithic global culture, Frank Schleier's Euro-calmness amidst the loud, frenzied discussion of the locals demonstrated that different cultures, like varying species, possess an inherent memory in their nature, or what one scientist called morphic resonance. An Austrian soul revealed itself through his thoughtful eyes.

Conversely, Professor Schleier could just as precisely spot the carefree spirit of an American marching down Hohenzollern Strasse in Munich or sight a lone American journalist at a Strauss operetta. While the popular media and global corporations decried such 'separatist' behavior as contravening a human collective conscience, Baruch summed up his thoughts in the final chapter of *Apocrypha Truth*:

So I call on each one of you to reject collectivity of the human mind, for to have as a goal conformity of conscience—that most deeply impregnated of thought—insures the perpetuity of mental bondage. Has not every tyrant longed for a people who accepted his reality? Has not every

demagogue called for unity? Don't be fooled by modern euphemisms—
they are only words. We should feel no shame for those greatest of
human conditions that we call diversity and intuition. When each indi-
vidual follows his own path to truth, we will discover a cooperative indi-
viduality, the sum total of that which will fuel our free spirits and lead
humankind to a new, passionate reality.

Using such intuition, Maggie, who had never met Frank
Schleier, grabbed Greg's shoulder and pointed.

"That must be him in the corner."

A second man seated at the table turned his curly black hair
towards the entrance as Maggie and Greg approached the professor.

"Is that Charley?" Greg blurted in disbelief.

Charley Hardeway, his short, curly black hair and coke-bottle
glasses looking down from the slightly elevated dining area of
the cozy West Egg Diner, strained his neck to see his former
employees ascending the two steps.

"Yes, it's me Greg. Very subtle."

"Sorry about that, Charley. I'm just surprised. I thought you
were in New York."

"You're right. Except today I'm in Chicago. They have these
things now called *airplanes*. Cutting-edge stuff."

Greg smiled like Maggie hadn't seen for ages. She felt Greg
got too caught up trying to please the boss. While Maggie took
pride in her work, she often considered leaving WNN to do some
freelance work now that her girl was out of school.

"So when are you going to come work with my fine, growing
company?" Charley asked sarcastically.

"Thought about freelancing, but figured I'd end up working
for the same assholes!" Maggie answered.

"Except they'll treat you even worse," Greg added.

"What ever happened to principle?" Charley chided.

"Principles are expensive," Maggie said dryly.

Maggie was taken by Greg's relaxed smile as he greeted the professor, who stood up and shook Greg's hand with one firm motion.

"Nice of you to come, Ms. Helbling," said the professor in a gentle tone of voice, motioning for Maggie to sit in the chair next to him. "Mr. Lancy, please understand that I couldn't speak in any detail at your office yesterday. Mr. Hardeway said he didn't feel comfortable in your building."

Greg laughed and put his hand on Charley's shoulder.

"Charley's always welcome in my office—if he can get past security."

The four of them laughed in unison.

"What can I do for you, Professor Schleier?" Greg asked.

"I'm in a very precarious situation. You see, I must trust someone at WNN. Mr. Hardeway told me I can trust you and Ms. Helbling."

Greg looked over at Charley, who raised his hands over his head.

"You got me. I did say he can trust you."

Frank Schleier continued: "Baruch is alive and doing fine. I know where he is. But I have some rather disturbing news as well."

Charley interrupted, "Hold on to your seats, you guys."

"We have evidence that your company ..." Frank Schleier paused, "plans to kill Baruch."

Greg's head jolted back, his eyes appearing to lift out of his head. Maggie was unable to move.

"M... Mr.... Schleier," Maggie stuttered, " I know that Jim Anderson won't get any Nobel Prize for ethics, but that's a pretty strong charge."

Charley impatiently joined in, "That's exactly what I said, Mag. Then I saw this."

Charley produced a series of photos showing Marco Van Wels entering the Oiltron building in Baku. Then there was a second series of shots showing Marco in a red convertible, entering the driveway of Scott McNally's house.

"I know that guy," Maggie yelled in disbelief. " He was on the helicopter with me when I went out to view the oil platform. He's an insurance adjuster."

Charley shook his head.

"If he's an insurance adjuster, I'm a warthog! He's an expert in corporate espionage from Holland. Ex-Interpol guy. Speaks something like seven languages and has a law degree. His name is Marco Van Wels. My source says he's the best."

"He did seem very..." Maggie searched for the right word, "*informed* for an insurance adjuster."

"This guy's in the deep know!" Charley said with conviction.

Greg had regained his composure after hearing the 'kill' word and asked, "OK, so he was in Baku, went to the Oiltron building, and checked out the rig. Maybe they hired him to investigate the fire?"

The professor leaned forward and spoke quietly.

"Mr. Lancy, was he trying to put out the fire when he visited my office in Munich?"

"And is it normal that an insurance adjuster would visit McNally *at his home*? Or that he would know Jim Anderson?" Charley added as a topper.

The four of them sat silently waiting, leaving only the anonymous background discussion and high-pitched chiming of ceramic coffee cups being cleared by a busboy. Each was hoping that the other would throw another card on the table. Charley broke the quiet.

"Here's the deal, you guys. Professor Schleier has more information—I've seen it. But before you see anything else, I've got to know if you're in."

Greg's relaxed smile vanished as he saw his whole career flash before his eyes.

"I've been here over twenty years. My son Jeff turns ten next week. If I try to bury NcNally, I'm gone."

Charley nodded, "No, Greg, we're talking about taking down the whole company, not just McNally."

"Are you saying WNN or the AZI-Group?" Maggie asked.

"I'm saying the whole fucking company."

Charley looked at the professor. "I apologize for my language. That's just the way we talk in New York."

"We didn't talk that way where I grew up," Greg noted to Charley's dismay.

"Thanks for sticking up for me, pal," Charley answered sarcastically and, taking a deep breath, continued. "Here's the short of it. If you don't help, your company is going to kill Baruch."

"How do you know that?" Greg asked, unconvinced.

"Question: who wrote that the Chinese would trounce on Hong Kong? Answer: me. Question: who nailed the brokerage houses for collaborating with the Federal Reserve on interest rates? Answer: me. In fact, who exposed the secret pact between the Federal Reserve and the International Monetary Fund? Final Jeopardy: which outcast editor predicted the Cubs would win a pennant?" Charley threw up his hands excitedly. "Greg, I know!"

Maggie looked at Greg,

"If you're in, I'm in."

"What do you mean by 'in'?" Greg asked Charley.

"It means that at some point in time we'll need your help. We need someone inside, mainly to access computer files."

"I'm not an expert, Charley. And you know how tightly sealed our MIS is. You couldn't slide a dime in the crack of their ass."

Charley smiled. "Thanks for the imagery. But don't worry. I've got that covered."

"How deep are you in this, Charley?" Maggie asked, like a caring mother.

"Up to my 20/60 goddamned eyeballs, Mag!"

Greg knew he was the one they needed. Turning to the small professor, he asked,

"Why should I trust Baruch? Maybe he—if he is alive— wants to access the WNN files for something else?"

"Mr. Lancy, I'm sure that you find this whole scenario ludicrous. I didn't want to believe it either, but for the simple reason that Stefan is my friend. Do you wish to see him, Mr. Lancy? Would that help?"

"Before I risk my future? Before I take on the most powerful organization in the multi-verse? Yes."

"So I take it you're in," Charley stated, like a salesman closing a deal.

Greg and Maggie, looking deep into each other's eyes, nodded.

The professor stared at the fifty-three-year-old reporter's worn jeans, herringbone jacket, and scared eyes.

"Mr. Lancy, Ms. Helbling, I suggest we go to my hotel room."

Charley pulled out a circular, leather money pouch he had received from his grandfather and paid the bill. He yelled at the waitress to keep the change, as he hustled after Maggie, Greg, and the professor.

CHAPTER 29

THE SCREEN ON THE PORTABLE GREETED SHARON TUCKER: "SEPTEMBER 7, 2013. The phrase of the day: 'Anything worth doing is worth doing well.' To view uncompleted tasks..." Sharon hit the ESC button with robotic precision, her eyes embracing the endlessness of Lake Michigan's chilly waters. Saturday allowed her to escape both office and home and be truly alone. For almost an hour she had sat motionless on the green wooden bench in a meditative trance. Her thoughts wandered past the water's horizon, thinking about what she would write for this week's editorial, or what was known internally as a web-a-torial. This weekly feature, a 500-word column of Sharon's insight, was her last creative refuge.

Reaching into her backpack, she palmed the stainless steel thermos and poured a cup of coffee into the black plastic top-turned-cup. She peeled off her bright patchwork sweater and, stretching her arms toward the sky, breathed deeply. The breeze picked up the combination of water, sand and sun, blending them with the music of birds into a fragrant fall perfume—nature's own aromatherapy.

She adjusted the screen to eliminate the sun's glare and began typing.

Draft I. Web-editorial for Sept. 9:

This post-Labor Day weekend along Lake Michigan's vast shore emits a strange, artificial emptiness. I say strange, because scanning north and south nothing can be seen but a stream of fitness buffs filing up and down the narrow boardwalk, bicyclist and skater barely avoiding high-speed collisions. I say artificial because it was only last week, on this very beach, that thousands of families huddled on blankets and celebrated what we call Labor Day. One weekend, thousands of passionate people uniting; this weekend, desolation. We are a peculiar species.

Much like America's Greek Revival of mid-19th Century, the late 20th Century witnessed a revival of its own; namely, a revival of the great works in Eastern philosophy. America took these holy works, turned them on their head, and called it the New Age movement. In those books I read a thousand times over about the unalterable growth of a collective consciousness among the peoples of the globe. It was the sixties without a cause and, to be honest with my readers, I believed it myself. I was young.

The New Age prophets claimed that we create our own reality, much like the families who filled this empty beach a mere five days ago. Similarly, we, according to them, created our own societal woes. These philosophical hacks, cherry-picking quotations from Buddhism, Zen, and any other scripture that made a good sound bite, told us how to free the human spirit. Now we find ourselves two decades free... alone on an empty beach, free from what? We are alone—"free" from our fellow man.

But we missed the entire foundation of freedom. Until Baruch, we focused on freedom as individualism. We reasoned that because government governs and leaders lead, we are not free. In truth, we have fallen subject to the basic premise of life: some will lead and some will follow. We shouldn't forget that the freest minds often rose out of the ashes of tyranny. And so today tyranny moves dangerously close to rising out of the fluff we call freedom.

In my old Atlanta neighborhood, the problem wasn't that we were black, or that we lived in Zone 3. The problem rested less in the people who led us into poverty than those who kept us there. We need someone to lead us out of the haze of capitalistic indoctrination into a more enlightened democracy. Will Baruch be that leader?

Sharon scrolled back to the top of the page and re-read her draft.

"Sister, this sounds like something Charley Hardeway would write," she said with her rich, streetwise accent.

Dropping her head, her arms fell limply on the wooden bench as she laughed in a soprano pitch. Barely getting the words through her laughter she sputtered, "Sister, get a hold of yourself! Save that draft for prayer meeting on Tuesday!"

Sharon sobered up and, starting over, wrote:

Draft II. Web-editorial for Sept. 9:

It was a century ago, in 1913, that Henry Ford introduced the assembly line. Two hundred years ago the steam locomotive appeared. And in 1713 man first saw the steam engine. History will probably note 2013 as the year of MED II artificial intelligence chip and the year that the central banks of Asia, North America, and Europe merged into one global currency fund.

But for those who have lived through this decade, the name Baruch will define this era more than presidents, technology, or central banks. For this singular man has forced us to question the path we're on..."

Sharon looked into the distance, typing as effortlessly as a concert pianist.

CHAPTER 30

MAGGIE, GREG, AND CHARLEY ARRIVED AT PROFESSOR SCHLEIER'S suite at the Raphael Hotel. The room was tidy, with no clothes lying around or anything else for that matter. The professor offered them a seat. Maggie and Greg took the couch; Charley snatched the wooden desk chair, which he turned around and straddled. From his briefcase, the professor took a screen, attaching it dexterously to a device that looked to Greg like an old external modem.

"This is a special satellite encryption device," the professor duly noted.

It had now dawned on Greg and Maggie that he was going to create a video link with Baruch. The silence was unbearable.

"Can I help you, Professor?" Greg asked.

"Can you divert and reconstruct an electronic signal so that the friendly American government can't locate Baruch?" he asked. The professor smiled gently saying, "I can," as he unveiled a gold-plated MED II chip from his suit coat pocket and inserted it in the box.

"I thought those chips were classified," Greg said.

"And I thought there was supposed to be a thing called free speech. Don't believe everything you hear, Mr. Lancy."

The professor focused back on the screen and mumbled

something in German. Waiting for the line to engage, he turned to Maggie: "You've been very quiet. Is everything all right?"

"I just don't understand why Baruch is hiding from the government. I thought you said the AZI-Group was after Baruch."

"You don't think that Jim Anderson and Haig Abku put together that deal in Baku alone, do you? The AZI-Group had lots of help, especially the American government, in putting that together."

"So they're after Baruch, too?" Greg asked, sounding skeptical.

"We're simply being cautious," Frank Schleier assured.

A series of rings emitted from the screen and the professor began typing. The screen blinked several times, then he clicked an icon. The video image of Baruch's table next to the stone fireplace appeared. There was some stirring in the background that became louder. Finally, the moment arrived: Baruch sat down in the small, wooden chair next to the fireplace.

"Hörst du mich, Stefan?" The professor asked in German.

"Yes, Frank. How are you?" Baruch answered in English, knowing they were not alone.

"Stefan, we will only be able to see you. It will be safer. I'm sitting here with Mr. Lancy, Ms. Helbling, and Mr. Hardeway."

"Thank you all for joining me. Do you now believe that I'm alive?" Baruch inquired with an understanding smile.

"Well," Greg hesitated a moment, not knowing what to call him, "this is Greg Lancy. We're glad that you're well."

"Thank you. How are you, Mr. Lancy?"

"A bit shocked. We listened to Professor Schleier's story and we would like to help, but we have a hard time believing that our company is planning to harm you."

"*Kill*, Mr. Lancy. They're planning to kill me. There's no need to play with words." Baruch continued, "Do you believe in a god, Mr. Lancy?"

Greg looked around the room. "Yes."

"Do you ever ask yourself how someone who calls himself God could create such an unjust world?"

"Yes, I suppose everyone has."

"No, Mr. Lancy. Only those who are repressed ask that question. Jim Anderson has never asked that question because he knows why our world is unjust. It's because people like you won't act to change it. Did you ever ask yourself how twenty thousand British soldiers controlled ten million Indians?"

"No, I don't believe I have," Greg answered shyly.

"Very simply because the British assumed that the masses were too weak, too pathetic, to rise up and take charge of their own lives." Baruch hesitated and waited.

"Mr. Lancy, do you think it strange that Professor Schleier had a video link all set up with a special encryption device for this particular connection? Don't you think I knew that you would not believe what we tell you? Or do you find it more convenient not to believe?"

Greg looked like a reprimanded schoolboy, a silly expression on his face. "Why should I believe that my company is trying to kill you?"

Baruch sat peacefully in his small chair and cocked his head inquisitively to the side. "Mr. Lancy, how long have you been the lead reporter on my case?"

"Six months."

"Do you believe I am a terrorist?"

"No. But the police do."

"Well, it's positive that *you* don't!" Baruch joked. "And you, Ms. Helbling. Did you find anything in Baku that looked like my work?"

"Not at all—no, nothing," she said nervously.

"If you simply look for the little truths, you will find the big truth."

Baruch paused and added apologetically, "I'm sorry I can't see all of you. Are you there, Charley?"

"Yes, Stefan. How are you?"

"Oh, very well. Thank you for your faith, Charley.

"When would you say that I became 'popular', Mr. Lancy?"

Greg was astonished at the fact that Baruch had called Charley by his first name and more shocked that Charley had called him Stefan. Answering Baruch, but looking inquisitively at Charley he replied, "June, 2010. There was a feature article about your appearance at the UN Convention on Spirituality—we ran it full distribution."

"Good. I want you go back to 2010 and look up all the news reports about me. "

Greg rustled about in his chair. "Why don't you just tell me what's there—it would save us both some time."

"Because, Mr. Lancy, I believe in you. I believe you will find the truth if you can remember that the truth never comes prepackaged. Take off the corporate mask for one day and look at those reports through your own eyes. Think your own thoughts, Mr. Lancy."

Baruch took a sip of water and continued, "Mr. Lancy, have you read my ... collection of thoughts?"

"You mean *Apocrypha Truth*?"

"Exactly."

"I've read it a couple times."

"Have you ever asked yourself what that first epitaph means?"

"You're referring to 'Some truths are so clear they become demons in an untrue world'? ... No, I never quite figured that one out."

Baruch flashed a stern look and stood up: "You're about to find out what that means. Good-bye, Ms. Helbling, Mr. Lancy."

Greg sat with his head in his lap.

"Are you all right?" Maggie asked.

Greg looked up with watery eyes. "Mag, just two days ago, in Munich, I was sitting on a park bench and I wrote that exact quote in my notebook. Next to it I wrote 'what did he mean?'"

CHAPTER 31

AMY LAURANCE SAT ALONE AT THE COUNTER OF THE PERPETUALLY busy West Egg Diner. She had seen Greg and Maggie scurrying into a cab, but didn't catch the other two people they were with. Being a recent college graduate and relative newcomer at WNN, she had never met Charley Hardeway; however, she read his articles every weekend. She felt Charley was an embittered, frustrated writer with no vision. The fact that Charley regularly lambasted Amy in his cartoons might have aided her strong feelings.

To be sure, Charley's assessment of the world clashed with that of Amy's, a post-Xer who admittedly judged her success by how much free time she had and how much her portfolio increased last month. Employed to attract the younger viewers, Amy enjoyed the luxury of her specialty, being the beautiful blonde who stopped any sane man from flipping to another channel. Being a specialist also limited her responsibility and reduced her level of stress. She laughed when Charley wrote that her job was 'less taxing than hosting home shopping television.'

The idea of increased specialization of the twenty-first century concerned Baruch. Perhaps because he had seen the manifestation of a hyper-specialized system in Austria, or what the Germanic people call *Fachidioten*, kindly translated as 'narrow specialists', Baruch openly encouraged people to be more balanced and less singly oriented. He was quoted as having said that 'character diversity keeps humans off the endangered species list.'

"Species that become too specialized perish," he declared succinctly. "The comfort of specialization has a lullaby effect."

Amy was only one of millions of specialists who ignored Baruch's advice. Her routine consisted of showing up on site, receiving a script, delivering it, and leaving. She did keep up on current affairs, at least on a superficial level, by reading several papers every day and surfing news banks before going to bed. For Amy, being conversant in subjects outside the realm of reporting sufficed. "There are no Renaissance people in this age," she wrote in a college paper titled *Humanism in the 21st Century*.

Amy fed off the rush of the spotlight. She loved reading a script, especially on location and surrounded by an audience. But she went home to an empty apartment, a place she tried to avoid as much as possible. Before work there was her 6:00 AM workout; after the evening report she would find a place to eat; before going home she'd often stop at a shopping center or entertainment mall. After she had exhausted every other opportunity, she'd go home.

A natural blond, 5'5" knockout with the body of a professional figure skater, she had no problem finding guys who wanted to take her out. But the courtiers were always corporate men like the ones she worked with. She liked a couple of the guys at WNN, but her contract prohibited her from dating AZI-Group employees.

"That takes 50 percent of the American male population out of the pool!" she had lamented with Maggie.

It was 12:30 PM as she flipped through a script for her 2:00 PM program, "The Politics of Politics", a weekly show that looked behind the scenes of political decisions.

It seemed that every year there were more shows ... about shows.

The young Italian waiter set Amy's hamburger and hash browns on the counter and gave her a friendly nod.

"Thanks," Amy said, winking at the young waiter.

"Looks good!" Marco Van Wels grinned. "It's nice to meet an American that still eats meat and hash browns. Grease, salt—good stuff!"

Taken back by the direct approach of the unexpected guest, the bubbly Amy could only look down at her plate.

"I'm sorry, my name is Jan." Marco's eyes penetrated Amy's entire being. Amy's dazzling eyes looked away.

"My name's Amy. And I usually eat fries—except they don't serve them here. And I usually don't talk to strangers," she added, still avoiding eye contact with the Dutchman.

"Pity, never talking to strangers. I never learned much from myself."

Amy blushed, and laughed softly. "So, Jan, is that your best pick-up line?" She slid a forkload of hash browns into her mouth.

Marco's long, athletic body tilted toward the counter, his elbow supporting him. Contemplating Amy's question, he set his head gently on his open hand. "My best line would be 'How about front row tickets to *Carmen*, dinner at Chez Jacques, and Champagne at Oak Park Beach...with a stranger?'"

He remained still, except for the sparkles dancing in his eyes and added as an afterthought, "Tonight."

Baruch may have had a visionary light, but Marco had a machismo that society said was out, yet Amy's instincts told her were in. Amy looked at the handsome, sculpted face of the tall, lean Dutchman and, not wanting to look too fragile, fired back: "OK, Jan. So you want me to go to *Carmen* with you tonight. Do you like opera, or are you just trying to get laid?"

"I truly do like opera and I would *never* try to take advantage of your weak nature," Marco said with an openly insincere smile.

"OK, Jan, you're on. What time?"

"Can you meet me in the lobby of the Drake Hotel at 7:00 PM?"

"I'll be at the Drake at seven if you tell me your last name."

"Is everything a negotiation with you, Amy? My last name is van Linden."

Marco touched her lightly on the shoulder. "Amy, I'm looking forward to tonight."

He began to head for the exit, when Amy, a napkin clinging to her blue skirt, ran up behind him. "Don't you want to know my last name?"

"Your last name is Laurance and you work at WNN," Marco said without hesitation.

A spooked look came over Amy's face. She started to ask, "How did..." when she was cut off. Marco put one hand over her mouth and, pointing at Amy's left breast, said comically, "Lighten up, Amy. I'm just a stranger, not a stalker. You forgot to remove your security badge. See you tonight!"

Marco, Amy's Jan, headed out the door, laughing loudly.

CHAPTER 32

GREG PULLED INTO THE DRIVEWAY AT 3:30 PM. JENNY SPOTTED GREG from her front office window and rushed out the door.

"Is something wrong?" she asked with a concerned look.

"Hi, honey." Greg gave her a hug. "No, nothing's wrong—except that Baruch claims that the AZI-Group plans to kill him."

"You're not serious," Jenny said, shocked. "You spoke with Baruch?" she asked in disbelief.

"Sure did!"

The two of them moved toward the front door of their suburban tract mansion and into Jenny's office.

"Jen, I need to use this place for a couple of hours, if you don't mind."

"No, of course not. Let me close this file."

Jenny moved past Greg and noticed a certain look in Greg's eyes—the look a child gets after finding out there's no Santa Claus.

"So, Baruch's alive. Is he here in Chicago?"

"I don't know. We had a videoconference. It looked like he was in a cabin, like the one we stayed at in Park City last winter."

"Are you sure it was him, Greg?"

"As sure as 'a' comes before 'b'!" Running his hands over his tired eyes he asked, "Can you please make me a cup of coffee, honey?"

He looked up at the ceiling. "The biggest event on the planet and it lands on my lap!"

Jenny messaged his shoulders. "Was he nice?"

"Baruch? Yeah, he's nice. Except he made me feel like an imbecile."

Jenny terminated the shoulder rub, moving towards the kitchen to brew some coffee. Her pleasant voice echoed through the house, "If he thought you were an imbecile, he wouldn't have contacted you."

Greg shouted into the kitchen, "He didn't contact me! Charley Hardeway did. Believe me, he thinks I'm an imbecile."

Still in the kitchen, Jenny said loudly, "Come on, Greg. He doesn't think you're an imbecile."

"Put it this way: He made me *realize* that I'm an imbecile."

The fingers of a maestro breezed across the digital keyboard. Greg didn't ever use voice recognition; he found he thought more when he wrote something down. He worked his way through a series of search commands and field definitions until the screen announced:

Search Criteria:

Original Feed Only\Contents=Baruch, Stefan Mostl, related\ Limited: 10/01/10-current\end. Please press enter or say 'yes' to continue search.

The high-speed processor hummed, searching all web sites, libraries, government files, and the likes. 'Original feed', by eliminating duplicate stories or re-writes of major wire services, made much more work for Jenny's powerful processor. Finally, tallying the results the screen displayed: "I have located 567 total media files."

"You haven't located anything. You're a damn computer!"

"What did you say?" Jenny asked, entering with a white, ceramic mug of coffee which she placed next to the screen.

"Nothing. I was talking to the computer."

"Well let me know when you two finish your discussion," she jested. Turning to the screen her eyes lit up. "567 files? You sure you don't want a *pot* of coffee?"

"Check this out, Jen. We're on this video link with Baruch. At the end of the interview he asked me about a quote in his book—the very quote I had written in my journal two days ago!"

"Coincidence is a powerful force. Maybe someone saw you write it?"

"No, I was alone in the park in Munich. It was 5:00 AM."

"Or he got ahold of your journal?"

"It's been in my bag the whole time."

"Greg, he must have known somehow."

"It was the *way* he said it, as if he knew what I was thinking. I feel like he's watching me right now."

Greg looked up, still straight-faced. "Honey, can you help me out?"

"Sure, boss. What do you need?"

Greg pulled his screen out of his briefcase and plugged it in. Typing and talking at the same time he laid out the plan: "I'm going to dial into WNN's internal system. I need to locate all of Baruch's articles in Walter Butwin's source file. Can you arrange it so the MIS guys don't know the search originated from my computer?"

Jenny smiled, picked up the phone and dialed WNN.

"World News Networks, how may I help you?" the female voice asked.

"Yes, I received a call from a woman in your MIS department. Her name was..."

"Oh ma'am, it could have been Ms. Wright or Ms. Childers," the operator said with a friendly southern drawl.

Jenny paused. "Oh yes, it was Ms. Wright."

"I'll connect you."

Jenny hung up and searched the WNN database Greg had now accessed. "Let's see. There she is. Ms. Wright."

"What are you doing, Jen?" Greg asked.

"Some low-tech hacking. Let's see if old Walter has nothing better to do on a beautiful Saturday afternoon than work." Jenny picked up Greg's secure phone and dialed WNN again. "Yes, Mr. Walter Butwin, please."

Greg listened to Jenny go to work.

"Hello, Mr. Butwin, this is Judy Fenz, Ms. Wright's assistant from MIS...Well, I'm doing fine thanks. Mr. Butwin, we have had a security breach and..." She was interrupted.

"No, sir, it was not a virus—it looks like a hacker. All files are intact, but we *are* changing all the personal access codes. Your new code will be phoenix/7755. I need you to verify your old access code."

Jenny wrote 'Saturn/8153'.

"Thank you, Mr. Butwin. That change will be effective at 8:00 AM Sunday morning."

Jenny hung up and shook her head. "People can be so stupid! It would be harder to scam McMillan's inflation technology than Walter!"

Greg laughed. "That was good. But won't he still see that I accessed the file?"

Jenny reached in her file drawer, pulling out a gold-plated MED II chip.

"Don't believe everything you hear," Greg said.

Confused, Jenny asked, "What?"

"The professor, Mr. Schleier, had one of those chips. I told him that I thought the government classified them. He told me not to believe everything I hear."

"Well, they are classified. That's why everyone wants them,

honey. They cost a thousand dollars with the software. The commercial version runs around fifteen thousand dollars."

"And it really works?" Greg asked.

"Sure, if you know how to use it. But most programmers don't even understand how it works."

"So how does it work?"

"We don't have enough days for me to teach you AI, Greg."

Greg had a blank stare. Jenny chuckled.

"AI—Artificial Intelligence. Remember what Charley says: 'If you don't know what it is, you don't need it'." Jenny gave Greg a conciliatory kiss on the cheek and asked, "Where do you want the trail to end? It has to be someone in the system."

"You may think I'm mean," Greg said grinning, " but how about Amy Laurance?"

"OK, but they *will*, eventually, be able to trace it to her."

Greg looked satisfied with that answer and gave Jenny a big kiss.

"You're the best!"

The couple turned to their screens and got to work.

CHAPTER 33

IT WAS 7:30 IN THE EVENING WHEN SCOTT MCNALLY ARRIVED BACK AT his mansion. He had called Maddie on the way home and she was at the door waiting for him when he arrived.

"Nice to see you, Maddie."

Scott entered the foyer and smelled a melange of rich fragrances that reminded him of Thanksgiving as a child in upstate New York.

"Smells good."

"I made your favorite: pot roast with dumplings and gravy. Oh, and I made a paper bag apple pie for dessert—your mom's recipe."

Scott had already discarded his suit coat, tie, and shoes, as he reached automatically for the bottle of Seagrams.

"The apple pie sounds terrific, Maddie. Let's just forget dinner and get to that pie," he said, laughing.

"No sir. This roast has been cooking all day," Maddie said emphatically.

Scott lumbered to the great room and dropped his weary body in between his leather recliner and the chinaware-covered TV tray. Pointing the remote at the wall of jumbo-sized screens he pressed 'Multi-source on'. His giant hand grasped the crystal goblet, shaking the ice cubes from side to side like a chime. Proceeding with his ritual, he continued to wiggle the goblet with one hand while he splashed Seagrams over the ice cubes with the other.

"Thanks for replenishing my supply of whiskey," Scott yelled at Maddie in the kitchen.

He heard a muddled response from the distance.

Scott thanked Maddie for everything she did. In fact, he appreciated Maddie more than anyone else in his life. She understood what he wanted and didn't ask anything in return. A divorcée, who had recently recovered from a drug addiction, she liked the fact that Scott's house offered a secure environment without the demands of a relationship. Both Scott and Maddie were happy in the confines of the stucco mansion on the hill.

Maddie placed a staggering portion of pot roast in front of Scott, who was by now lost in the sea of media screens covering the same news: Baruch was a terrorist. A WBG cable station aired a report featuring an investigator in Baku. One of WNN's interactive talk shows interviewed experts who gave psychological profiles and evaluations of Baruch. An independent station delved into the question of Baruch's possible association with the Scientology movement.

Scott zoomed in on competitor WBG's International Satellite broadcast. Todd Zone, who had worked for Scott several years ago as a sportscaster, stood with a large image of Baruch behind him:

"Baruch's mysterious past has become more transparent the last twenty-four hours. Based on a source at the CIA, Baruch is possibly an 'invention' of an anti-capitalist terrorist group looking to define a New World Order. In another breakthrough, an expert pathologist has expressed doubt that Baruch wrote the book *Apocrypha Truth*. Instead she believes that Baruch's deceased father, a doctor of philosophy, wrote the book as early as 1982."

"His dead father was a psychiatrist! His foster dad's a philosopher!" Scott pointed out to the nonattentive Todd Zone.

Shaking his head and grinning, Scott took a bite of the juicy, shredded pot roast and mumbled, "Mike McMillan, you fucking genius. Why didn't Walter come up with that spin: an unnamed source and a dead philosopher in the same story. It's like 'yeah, go prove this *isn't* true!' You gotta love it!"

After laying waste to Maddie's pot roast, Scott set his plate on the coffee table and sifted through his mail.

"I'm waiting for the paper bag apple pie!" he shouted in anticipation, working through the junk mail, bills, magazines, and one unstamped, blank manila envelope. He cleared his throat, opened the envelope, and grasped the lone content—a high-speed videodisk. Moving quickly to his office, he inserted the disk and waited.

His eyes exploded as Baruch's face came on the screen.

"It's September 7. In order for you to know that I made this video today, I'll remind that your 2:00 o'clock show opened with Ms. Laurance saying, 'Baruch: a spiritualist or a terrorist'. If you didn't see that, then just trust me."

Baruch's delivery was calm and confiding.

"Mr. McNally, I apologize that I never had the opportunity to speak with you personally. The events of this past week have made that all but impossible. Let me begin by saying that you cannot wish me away, any more than you can destroy me. With every blow you strike against me, my vision becomes clearer, more powerful."

Baruch paused and took a sip from his glass.

"Do you hate me because you perceive that I exert more power than you do? Does the idea of a god offend you? But let's be honest—the media has been playing god, not me. But your god is weak; your god disappears every time someone presses the off button. My God can be found in a single flower petal of the most remote field."

Baruch's eyes wandered toward the ceiling, as he took a deep breath.

"This all raises an interesting point. Imagine you controlled the media and religion; that is, even when a viewer turned off your station, he would still be tuned into your message. Wouldn't that be the coup of the century: a media mogul with his own messiah? That would give you complete control of the human mind, wouldn't it?"

Baruch angled his face more closely to the camera and continued:

"Mr. McNally, whether or not you believe a god exists doesn't matter. You do believe in something—we all believe in something. Is it your job, money, or yourself? You're a man who likes to be in charge. If you are in charge, why can't you stop me? Do you not find that strange?"

Baruch gave the deep penetrating gaze that had made him so famous.

"Before you try to ruin both of us, ask yourself one question: 'Who created Baruch?' The answer can be found much closer than you think."

Baruch relaxed his facial expression and asked in a more conversational manner,

"Did you enjoy your pot roast, Mr. McNally?"

Scott tightened his red face and yelled, "Maddie, come here!"

"Yes? Are you all right, sir?"

"Maddie, was anyone in the house today?"

"No, just a courier who delivered a package."

"What did he look like, Maddie?"

"It was a she. She was a young girl wearing a baseball cap."

"Never mind. Sorry to have scared you like that, Maddie."

Maddie left Scott's office breathing heavily and shut the door behind her.

CHAPTER 34

AMY LAURANCE MOVED SMOOTHLY DOWN THE AISLE OF CHICAGO'S new Symphony Hall and lowered herself into a red, velvety chair in the front row, directly in front of the orchestra pit, where the string section tuned their instruments. She wore a short, black satin dress that looked more like a negligée. Her breasts could be seen from the side and when she crossed her legs, the lower part of her buttocks were exposed.

"I met this total stud today. We're going to see *Carmen*. He's definitely bedable!"

Amy had recounted her encounter with Marco to Maggie before leaving the office.

Maggie, intent on figuring out the Baku-Baruch connection, could only muster the words, "How nice for you."

Marco, wearing black pants, a gray shirt, and a green, checkered jacket could have just come off the catwalk. He ran his fingers through the timeless style of his slicked-back black hair, his hand moving down the back of his muscular neck. A set of broad shoulders ran over onto Amy's seat.

"So what do you do?" Amy asked.

"I'm a freelance detective—I inspect insurance claims," Marco said modestly. "And how about you? I know you work for WNN."

"Well, do you ever watch TV?"

"Rarely," Marco confessed.

"Well, that explains it. Normally, everyone knows me because I'm an anchor for WNN. In fact, this afternoon at the diner I thought you were another guy looking for an autograph."

Marco laughed and touched Amy's knee. "I don't have heroes. Never did. I prefer plain old people."

"Heroes can give people something to shoot for," Amy said in an understanding voice.

"Normally, they get shot *at*," Marco said snidely.

"Well, I like having heroes," Amy concluded. Then she asked, "Where did you say you were from, Germany?"

"No, the Netherlands."

Amy talked about her short stint in Amsterdam as an editor for WNN during a summer internship. Marco, not paying much attention to what she said, nodded his head at regular intervals and threw her a sparkly-eyed glance from time to time. He looked at her brown skin, thin legs, and tight breasts. Amy broke his concentration and added

"How long are you staying in Chicago, Jan?"

For a moment, Marco forgot that he *was* Jan.

"Oh, the way it looks right now, only two or three days. I've almost wrapped up my work here. "

As he finished his sentence the lights went out and a violinist broke the silence, striking a couple of notes with his bow.

♦ ♦ ♦ ♦ ♦

"That was depressing," Amy summarized, as she and Marco exited the patterned carpet of the Symphony Hall lobby.

"Yeah, but life resembles *Carmen*—we have to make tough choices. Sometimes, we make that choice and it ends up in tragedy. And some people, well, just don't make it."

"But she didn't have to die!" Amy answered.

"She was a gypsy who worked in a cigarette factory and stabbed a coworker. Then she seduces this soldier away from his lover, gets him thrown in jail, forces him to renounce his title and then join a group of bandits." The normally cool Marco was worked up. "That's why art is such a dangerous thing. It can twist the truth. And the truth is—she deserved to die!"

"And the woman that played Carmen was no Maria Callas," Marco continued.

Amy looked confused. "Maria who?"

"Maria Callas was a famous singer. Some say she was the best," Marco stated factually as the valet parking attendant brought Marco's convertible to the front of the Opera House.

Two hours later, the good-looking couple was enjoying the second seating at Chez Jacques and waiting for dessert when Amy, tipsy from the wine, said, "I've met a lot of guys, Jan, but you're really cool."

That one sentence gave Marco an insight into the real Amy Laurance—the immature, insecure twenty-five-year-old who paraded around by day as America's power reporter. He liked this Amy as a person, although he liked the Amy at WNN as a sex icon.

"I've enjoyed this evening, Amy. It's been very relaxing."

The convertible headed back towards the Drake Hotel with the cool September air blowing Amy's blond hair into the back seat. Amy took Marco's right hand and placed it on her thigh, securing his hand with both of hers.

"Turn left here," Amy said.

Marco veered left toward Lake Michigan and continued driving east. Amy released her seat belt and slid over next to Marco, kissing the tight skin on the side of his neck. Marco obliged her by putting his arm around the back of her soft dress and pulling her even closer.

"Pull in at that entrance."

Amy pointed to a small driveway that led to a gate: Oakmont Boat Club.

"It's locked," Marco said sadly.

They embraced and Amy almost crawled over the steering wheel on top of Marco. Reaching back to the passenger seat, her breast in Marco's face, she grabbed her purse and pulled out a key chain, dangling it hypnotically in front of Marco.

"It's not closed if your dad's a member," Amy clarified.

She gave Marco's cheek a quick kiss, jumped out the top of the cabriolet, opened the gate, and waved Marco in as if she were bringing an airplane into the gate.

She pulled Marco out of the car and together they ran to the pier.

"Some great fall weather," Marco said, as he lifted Amy up to his 6'3" frame, his two hands clenched firmly under her dress. Amy's hands moved through Marco's thick hair and stared into his eyes as if she really knew him.

"Welcome to our boat," Amy declared, pointing to a forty-two-foot teakwood sailboat behind them. She wrapped her legs even tighter around her Jan and looked him in the eyes.

"God, do I want to fuck you!"

CHAPTER 35

THE WEEKEND OF SEPTEMBER 7 PASSED LIKE ALL OTHERS. THERE WERE stories to tell and stories to bury by the AZI-Group employees who were anxious to get back doing what it was that they did best. Sharon entered the glass-framed corner office, set down her purse, and headed straight for her screen. The screen greeted her.

"Good morning, Sharon. It's 7:45 AM on September 9, 2013. The motivational word for the day..."

Sharon hit 'escape'.

"Honey," she said looking at the screen, "if there one's person I don't need advice from, it's you."

She went into her mailbox and saw several memos from Scott and Walter. Before she could read anything, she was interrupted.

"Good morning, Sharon," Greg announced. "How are we doing this morning?"

"I'm not doing anything, yet. Cup of coffee?"

Sharon poured two cups from the shiny, stainless steel thermos.

"Greg, if I get one more memo about Baruch, I'm going to go shoot him myself."

Greg sat down across from Sharon.

"I'm joking, Greg," Sharon responded to Greg's grim look.

"Sharon, I was doing some research on Baruch last night."

"Who wasn't?"

"No, I mean some *serious* research."

Greg pulled a handful of documents from his leather case and threw them indignantly in front of Sharon.

"I find it interesting that up until a couple of months ago you were editing the stories that went to Walter Butwin."

Unfazed, she shot back, "First of all, Walter edits the stories. But did they come through my office? You're damn right. The man himself came in here and told me to compile all stories on Baruch."

"So why did they come to you?"

"Good question. When the reedited versions came back, there was stuff in there I'd never seen."

Greg pointed to the page on top of the stack.

"Like this story dated June 13, 2010, the Sunday edition: 'The Man They Call Baruch'. You submitted it. Where did you get this info about Baruch taking Europe by storm? I can't find anything to substantiate this report, and I searched every damn European paper."

Sharon shot back, "Hey, when the man tells you to run with a story, you run with it."

"The man? Do you mean Scott?"

Sharon laughed. "Scott's the only one that thinks he's the man. The stories came from the AZI-Group. They told me this was a government case and there had to be tight security."

"Did the stories come from Jim?"

"I got my undergrad in political science, Greg. Wanted to be a lawyer. The more I learned about law, the less I liked it. But I never forgot one lesson: people who have real power don't need to use it. The only reason they need us is to carry out their grand schemes. Ever hear of British Common Law?"

"Yeah, that was Henry—right?"

"Exactly, the Magna Carta. Invented to ruin the nobility and prop up the king. But they teach us in school that it was the first step toward democracy."

Sharon filled her half-empty coffee cup.

"The point is, people like Jim use us as they see fit. I have no clue why those stories ran through my office. I'm smart enough to understand that, Greg."

"So you're not going to tell me?"

Sharon got that streetwise look on her face. "It was a fella who looked remarkably similar to Jim, if that's what you want to know." She added suspiciously, "Greg, my woman's intuition tells me you're up to something."

"I don't know what I'm up to. But let me tell you that someone visited me yesterday and spouted some interesting theories. Do you want to hear them?

"I can't wait!"

"This someone told me that I should check the origin of all the stories on Baruch. I did. And every one of those reports sitting on your desk comes through this office. Then I'm told that a corporate espionage specialist paid to go after Baruch is on WNN's payroll. More interesting, though, is what I found out last night. Did you know that Jim Anderson met Baruch at a conference in Brussels?"

"And what does that prove?"

"It only proves that Jim has known him since—are you ready for this—2010!"

"Now that's strong, Greg. That's real strong."

Sharon threw her hands up in the air. "Here's what I know. I'm told the government has classified Baruch as a threat to national security. They tell me all stories come through me. Then a few months ago, you take over."

"Why not send the stories directly to Walter? That's what I find strange."

"Because Jim always distances himself. That's why."

"But what is he distancing himself *from*?"

"He's paranoid, Greg."

"Think about it, Sharon. In June 2010 no one even knew who Baruch was! Why all the hush-hush? Why would the government be involved?"

Sharon shrugged her shoulders while Greg sipped his coffee.

"We broke every story, Sharon. Where was WBG? Where were the independent stations? They didn't break one goddamned story! Think about it."

"Greg, Baruch's probably dead. Just drop it!"

"He's definitely not dead, Sharon."

"Sounds like you've seen him."

Greg stood up and gulped the remaining coffee from his cup.

"I can neither confirm nor deny that," Greg said, shutting the door behind him. No sooner was the door shut than he reopened it and stuck his upper body through the small crack.

"Sharon, have you ever seen this guy?" He held up an 8 X 11 inch photo of Marco Van Wels.

"Yeah, he's doing some work for Scott."

"Sharon, I hope you're not holding back on me, because this is getting really heavy!"

CHAPTER 36

THE LANKY IRISHMAN, PONYTAIL PULLED NEATLY BACK, STEPPED INTO the spectacular elevator, admiring the lacquered mahogany panels, handcrafted moldings and tightly woven green carpet. As the door closed, the marble-filled lobby of the WNN Tower disappeared. A young security agent inserted his shiny, metal card into a gold-plated slot, illuminating the button for the tenth floor.

"Please confirm your security code," the friendly digital voice stated.

The guard entered a code and the elevator ascended to WNN's tenth floor.

Waiting for the elevator to move, his hands tucked behind his back, Mike McMillan spoke to the uptight guard. "Is this a board room or an elevator?"

The guard smiled, "Yeah, they remodeled it last year. It's reserved for executives and senior reporters."

The elevator door opened. Looking at the elegant furnishings of the waiting area the guard snapped, "Ask me if I got a raise last year. Who knows—maybe this year!"

"May you have the strength of ten," Mike said pleasantly, bowing his head courteously to the confused guard. "Means 'good luck' in Irish," Mike whispered.

As he stepped onto the tenth floor, another guard met Mike and escorted him past the receptionist and down a long hallway.

He heard the strokes of keyboards bolting through the calmness of what Charley had named ' the JAPE'—Jim Anderson's Penile Extension.

Exiting the door marked 'Men', Greg turned swiftly onto the plush carpet of the hallway and collided with the warm-weather stranger, who wore beige pants and a white, short-sleeve T-shirt.

"Excuse me," Greg said, stopping in his tracks.

"You must be Greg Lancy," the man with the Irish accent shot back.

Greg's eyes gave away his amazement. "Mr. McMillan. It's a pleasure to meet you."

The guard looked anxious as the two men shook hands.

"You do fine work, Mr. Lancy. Maybe one day you'll work for the good guys!"

"That's very kind of you, Mr. McMillan."

The guard tried to get the guest moving towards the offices, but Mike turned back and, with a warm smile, added, "That's an open invitation. And my name's Mike."

Back at his desk, Greg stared at the security memo flashing on his screen: "Mr. Mike McMillan of WBG will arrive on the tenth floor in three minutes. Please use proper operational procedure."

Somehow between his office and the toilet Greg had missed the security call. He immediately shut his door, which covered the only 'operational procedure' he was aware of.

"Meeting Baruch and Mike McMillan within twenty-four hours...Wow!" he said, smiling as Maggie dodged into his office.

"Did you see the message?"

"Yeah, I ran into McMillan in the hallway—literally."

"Well, what did he say?"

"He offered me a job!"

Greg's face radiated. The security monitor blinked: "PLEASE SECURE ALL DOORS."

Greg got up and shut the door, again. Pointing at the screen he added, "It's the information age, and MIS has all of it."

"Yeah, I know. As if the almighty computer were some secret metaphysical entity that only MIS tech-heads can understand."

"If it's so technical that only twelve guys on the planet can figure it out, it should be safe," Greg contributed.

Maggie shook her head: "The tech-heads. If those kids fell, they would miss the ground!"

"Yeah, it's kind of funny. McMillan invented that operational software—you know, inflation technology—the MIS goons are using. Like McMillan needs to steal something from them!"

"So what did you say to him?" Maggie wondered out loud.

"Not much. The security guard grabbed him as if he were a prisoner."

"How did he look?" Maggie continued with a big girlish smile.

"Ponytail, T-shirt, beige pants..."

"No. How did he *look*?" Maggie interrupted.

"If I were a girl, I'd do him!" Greg said in a heavy Bronx accent.

"That's terrible," Maggie said, still smiling.

♦ ♦ ♦ ♦ ♦

"Mr. McMillan, sir," the security officer presented the visitor to Jim Anderson.

"Hello, Mike. Nice to see you in Chicago."

Mike entered Jim's stately office, the place where Jim had spent most of his waking hours before moving the headquarters to Baku. The door clicked shut and the globe's two power brokers were alone.

"Todd Zone has put some great spins on the Baruch reports," Jim praised.

"Ah, just the luck of the Irish, I guess," Mike said humbly.

"What brings you to Chicago?"

"I had to stop by our chip factory..." Pausing and rubbing his temples Mike continued, "So I thought it was better to deliver this news to you in person."

Jim's face expressed concern as he watched Mike light a cigarette.

"Mind if I smoke, mate?"

"Not at all. In fact, I'll have one."

Mike offered Jim a hand-rolled cigarette from a silver case.

"What's that inscription on the cigarette case, Mike?"

"It's an old French saying: '*Ce n'est pas important ce que on fait, l'important est ce que on a le pouvoir de faire*'," Mike recited in beautiful French.

"And that would mean in English?" Jim asked.

"It's not important what one does, what's important is that which one has the ability to do'."

Jim grinned. "Touching. I didn't know you speak French."

Mike poured himself a cup of coffee and took a seat across the walnut table.

"Oh, Jim. There's all kinds of things about me you don't know."

Jim seemed curious, but passed.

"What's the big news, Mike?"

Mike crossed his legs, obviously uncomfortable in the small, short chair. Uncrossing his legs and standing up, he said, "Jim, the FCC visited me yesterday. Then the World Media Regulatory Group, the FBI and the CIA contacted my legal department. They started asking a lot of questions."

Jim looked surprised. "What's that all about?"

"They want me to produce some evidence that Baruch blew up that rig. I guess the CIA wants to get him and the FCC wants to get me."

Jim, looking anxious and unprepared, glanced down at his desk and searched for the right words.

"Hey, Mike. I gave you that file with the report from the Baku police and the insurance company. Didn't you get that?"

"Sure did, Jim. The CIA says that the report's a crock. They say that Interpol's report indicates a maintenance problem. I'm not an expert on oil rigs, Jim, but I do make it a practice to keep the CIA out of my office."

Mike lowered himself back into the chair and put his elbows on his knees.

"Did you know that the FBI is protecting Baruch?"

"Come on! You're not serious, Mike?"

"They claim somebody has put out a contract on him."

Jim listened in disbelief. Mike continued, "I'm telling you what they told me... and I'm pulling the Baruch stories, mate. I agreed to a formal retraction and the FCC agreed to stay out of my office. I came by to warn you."

Jim reflected. "Those reports from the Baku police have to be accurate. Mike, we had a private inspector check it out before I ran with the story."

"Listen, I'm not going to ruin my media group over Baruch. Anyway, he's good press."

Jim rubbed his own neck with one hand and tapped the desk with the other.

"OK, Mike. How long can you hold off on a retraction?"

"They want me to run it today!"

"Can't you stall?"

"Come on, Jim. When a celebrity gets caught with a hooker, we have a full report within ten minutes. What... am I going to tell them that I need a week to issue an apology? It'll have to be a damn long one!"

Jim leaned back in his chair, let his head fall back, and

breathed deeply.

"Can you wait until the evening news tomorrow?"

"Sure. I'm a good enough salesman to get us thirty-six hours."

"Mike, I'm certain that I can substantiate those reports."

"You've got until 6:00 PM on the twelfth. May you have the strength of ten," Mike said with a rich Irish accent.

"Oh yes," Mike said as he stood up, "there's one other thing I want you to know, Jim...as a friend. Some interesting documents found their way onto my desk. My reporter says that BNG and Haig Abku were involved with the Kirov drug cartel. The reporter has some evidence."

Squinting and exhaling as in pain, Mike continued, "Anything I should know before I run with this, Jim?"

Jim smiled and studied his youthful competitor.

"For five years they've been trying to find something that isn't there. Tell your reporter 'I wish them the luck of ten.'"

Jim moved around the desk and extended his hand. "Thanks for your understanding, Mike. I'm sorry you were put in this awkward position."

With one hand on the doorknob, Mike admired his silver cigarette case and, smiling playfully, said, "Awkward position? Nah, I'm just having fun. You're the one trying to take over the world."

The security guard buzzed open the door and escorted the visitor to the elevator.

Moving quickly to his desk, Jim grabbed his secure phone line.

"Scott, Jim. I need you in my office—pronto."

CHAPTER 37

GREG LEFT THE OFFICE SHORTLY AFTER CRASHING INTO MIKE McMillan, heading to his posh West Side suburb where he had a lunch appointment with Charley. Outside the door he could hear Charley, Maggie, and Jenny roaring with laughter.

"I must have missed a good one!" Greg commented as he opened the door.

Jenny tried to speak, but was laughing so hard that she could only gasp, "He kills me."

Maggie jumped in: "Remember the look on Scott's face when he opened Charley's present at Christmas and it was a huge banner?—'I fucking quit'."

Greg laughed along. "But the funniest thing was that Scott thought you were joking, Charley. And then you said 'No, really. I fucking quit—Merry Christmas!'"

Greg could remember the entire staff holding champagne glasses and standing around the beautifully decorated Christmas tree in the conference room. Scott had been loose from the bubbly and thought the banner to be another of Charley's tasteless jokes.

"You know, Charley, to this day Scott still can't understand that you quit over principle. He must have said a hundred times: 'Question: who could have made two million in preferred stocks if he'd just shut his mouth? Answer: Charley the weasel.'"

Still in stitches, Jenny got up from the couch and headed to her office, leaving Maggie, Charley, and Greg to do their thing.

Charley continued Greg's thought: "That's McNally. He'd jump on a grenade if it increases the stock price. That's the bad thing about employee stock benefits—it makes the employees more ruthless than the fucking owners. Golden handcuffs, what a crock of shit. They should call it what it is..."

"Multilevel greed," Maggie interrupted, "that's what Baruch calls it."

Greg set down his briefcase and sat on the ottoman across from Maggie and Charley. "So, Mag, did you tell Charley who I ran into?"

"I would have taken the job offer on the spot," Charley jumped in, "because he's the only one on this planet with integrity."

"Yeah, Charley. It's not the same without you," Greg chuckled.

"We both know I was a pain in the ass. But we did have some fun; that is, before the AZI-Group brought in their umpteen trillions of dollars and Jim 'the figurehead' Anderson."

"Come on, Charley. You think Jim's just a figurehead?" Maggie prodded.

"Think? I know! Remember the 'thing that owns the thing' theory, Mag. Who owns Jim? The AZI-Group. Who owns them? Institutional investors. Who owns them? The banks. Remember, Greg, it always ends up with the banks."

"You and McNally are the only ones who buy the bank conspiracy," Greg teased.

Charley became serious. "So you want to open a book distributorship. Where do you get the money? Say you have financial problems. Who starts moving in on your stock? I'm telling you, Greg, if the banks don't underwrite it, it doesn't happen."

Greg looked at Maggie. "I'll sit this one out," she joked.

Seizing the moment of silence, Greg asked, "So, do the banks own Baruch?"

"That's the reason I like Baruch, Greg ol' buddy. Baruch has used the system and beat it at its own game."

"What's that supposed to mean?" Greg asked.

"It's simple. You've read his book. He talks about the hyper-consolidation of the media, the lack of spirituality, and the twisted object of people's desires. So he finds a solution — himself. He perpetuates himself through the media and becomes such a big story that they and their endless money grabbing make him even bigger. But then the media figures out that people are actually listening to his message. You see, we journalists expect people to listen, but not to think. Somehow Baruch got people thinking about everything going on around them. And trying to pin him to this oil fire was really dumb. You don't build a guy up for five years and then say 'Just kidding, he's really a terrorist!' Where did you guys learn to write a story?"

"Charley, I heard the way he addressed you yesterday. You're the first one—besides the professor—who he's ever called by his first name. How long, Charley?"

"Once you're in, Greg, it's going to get deep."

"I'm already in," Greg said, handing the electric New Yorker a twelve-inch stack of papers. "These are all the records you asked for yesterday."

Charley smiled like a schoolboy. "Greg, buddy, you're a champ."

"So how long have you known him?"

"First, tell me what you know, Greg. That's part of the rules."

"What rules?"

"My rules."

Greg had an all-knowing air as he spoke. "WNN broke every

one of those stories; Jim Anderson has known Baruch since 2010; WNN made Baruch."

Charley threw Greg one of his big loving smiles. "Greg, congratulations. To think that I told Frank that you wouldn't figure it out."

Greg's look went from all-knowing to all-confused.

"You knew all along?"

"Sorry, but I was sworn to secrecy. Would you like me to fill in the spaces of why and how your loving, caring organization got the inside scoop on Baruch?"

Greg nodded. "You little bastard. How long have you known this?"

"Oh, a while."

"What's a while?"

"Years."

"And you kept it inside all this time. Did Baruch write those articles, too?"

"No way, Greg. Baruch doesn't own me any more than I own him."

Maggie leaned forward on the couch. "Tell me, Charley. Those pictures of Marco van Wels you showed me yesterday. I noticed something interesting. There aren't any tall buildings around the Oiltron offices in Baku, yet the photos were aerial shots. A friend of mine said they could have been taken from a reconnaissance satellite."

Charley chuckled. "So you're still trying to shoot down Baruch. For those types of photos you need a very special satellite, either a sun synchronous polar orbit or a missile projected satellite."

"And how do they work?" Maggie asked.

"The sun synchronous polar orbit satellites are the ones that they use for weather. The government, WNN, WBG, and a hundred other organizations and countries have polar orbit satellites. But the best satellites are ones that you don't know are there. That's why for the really good photos the military shoots a satellite from a missile. It only orbits for a while, but nobody can track it."

"This is bizarre. We've got someone on the heels of Marco Van Wels—the guy tracking Baruch. So who's hunting the hunter, Charley?" Maggie inquired.

"Mag, Greg, you're not *even* going to believe this."

CHAPTER 38

SCOTT, LOOKING CONSPICUOUSLY OUT OF PLACE OCCUPYING THE SEAT Mike McMillan had sat in only a few minutes ago, observed Jim who removed his jacket, revealing dark perspiration stains under his armpits. Jim said harshly, "Scott, I hope you have a good story to tell me about our friend Marco."

"You want a good story? The CEO of a major corporation feeds news stories—576 of them—around the back of the president. The same CEO miraculously uncovers the secret of the world's most wanted man."

Scott fired a look of disgust.

"You want to know about Marco? The Marco who called me this morning and said he's off the investigation?"

Jim smirked and offered a warm gesture.

"Scott, I've been hoping this Baruch story would magically disappear, but it's only gotten worse. I think we've both held back too much information—I'm certainly as guilty as anyone is. OK, I give you the entire scoop; you give me the scoop. We find a solution and it stays between these four walls. Is that a deal?"

Scott's clenched fists relaxed and he slid his chair away from Jim's desk.

"OK. All the secrets are on the table. You've got honors."

Jim laughed. "This is embarrassing." Rubbing his forehead he continued. "It's May 2010. I'm at a conference in Europe. They show a speech by Baruch in a highlight film—he had been at some spirituality conference. Anyway, Baruch and I meet at a tea party that evening and he starts spouting out his various themes—the void in world religions and the likes. He tells me he's got the answer."

"You're not going to tell me he works for us," Scott shot out.

"If you would have asked me a year ago, I'd have said yes. Put yourself in my shoes...I figured he's no threat. He's only a visionary with no one behind him."

Jim took a gulp of iced tea. "The ratings in 2010 were abysmal. Our stock flattened out. We needed a feature event, an event where we controlled the spin. So, to make a long story short, I put Baruch on the payroll."

Scott looked shocked, grumbling and laughing simultaneously.

"Boy, and I thought I had some heavy shit."

The pitch of Jim's voice raised: "It was working. You have to understand the genius behind the plan, Scott."

"I'm listening."

"Every protagonist needs an antagonist. Do you think that Liberals hate Republicans; that militants despise the government? On the contrary, militants feed off the government. The more repressive the government becomes, the more power the militants gain."

Scott bit his lip and shook his head in disbelief. "So Maggie was right."

"What do you mean?"

"Maggie Helbling figured it out months ago. She guessed that someone was creating Baruch as a diversion."

Jim threw his hands up in the air. "I didn't know that the guy would turn on us—goddammed scumbag...and that book just had to become the number one seller on the planet!"

"Well come on, Jim. With us promoting it, that didn't hurt his chances!"

Jim tightened up and pointed his finger at Scott, almost touching his nose: "This guy has a master plan! Now he's putting us out of business. He owns us."

Jim appeared drained. "OK, Scott, that's my confession."
Scott breathed deeply and exhaled through his nose.

"My story starts six months ago when I hired Marco Van Wels. When you put out the word that Baruch had to go, I took it seriously. If you would have told me this then, I would never have started this fiasco."

Jim shrugged his shoulders as Scott searched his memory.

"As Marco starts closing in on Baruch, the oil rig goes up in Baku. Marco comes to me with the idea to set Baruch up—he says he has great contacts in Baku and that he can point the explosion at our spiritual friend. Well, we run with it and it's a bull's-eye. Baruch's a terrorist."

"No, Scott, it's not a bull's-eye. Didn't even hit the target. Interpol and the CIA say it wasn't an act of terrorism. WBG was forced to retract the stories on Baruch. You need to find your friend Marco and find a way to make this story stick, because if you can't, Custer's last stand is going to look like a fucking picnic."

With a face red enough to match his curly Irish hair, Scott said matter-of-factly, "I'll figure something out."

Prying himself out of the small chair, Scott pondered: "You were going to turn Baruch into the anti-AZI-Group. You had the protagonist and antagonist on the same side. That was a ballsy plan, Jimbo! A fucking *ballsy* plan!"

Ignoring Scott's input, Jim said briskly, "OK, you've got thirty-six hours until WBG issues their apology and blows the lid off this kettle. I don't want that to happen."

Scott snapped his fingers.

"I almost forgot. Baruch sent me a message Saturday."

Reaching in his pocket, Scott placed the videodisk on the desk. "Jim, this guy is really good."

CHAPTER 39

THE DARK, HANDSOME AUSTRIAN DISPLAYED A SOMBER FACE, AS A group of large men wearing FBI jackets ushered him down a littered, pungent alley to the single steel door marked WBG SECURITY ENTRANCE. The group huddled near the closed door in the chilly morning shadows of McMillan Business Park in downtown Los Angeles. The heavy steel door opened and two agents secured the entrance. Another agent checked the freight elevator and signaled that all was clear.

They led Baruch down a narrow hallway with scratched walls and archaic vinyl floor tile. A hallway normally reserved for janitors and catering crews temporarily housed the most talked about man on the planet.

"Is this necessary?" Baruch asked.

"Sir, the president of the United States wants you protected," the agent stated.

The door at the end of the hallway opened to the luxurious office space of WBG's executive floor, which had been emptied out minutes earlier by WBG's own security force due to a 'gas leak'.

"Sir, please stay between us at all times," the short-haired marine-turned-FBI-agent advised Baruch, who seemed to absorb all that was around him like air absorbs a fragrance.

Two heavy wooden doors with a sign 'Recording Studio: VI'

opened to a group of WBG security guards, or 'brownshirts' as they were called by insiders.

Moving through the guards, a well-dressed, broad-shoul-dered man approached Baruch.

"Please have a seat."

Todd Zone gave a firm handshake and motioned politely for Baruch to move into a comfortable black leather chair on the set.

"Thanks, Mr. Zone," Baruch's deep, rich voice echoed.

The two WBG brownshirts scurried behind Todd, placing glasses of ice water on the cork coasters that nicely matched the mahogany table.

"It's an honor to meet you, Baruch," Todd said with confi-dence. "Sorry about those reports we ran the other day."

He set his folders down on the second black chair adjacent to Baruch.

"The pleasure is entirely mine, Mr. Zone. And those stories... if you make me look too good, people won't believe it," Baruch replied politely with a soft grin.

He sat peacefully, his elbows propped on the armrests and his hands loosely intertwined, as if he were praying. The FBI agents spoke with Todd Zone in the opposite corner of the room. Todd, an all-American linebacker at USC in his college days, made the FBI agents appear very average in size. Although now a polished anchorman, Todd's face still exposed the intensity of an all-American athlete.

The FBI agent advised Todd, "As soon as the interview ends, you come out alone. Then we'll clear the floor and escort the gen-tleman out of the building."

Turning to Baruch, the agent asked, "Sir, would you like us to leave an agent here with you?"

Looking at the size of the WBG anchor, Baruch assured the officer: "No, I'll be quite fine with Mr. Zone."

The half dozen FBI agents shut the door. Todd Zone walked over towards his guest. "Because of the security issue, we'll use these two still cameras. Then I'll splice them myself to insure that no one has access."

"That suits me, Mr. Zone," Baruch concurred.

Todd positioned the cameras, commandeering the mixing board like someone who felt at home with his trade. He lowered his huge physique gracefully into the chair and, using the remote to zoom one camera on himself, commenced:

"Ladies and gentlemen, we are about to experience a historic event. There have been many rumors about the spiritual leader, Baruch. Just one week ago, he was interviewed by WNN on a live satellite broadcast. Then he disappeared. Many said a religious group had kidnapped him. Some even accused the business community. Then came a shocking report from WNN indicating that Baruch was behind the explosion at the AZI-Group's Baku oil facility. WBG has obtained information from Interpol and the CIA that no connection exists between Baruch and the incident in Baku."

Todd maneuvered the lens to a wider angle.

"We at WBG believe in the public's right to know. Therefore, we made an offer to one of Baruch's closest friends for Baruch to appear on WBG's World News, uncensored."

The second camera showed a very healthy and alive Baruch—the twenty-first century David who had dared challenge the world's most powerful organizations with their own weapon: words.

Todd Zone commenced the interview.

"Baruch, this has certainly been an eventful week. Can you tell us how you've been coping with the situation?"

Chapter 40

Scott McNally sat at the bar of the posh Drake Hotel.

"This place reminds me of a country club," said Scott, as he flirted with the attractive young lady behind the bar who barely looked old enough to drive.

"Yeah, it's kind of snooty," she agreed. Her eyes gazed past Scott, sizing up the male object approaching.

Scott spoke loudly: "Judging by the sparkle in this young lady's eyes, that must be the mad Dutchman standing behind me."

"Bingo," Marco responded playfully.

Scott stood up and led Marco to a deep, oak table in the corner of this nineteenth century remnant.

"Scott, I hope you're not here to discuss the Baruch issue."

"Yep, I am—and so are you."

"We've known each other too well to start threatening one another." Marco tapped Scott on the shoulder and kept a friendly demeanor.

"OK, Marco, agreed. But I had a meeting with Jim this morning. The CIA and Interpol have refuted your report. WBG is retracting all their stories as of Wednesday as are we. That is, if we can't verify your report."

The pragmatic Marco from Amsterdam flashed a confident smile: "If you think that I only had Plan A, you underestimated me." Marco squinted and pointed his finger at Scott. "But *why* were Interpol and the CIA checking this out? I mean, I covered all the official protocol. Someone with some clout had to file a request for that case to be opened. Believe me, this case was solid."

With a puzzled expression Scott lifted his shoulders and countered, "Does it really matter? The fact remains that they're on to it. So what do we do?"

Marco roared, coughing from intense laughter.

"What's so fucking funny?" Scott asked with an irked tone.

"Oh, Scott. You big corporations are all the same. You have all this power, but you get pulled out of your little world and you can't punch your way out of a paper sack. All your billions of dollars and thousands of employees together can't do what I can. It's charming!"

"Alright, you got your 'Marco the Great' speech in. So, what do you suggest, Great One?"

Fighting off laughter, Marco gathered himself. "First thing you do is blame the Baku police for providing false information. Write an apologetic sob story for your little hardbody reporter to read on WNN. Make sure you blame the Baku police and no one else. Then count on me to take care of the rest. Scott, do not—I repeat, do not—mention me in any news reports or I'm a dead man...and I won't die alone."

"So what are you going to do? This isn't like ordering out Chinese for lunch. If you don't deliver, we're fucked, my friend!"

"The Feds are protecting Baruch. Before I do anything, I need to make a few calls."

Scott jumped out of his chair and placed his hands on his face.

"Do you mean the FBI is protecting him? Why would they do that?"

"You media people aren't as bright as I thought," Marco lifted his lean figure and placed his powerful hands on Scott's shoulders.

"You need to open your eyes, man. Has it ever occurred to you that Baruch never goes after the government? He'll go after religion and business, but never government."

There was a long silence. Scott now had to be the sap who asked the question to the almighty 'boss'.

"Why?"

"Because, believe it or not, governments like the world broken up in disunited little pieces. For bureaucrats, chaos justifies power. Do you think they like this global consolidation stuff? Hell, Scott, they're just along for the ride—grabbing a little power here and a little power there. They want to see the AZI-Group fall hard. And if Baruch gets too much power, he'll go next...and he knows it. You should read his book—it's all there!"

Marco released his hold on Scott and headed out the front entrance of the Drake.

"They can't afford to bring us down! We're the American economy," Scott yelled.

Marco stopped in his tracks. "You're right, the government won't bring you down. Baruch will."

CHAPTER 41

TODD ZONE TURNED OFF THE CAMERA AND ASKED, "BARUCH, CAN WE start over again? That was a terrible introduction."

"Please, you're the expert, Mr. Zone."

Todd turned off his linebacker intensity for a moment and switched on the light-hearted, fun-loving ex-sportscaster.

"We've all heard the rumors about *the* spiritual figure of the twenty-first century: Baruch. There were rumors that he was dead, or kidnapped, or belonged to some terrorist group. Despite all the words recently written and spoken about Stefan Mostl—the man we call Baruch—he has escaped this row of accusations unscathed, vindicated of all charges by the U.S. government. When I was a sportscaster, there were certain figures I interviewed who conveyed power through spirit. I'm glad and honored to have a man of power and spirit with us today."

The camera focused in on Baruch.

"Baruch, maybe you can begin by telling our viewers what you've been up to the past week?"

"Certainly, Todd." Baruch dropped his head, breathed deeply, and challenged the camera with his eyes.

"Angry individuals and groups who clamor for power have driven me into hiding by threatening my life. This week has reminded me how urgent my work is. I do not clamor for my own life any more than I clamor for personal power. But when I go, truth, love, and faith must be on the right path."

"Are you saying, Baruch, that someone has actually made threats?"

"Yes. Unfortunately, they fail to understand that by focusing on my destruction they insure their own."

"Who are 'they?'"

"Take your pick—government, virtual corporations, religious fanatics. The better question is: why?"

"Well, some people say you're an anarchist, others say you're a socialist. How would you describe your political orientation?"

Baruch hesitated for what seemed like an eternity. Todd, however painful it was, sat and took the silence like a linebacker taking a crack-back block.

"Mr. Zone, you have just described one word that means a political void: anarchy; and a second word that describes an economic model: socialism. Any manmade model is inherently dangerous. Take capitalism: Is this not just another philosophy, a best guess, at how the world should be? Is blind faith in a human invention any less dangerous than faith in the force that created us? Politics is simply the vehicle a group of individuals uses to control another group. In that sense of the word, you may consider me apolitical."

"So you're going to dodge the question?" Scott asked lightheartedly.

"Contrary to what many think, I do like a free market system. What scares me is when we confuse capitalism with democracy, and wealth with freedom. We can have capitalism and wealth while still being repressed. At what point does capitalism become a tool of tyranny?"

"I'll let you answer that question," Todd responded.

"When a single individual from a small village in Austria is forced into hiding because he questions an economic model; when the free market's 'invisible hand' gains a chokehold on personal liberty."

Baruch continued, "My sole purpose, Mr. Zone, is to make minds move. And virtual corporations fear this one abstract power more than anything."

Todd looked at his notebook.

"In *Apocrypha Truth*, you discuss at great length the virtual corporations who you refer to as cartels. Do you recognize a distinction between the cartels of the industrial age and the modern virtual corporation?"

"That's an excellent question, Mr. Zone. The difference—or distinction—is that the virtual corporation exercises much more power than a cartel ever dreamed of. It is more important to own the mind than to conquer it. Several million workers pledge their allegiance to a corporate philosophy—a philosophy subject only to the laws of economics. These same companies then turn around and externalize their message via their vast holdings, media channels and the likes. It's ironic that we as a society scrutinize spiritual leaders, visionaries, and the Bible more than we scrutinize the moral consequences of corporate philosophy."

Baruch extended his arm, palm upward as if to say, 'And you're part of it.' He continued, "And the media acts as the arbiter, keeping the focus off themselves and on everyone else. When was the last time you saw a major media group investigated?"

"But you are admittedly trying to 'make minds move'. Aren't you ultimately pursuing ownership of the mind?"

Baruch appeared amused. "Specialize or die. Never be satisfied with what you have. Buy happiness. These are the slogans of your New World Order, slogans that were sold to the people of the world via slick ad campaigns, the same way you brand a soft drink. Is this how *advanced* we are? Where do we go from here?"

"So you're not pursuing ownership of the mind?" Todd persisted.

"I'm not a prophet. My goals are more modest, more practical."

Todd glanced again at his notebook. He appeared to enjoy this tête-a-tête with Baruch.

"How do you respond to those that say a religious world got us into centuries of wars and the secular, capitalistic world pulled us into prosperity?"

Baruch smiled, unleashing a bit of arrogance. "People, not abstract institutions or intellect, set events in motion. 'Religion' cannot start a war any more than a virtual corporation can ruin our planet. In fact, an enlightened virtual corporation could indeed help the planet. I long to see that day."

The two went on to discuss topics as abstract as the essence of a universal god, the popularity of unity theory and more concrete ideas, like the failure of the European Union and consequences of harmonized labor in developing nations.

Baruch was tireless in his passion to debate any issue Todd Zone brought up.

Asked why the European Union was struggling, Baruch stated simply, "Because the people don't want it to work."

After exhausting every question he served up, Todd eyed the final question on his notepad. "Baruch, what has been the most significant human change in your lifetime?"

"Human evolution has been one of stepping-stones—a progression not apparent to us, yet perfectly clear to higher sources. This question is impossible to answer."

Restating the question Todd asked, "What then would be one particular event that has changed our world?"

"There is no short answer."

"We have time," Todd assured.

"In the early days of American democracy, government put the ball of destruction in motion by separating church and state. While the idea may have been noble, this church/state issue was hijacked by power-seekers looking to change the country's social fabric: in order to grab power they had to destroy the hold that religion possessed. Once that was accomplished, the governments began consolidating their position by self-created crisis. In the late twentieth century, the tides changed and the private sector swung the power to their side: business mutinied and took over the ship. Now we had a populace stripped of their religion, suddenly accountable to the new kid on the block: the virtual corporation. Like Napoleon crowning himself emperor, the business community seized control and then proceeded through careful manipulation to sell the populace on the most destructive idea to penetrate the human mind: 'that's business'."

Baruch leaned across the mahogany table and pointed at Todd.

"Those words erased humankind's most precious collective achievement: integrity. What are we without integrity? How far our belief system must have digressed to see people turning to chanting, crystals, and any other superstition, just so they can get out of bed in the morning."

Appealing to the viewers, Baruch asked, "How many of you have used 'that's business' to justify your actions? If what you are doing is right, why justify it? Be aware that the era of global consolidation used the addiction of physical comfort to pry from you your mental liberty. Unless we once again learn to think our own thoughts, the worst is yet to come."

The power and conviction of Baruch's words reduced Todd to just a nice guy who happened to be in the same room. Todd had kept the interview on track, asked the right questions, and stayed out of the way.

Baruch said sincerely, "Mr. Zone, I appreciate your kindness. I would like to thank you from the bottom of my heart."

Baruch stood up and shook his hand. Todd's emotions were running so high he didn't know whether to give a fist pump or cry. He clicked off the cameras with the remote and gleamed with excitement.

"That was phenomenal—that was real powerful."

Baruch penetrated Todd's innermost feelings with a fixed stare that no artist could paint.

"Todd, this is not a football game you win or lose. The very future of those millions of viewers lies with you and your company."

He touched Todd's massive arm. "You did well, Todd. God be with you."

Baruch knocked on the door and an FBI agent escorted him to the freight elevator.

CHAPTER 42

"WHY ARE THEY PROTECTING BARUCH, MARTIN? I'M NOT ASKING FOR details, just tell me why."

Marco stood on the cold granite floor of Chicago's Union Station clenching a pay phone in his hand and covering his other ear to dampen the noise of trains and intercom messages. The entire afternoon had been spent networking with the Baku police force, Interpol, and, now his buddy at the FBI, Martin Pena.

"Martin, forget why they're protecting him. Just tell me where I can find him."

This was the sixth pay phone Marco had used this evening. Even though he was sure every public line could be tapped, his Interpol experience taught him that switching pay phones made satellite interception almost impossible.

"OK, Martin. So he went to Los Angeles airport. Never mind, I know where he is. Bye."

Marco ran up to street level, jumped in his car, and sped off.

♦ ♦ ♦ ♦ ♦

At 8:00 PM, Marco was at Scott's home sitting in the same chair from which he had shocked Scott just forty-eight hours ago.

"Marco, are you sure he was at WBG today?"

"Scott, why would he go to LA if not for WBG? I mean, there

were reports of FBI agents all over the building, and they evacuated the tenth floor sometime between noon and 2:00 PM."

"Wait a minute." Scott indicated for Marco to be quiet as he turned up the voice of Todd Zone on the monitor on his desk.

"And WBG's information confirms that the BNG bank in Baku was facilitating transactions for the Kirov drug cartel as early as 2008. According to sources, Interpol has issued an arrest warrant for Haig Abku, president of Oiltron Industries, and former mayor of Baku. Mr. Abku is reported to be an operative for the Kirov cartel who used his position inside the AZI-Group to place drug traders in key positions. AZI-Group CEO Jim Anderson declined comment until he has been briefed on the situation."

Marco took a sip of scotch and pointed at Todd Zone.

"Why don't you tell them the truth. Jim Anderson doesn't need to be briefed. He's the one who covered the whole thing up in the first place."

"Why would he do that?" Scott asked in disgust.

"He needed to close the Oiltron purchase. When Oiltron's stock fell, some Baku locals were trying to put together a deal with a Russian consortium. Haig Abku led the Baku trade delegation and Jim needed him to get Oiltron. It was a simple business deal: Jim wanted Oiltron, and Haig wanted to be a player."

"You mean Jim *knew* that Abku was involved in illegal businesses at the same time he was running Oiltron?"

"Like I said earlier, sometimes you media guys aren't all that smart."

"So was BNG involved in the Kirov drug deal?" Scott wanted to know.

"It's complicated. The U.S. government wanted Oiltron in American hands for security reasons. The CIA was using the Kirov family to carry out contracts in the Middle East. And Haig, when he was mayor, took payoffs from the Kirov family in order to buy influence in Russia. In other words, they were all one happy family."

"Where does BNG fit in?"

"There were some Kirov operatives working there. Interpol was ready to bust them when Haig threatened to blow the Oiltron deal. That's when we closed the file on BNG."

Marco laughed. "To be honest with you, I still don't know exactly who was working for whom!"

Scott swirled his goblet in circles, whiskey clinging to the sides of the glass.

"So what's your plan?"

"Baruch's book made the Catholic Church's banned list. Well, I have documented several threats against Baruch from..."

Scott jumped in and barked, "Oh no! Character assassination is one thing, but I am not in the killing business."

Marco remained cool, as always.

"Here are the facts, Scott. People expect him to get assassinated. Hell, he prophesied his own death in his book. It's only a question of who and when."

Marco reached deep into his corporate experience:

"Your stock has lost twenty percent in the past twelve months. Your viewership is plummeting. Ad revenues are off. Why? Because you're no longer in control of your business. You thought giving Baruch that twenty minutes with Amy Laurance would shut him up? He's playing with you guys. My money says he cut an interview with WBG and is prepared to serve you and Jim to the world on a platter. Hell, Jim's already half dead if this thing with Haig blows open."

Scott sat silently and shook the ice cubes in his whisky-less glass.

"Bottom line, Scott. Baruch is carrying a stronger message

than your station and he knows too much. That's bad for business."

Scott thought back to the video he had received at home. No matter how hard he tried, he couldn't get that damn message out of his mind. He was lost in his thoughts and Marco rolled on.

"Scott, when your competition gets out of hand, you have to squash it."

"Marco, I won't be involved in killing an innocent man."

"I understand that. I only want to make sure that no one feeds me to the wolves."

Scott put his head on his knees and locked his hands behind his head.

"Marco, you weren't here tonight. I don't know you. Now, get out of here!"

Marco walked out onto the plantation-style porch and opened the trunk of his car. He pulled out a phone headset that was attached to a scrambling device, and ran around the side of the house until he came to the phone box, where he quickly matched the frequency of the secure line and dialed.

Speaking through a voice modulator he said, "This is Wild Boy. Identify yourself. Have you located the target? Fine. You are authorized to take out the bird."

Marco hit 'save file' and ran for the car.

CHAPTER 43

THE WNN TOWER STOOD QUIETLY IN THE PREDAWN DARKNESS OF downtown Chicago on Tuesday, September 10, 2013. The brilliant whiteness of full-spectrum lights illuminated the barren hallway of the tenth floor, where, in the corner office, a cadre of high-priced lawyers huddled around the desk of Jim Anderson, the aroma of coffee filling the air.

"No way, Bill. Go to Baku and take a chance of getting arrested? I don't care how good a PR move it is," Jim told his longtime attorney, Bill Wickes.

Bill Wickes, who had the polished look of a distinguished statesman, coifed his silver hair and listened.

"Here's how we spin it. For now, we're behind Haig, because we don't have any idea what they know. We'll put a card on the table when they do. Walter Butwin's on his way in to work the media angle."

"Walter Butwin, WNN's weapon of mass distraction," Bill Wickes joked.

Jim grinned and continued devising the game plan. "In the meantime, get the list of all the Azeri politicians we own, and start working them."

"May I suggest that we freeze all the Kirovs funds? It'll look like we're cooperating, and give us some leverage if the Kirovs try anything unscrupulous," one of Bill Wickes' young prodigies said matter-of-factly.

"Excellent," Jim conferred.

In his slow, deliberate speaking style, Bill added, "Jim, we'll contact you in any case before we make any comments for the record. But you need to understand that some Azeri politicians have mud on their faces, and they'll be looking for a sacrificial lamb. My advice is to let Haig fall."

The young attorney beside Bill Wickes added her concern, "The longer you stay with Haig, the more it's going to appear that you're protecting him. Legally, that raises a red flag."

Jim gestured with his hands, commanding attention.

"Listen. Haig will not fall, because if he gets desperate he'll talk. So we stay put for now. Your job is to let Haig know that he's safe."

Jim stood up and looked around the table. "Find those investigators in Baku and break them. And frankly, I don't care how you do it!"

Returning to his chair, Jim said calmly, "Thanks, Bill. I've got to take care of some other business now."

Bill added hesitatingly, "One last thing, Jim. What are you going to do with Baruch?"

Throwing up his hands, Jim replied, "What am I going to do? I'm going to let him be a hero!"

Bill shrugged. "Whatever you say."

He and his team of attorneys gathered their briefcases and filed out of Jim's office.

Jim's attention turned to the oversized monitor, where he punched up the previous day's summary of the financial holdings, energy division, news channels, and the rest of the potpourri that made up the AZI-Group. While analyzing every piece of every division with painful detail, WNN remained his baby. Because even though the energy division fueled the AZI-Group's profits, it was WNN that fueled Jim's legacy.

Today, with so much on the table, Jim flew threw the reports, glancing at only the short summaries provided by each division. He began to stand up, when he saw the flashing mailbox, reminding him to check his mail.

He had read most of the mail before Bill Wickes had arrived at 5:30 that morning. One new message, however, caught his attention.

NEW MESSAGE/RECEIVED TODAY AT 6:30 AM/SOURCE: UNTRACEABLE.

He clicked 'open'.

Baruch's fixed image flashed onto the screen. He began to move.

"Jim Anderson, I believe you remember me. Let me first say that your friend Haig Abku is finally where he belongs. Interpol, the CIA, and the Baku police know everything—down to the payoffs you made to secure the Oiltron deal. Don't bother asking how this happened. Like the thousands of lives you play with every day—people who never know why their lives turn out the way they do—you'll never understand."

Jim was struck by the casual tone of Baruch's voice.

"Do you remember Kubitz Furniture? It's a small manufacturing company outside of Vienna that you purchased last year. Do you remember? Or are you really that oblivious to the number of lives you touch? Let me bore you with a few details."

Jim punched up the numbers on Kubitz Furniture in the corner window of his screen as Baruch spoke.

"They manufactured Kubitz chairs, the very ones you have at several of your European offices. The Germans took over the factory in 1942, and it was destroyed in 1945. Werner, the only surviving family member, rebuilt the factory with remarkable skill. Orders increased every year. But last year, BNG Bank—the same BNG Bank that launders drug money for the Kirov family—released a negative credit rating. This caused cash flow problems, so BNG Bank took over the directorship of the company, which they sold to you at an excellent price. I remember your words: 'Our subsidiary today purchased several undervalued assets in Europe.' But that's just business, isn't that right?"

Jim, putting both elbows on the desk and pressing his thumbs against his temples, became increasingly absorbed by Baruch's monologue.

"You should know that you inspired me, Jim. You and your con! Convincing people that global consolidation was some unstoppable force! You were very clever. In fact, I wouldn't have figured out your plan to create this homogenous global consumption machine if not for a certain gentleman who visited my academy several years ago. He explained how business had consciously raised global consolidation to a mystical abstract, a god who had to eliminate anything that got in his way, be it churches, government, or people's souls. Or be it Werner Kubitz."

Baruch took a deep breath.

"The greatest things on this planet were conceived by human minds, even the calculator with which a scientist makes great formulations. Yet this process of human thought, our human technology, is either created or confined by the very objects we desire. Your objects of desire, Jim, are unacceptable."

Jim, forced to look at Baruch's magnetic eyes, fumed with anger.

"Power was never meant to be controlled by one person. Not you; not me. Our species excels through diversity. Someone who works in ways you will never understand has preordained a divine chaos. And no matter how much you try to package the human race into controllable compartments, there will always be people like me."

Baruch relaxed and smiled, as if struck by a fond memory.

"Do you remember what I told you in Brussels when we first

met? I laid out for you how to secularize the world, drive wedges into people's belief systems, and intimidate your employees. You see, Jim, I needed an antagonist. No story ever works without one. How quickly you were converted. Oh yes, the objects of our desires."

Jim looked petrified.

"Reliance on persuasion is your fundamental weakness. You will never be able to command faith. Only God, whether alone or through mortals like me, commands faith."

Baruch lifted himself from the wood chair near the fireplace.

"Consider this the end of our business relationship. May God forgive both of us."

Jim's trembling hands hit the 'save' icon. His screen spoke: "Access code required to download encrypted message."

Flustered, Jim typed in 'Baruch' as a wild guess.

"Improper access code. Message destroyed."

Jim hugged his monitor and cried, "God damn you, Baruch!"

A voice came over his intercom. "Mr. Anderson, a gentleman from the FBI would like to see you. He says it's urgent."

CHAPTER 44

JIM ANDERSON QUICKLY COMPOSED HIMSELF. THE FIRST FIGURE THAT entered his office wasn't a cold, angular FBI agent. Instead, an attractive middle-aged woman moved slowly past the WNN security guard followed by a senior reporter with shaggy brown hair and a boyish build.

"Maggie, Greg, what are you doing here?" Jim asked, as if his mother had returned from the grave.

Maggie and Greg each took a seat on the couch against the wall while a tall, fit young man with a crew cut and a gold crucifix earring answered for them.

"Mr. Anderson, I'm Agent Duarte with the FBI. Mr. Lancy and Ms. Helbling have agreed to cooperate with us."

Jim jumped at the too-young looking agent, "Cooperate? What the hell's going on!"

Agent Duarte and Jim were the only two standing. The stern FBI agent moved within six inches of Jim Anderson's nose and stated: "Mr. Anderson, we have evidence that your organization is involved in activities aimed at harming Stefan Mostl."

"Come on, Mr. Duarte. Are you serious? Why would we wish to harm Mr. Mostl?"

It seemed strange whenever Baruch was referred to by his given name. The agent backed away from Jim, having made it clear that he was serious.

"Here's a copy of the indictment against Oiltron Industries which we'll present to the Justice Department today."

Jim grabbed the document in disbelief and read some of the headings.

"Drug trafficking? Money laundering? Intimidation? ... Come on, Agent Duarte, we're talking about a guy who wrote a book and happens to be hot right now. Do you really want to start a legal battle with me?"

"Those charges have nothing to do with Stefan Mostl, sir. This is a separate order-to-appear concerning alleged threats against Mr. Mostl."

Jim Anderson rubbed his eyes, appearing fatigued.

"This is insane. First the CIA accuses Mr. Abku of aiding a drug cartel and, on top of that, we're supposed to be assassins. Sounds to me like politics, Agent Duarte. Did Jerry Bates contribute more than I did?"

"We'll leave the BNG case to the courts, Mr. Anderson. But looking at Mr. Mostl, we have leads coming out our butts. We've found over five hundred news stories that all originate from the same source. There are tapes of you and Mr. Mostl. And we have a phone call that sounds like a contract on Mr. Mostl's life."

"A fallacy of misplaced concreteness," Jim stated.

"I'm sorry?" the agent asked, confused.

"It's a leap in logic where you take little pieces and use it to construct a proof."

"These aren't little pieces," the agent said, flipping through his files. He spotted what he was looking for and continued: "Let's begin with Ms. Sharon Tucker. She breaks every story without ever leaving the building. Then we have your direct subordinates in Chicago and Baku falsifying documents to implicate Mr. Mostl in the Oiltron fire. We have officials in Baku receiving bribes to associate Mr. Mostl with Human Race..."

Jim cut him off. "Ms. Tucker's job is filtering stories. And as for information, bribes are still legal in some countries."

"Mr. Anderson, I wouldn't waste the time of someone as important as you if all that I had was flimsy evidence."

Agent Duarte reached in his case and held a recording in his hand. He pressed 'play'. "This is Wild Boy. Identify yourself. Have you located the target? Fine. You are authorized to take out the bird." The voice was Scott McNally's.

Jim stood paralyzed as the agent spoke.

"That call came from the home of Mr. Scott McNally. And what I have here is a complete testimony—with various audio and videotapes dating back to June 2010—from a Mr. Stefan Andreas Mostl. It appears Mr. Anderson, that someone would like to see Mr. Mostl dead. It would appear that that person is indeed in your organization."

Jim moved to his desk and clicked the speakerphone. Speaking in a monotone, he ordered, "Get the legal guys in my office right now.... And get ahold of McNally."

Jim studied Greg and Maggie sitting on the couch and said in disgust, "We pay you guys to report, not think. If you want to be a hero, join the fuckin' marines."

He turned his back and stared out the window at the vastness of Lake Michigan. "Just get out of here."

The FBI agent remained motionless across the room from Jim, who waited to be connected.

"Yeah, Scott. This is Jim."

Scott was still at home, rummaging through stacks of files in his study.

"Scott, I've got the FBI in my office. I just received some extremely disturbing news. I need you and Mr. Van Wels in my office now.

"What do you mean you don't know where Mr. Van Wels is?

Find him!"

Scott rushed to put on a tie, laced up his shoes, and headed for the car. As he opened the door to his German roadster, Maddie flew out on to the patio.

"Mr. McNally! Mr. McNally, you have a call."

Breathing as if he had run miles, Scott gasped, "Take a message!"

"It's Baruch."

Scott ran back up the stairs and grabbed the phone from Maddie.

"Yeah, this is McNally."

"Hello, Mr. McNally." Scott recognized the melodic tone of Baruch's voice. He listened intently.

"Mr. McNally, I've already recorded all pertinent events related to WNN's activities, and WBG has live videotape—a kiss and tell, if you will. You're a businessman, so let me explain how the arrangement works. If I should die, everything goes public—you go to jail. If I live, only a normal interview is aired and you walk."

There was a pause. "Are you there, Mr. McNally?"

"Yeah, I'm here. Why me?"

"It's all of us. You don't know who I am, do you?"

"Yes, I know who you are!" Scott shouted in an agitated voice.

"Remember that the small consists of the larger and the larger of the smaller. It takes evil people to make a corporation evil. Prove to yourself that good rests in your heart. And please don't act only to save yourself from going to jail. You must understand that I'm trying to save you from yourself. May God bless you."

Scott tried to get in a question, but only the dial tone was listening. He hit a preset button.

"Jim? Scott here. I think Marco Van Wels intends to kill Baruch. I'm on my way to the office."

CHAPTER 45

SHARON TUCKER ENTERED WALLY'S WORLD AND FOUND THE STUMPY editor busy typing behind his high-tech desk.

The Kirov drug cartel secretly plants agents in leading banks around the globe, appeared on the screen.

Sharon waved her finger and preached, "No, Walter. That will not be the lead story tonight. I won't authorize it."

"You're way out of your league on this, Sharon. Just back off," an indignant Walter said. "If you have a problem, talk to Jim."

"I didn't talk to Jim, Walter. But I *did* talk to the legal guys."

Sharon pulled out a legal-sized document and handed it brashly to Walter's outstretched hand. Walter's eyes spoke volumes.

"They can't suspend me!"

"Well, you sure didn't do anything right. When you accepted the stories on Baruch, stories that you knew to be false, you broke the law. Feel lucky that we only listed insubordination as the grounds for suspension."

Walter reached for the phone, but Sharon stopped him. "Now, listen good, young man. I could have had you fired. However, one, I need you gone *now* and, two, I understand that you're just caught in the middle of Jim's game.

"The suspension takes place immediately," Sharon added.

Stuffing papers into his briefcase and fuming, Walter remained suspiciously silent. Sharon interrupted again.

"You'll have to leave all those papers here, as well as your briefcase, keys, and access cards," she said, pointing to the document.

Walter handed over his keys, like a teenager who had just been grounded.

"Walter, I came dangerously close to falling into the same trap that you're in. Do you really like what you see going on around here? I don't."

"I can't believe that *our* legal guys signed that suspension," Walter mumbled.

"They had no choice."

Sharon threw him a warm, understanding glance and added, "Come on, I'll open the elevator door for you."

They approached the foyer and heard the bell of an arriving elevator car. Scott's black loafers stepped off the olive green carpet of the wood-paneled elevator. Still breathing heavily, more from anxiety than physical strain, Scott spotted Sharon and Walter.

"Where are you going?" Scott asked.

Walter swung his head from side to side and answered in a soft voice, "Don't ask, Scott. Just...don't ask."

"This is the heaviest news day of the century. I need you both in the meeting right now," Scott insisted.

"I'll explain in a minute," Sharon told Scott.

Confused, Scott marched down the hallway into the conference room, opening the door to the intense debate of the Red Team.

"Have a seat," Jim said forcefully.

Scott felt the emotional heaviness of Maggie and Greg, both of whom had been invited by Jim, on Bill Wickes advice, to remain involved in the investigation. "Keep close to your friends, and even closer to your enemies," Bill had reminded Jim.

"We have to find Marco," Scott said, sitting across from Amy, "or Baruch is history."

"How do you know that?" Jim asked.

"He—I mean Marco—was at my house last night. He told me."

Jim closed his eyes and dropped his head. He spoke quietly.

"That's marvelous, Scott. You and Marco spent last evening together discussing the murder of Baruch."

Then realizing the force of his own words, Jim shouted, "Do you realize that if Baruch dies, they're going to think I did it? Motive. Jesus fucking Christ. Do I have a motive!"

"Come on, Jim. Marco *told me* he's going to do it."

"Sure, Scott. Marco's just going to walk in court and say, 'Yep, it was me. I did it. Everyone can go home now.'"

He scanned the faces of Greg, Maggie, Walter, and finally Amy.

"So why is your voice on this tape?"

Scott listened and burst out yelling, "I never made that call! That's not me."

Jim picked up the phone and pressed a preset dial.

"Do you have the results? Yeah...OK...What?"

Jim disconnected the line and began pacing. His head shook, as he seemed to work himself into an emotional frenzy.

He spoke loudly: "The tape was manipulated. The digital trace of the voice doctoring comes from this fucking building!"

Jim looked angrily at the silent members of the Red Team.

"Wake up, people! We've been set up. Who knows, Marco could've been in on the whole thing."

"Hey, I don't even know who Marco is," Amy replied to Jim's scowl.

"Then you're the only one who doesn't know the flying fuck-ing Dutchman, Amy."

Scott plopped open his briefcase on the table and, in one motion, slid a file across the table towards Amy. She reached to her left and retrieved Scott's stray shot.

Her eyes revealed total surprise.

"This is Marco?" she grimaced, surveying the inquisitive looks of her colleagues. "He told me his name was Jan—I went to the opera with this guy Saturday night!"

Jim turned red with anger. "Scott, I told you she was too young for this scenario. She screws up the Baruch interview. Now, she sleeps with the guy who's going to kill him—and ruin me."

Jim approached Amy's chair. "How could you not know Marco? Is anyone home? I don't know whether to fire you or feel sorry for you."

Scott looked across the room at Greg and Maggie. "I'd like to know how you guys found out about Marco."

"When Baruch first told us about his theory, we were shown photos of Marco," Greg stated.

"Baruch showed you? Personally?"

"No, it was a video link."

"Thanks for telling me, Greg, buddy," Scott said in dismay.

Jim lit up.

"Baruch is out to get us. He thinks we're out to get him. We know that Marco's not with Baruch. So whom does Marco work for? That's what I want to know."

"He took out my dad's sailboat, today," Amy said, covering up her tears with cupped hands. "He may still be there."

Jim, smiling in disbelief, said, "So, Amy, did you make him a picnic basket, too?" He dialed the number on the card in front of him.

"Agent Duarte. Yeah, Jim Anderson. It appears that Marco Van Wels could be at the Belmont Club - Slip...?" He looked at Amy for guidance. "Slip 152. Last one that saw him at our organization was Scott McNally - last night here in Chicago. You're welcome."

Jim hung up, raised his hands to the heavens, and confessed, "Man, did I ever fuck this up!"

♦ ♦ ♦ ♦ ♦

Back in his makeshift office at the special investigations department of the Chicago Police Department, Agent Duarte stuck his phone in his pocket and sat in his Kubitz low-backed chair. An officer in street clothes entered. "Sir, there's a Mr. Marco Van Wels here to see you."

He rolled his head back in his shoulders. "Bring him on, Officer."

"Call Jim Anderson at the WNN Tower and inform him that we've found Mr. Van Wels," he instructed his assistant over the pager.

Marco walked up calmly, eye to eye with Agent Duarte.

"Hello, Cory, I heard you guys were trying to track me down."

An admiring grin broke the serious demeanor of Agent Duarte. "You never cease to amaze me, Marco."

CHAPTER 46

BARUCH HAD MET FRANK AT THE LA AIRPORT FOLLOWING THE WBG interview. Accompanied by a FBI agent, they were flown by military plane to Chicago where an informal discussion was planned with Jim Anderson the next morning. Nearing O'Hare Airport, Frank and Baruch's muddled conversation was inaudible to the curious FBI agent. A black limo met them at the far east runway, where they were hustled behind the black glass by a formidable bodyguard. The car halted briefly at the employee security gate and then skirted toward the city, the setting sun at their rear.

"Thanks for meeting me, Frank."

Baruch spoke German with Frank, although they assumed that the special agent spoke German as well.

"Frank, do you believe in an absolute truth?"

Frank stared out the window as he spoke. "We seem to always come back to this topic, don't we?"

"In today's world of chaos and superstring theories, I believe it to be a good question."

Frank contemplated.

"I'm not so sure."

"Don't give up on me now, Frank. The establishment wants us to believe there's no truth," Baruch said, as he patted Frank boyishly on the head and continued.

"But the flaw of new sciences—Chaos, Superstrings, you name it—is that they can never account for the infinite world they suggest, because their machines would have to have infinite capacity. So long as they dismiss the human technology, they will never see what I have seen."

Baruch laughed at his own words.

"Humans. We believe in theories that we can't explain...Yet I'm an outcast for claiming that each person can find an absolute truth. "

Frank looked curiously at his former classmate. "What is your truth, Stefan?"

Looking at the FBI agent, Baruch spoke in dialect: "Every day is a carrefour, a crossroad. Like the rays of the sun, this day can move in endless directions. But once we choose a direction, we can never again return to that point. The global consumerism our world chose was only one ray of the sun's vast light. While we may not be going in the wrong direction, I believe we have boarded the wrong train. And we can only change our path by changing the object of our desires."

Baruch's eyes watered as he spoke. "Frank, what I've experienced on this planet is something so beautiful, so intellectually perfect that I hope only to free the human spirit, be it only for the briefest moment, so that it may consider choosing a different path."

Their eyes met and both men smiled.

"And this was all your plan?" Frank probed.

"You overestimate me," Baruch smiled and put his hand on Frank's forearm.

The black limousine raced through downtown Chicago, and approached the Federal Building.

"Aren't we going to the hotel first?" Frank asked.

"No, instructions are to go directly to the Federal Building."

Baruch still had his hand resting on Frank's arm as he meditated. Opening his eyes, he pointed out, "Frank, you never asked me why I changed my name to Baruch."

"I read your explanation, Stefan."

"There's more to it than that story. Do you remember when we were kids and Anne was going to jump from your father's grain silo because she was pregnant."

Frank nodded his head. "Of course."

"Do you remember that she didn't speak for two days, and then she claimed I said 'I'll always love you'?"

Frank bit his lower lip and shook his head in assent.

"Frank, I didn't say anything to her. I took her hand, and felt a force more powerful than nature. I could see everything—mountains I had never skied, books I hadn't read, and stars I didn't know existed. My mind, for that instant, unified an unexplainable totality, a perfection, an absolute."

Baruch eyes looked into some distant place.

"After I walked her home and climbed the hill to our place, a man I had never seen before—an elderly man with overalls and leathery skin—came out of nowhere. He said, 'Be a servant to your generation. You are the blessed one, Baruch.' I just watched the old man disappear up near the caves."

Frank's eyes welled with tears, his face twitching as he tried to contain his emotions.

The wheels of the car let out a screech, the limousine pulling up the alley to the back entrance of the closed Federal Building. The agent spoke into his headset, watching the two Austrians stretch their weary limbs. "I'm here with the two subjects. Yeah, release the security door."

The agent escorted Frank and Baruch toward the back entrance as the door let off a loud buzz. The buzz was followed by a series of shots that echoed through the alley. The terror of the noise propelled the three men to the cement, the agent pushing Frank and Baruch out of the line of fire.

The agent rolled against the side of the car closest to the building and raised his gun above the car hood, aiming at an adjacent dumpster. Like a trapped animal, the agent flung his head from side to side. The only noise was the sound of his black shoes scuffing along the concrete.

Enraged, he yelled, "This is a goddamned alley! Where are they?"

Still giving cover, he moved backward to the security door and found Frank sitting against the wall, covered with blood, holding Baruch on his lap.

"Oh, my God!" the agent screamed in his headset. "We've got two men down behind the Federal Building. Suspects have not been spotted. Get an ambulance. Get backups."

The agent moved to the limousine and pounded the roof as he yelled at the dead driver.

"You motherfucker! You changed the route!" The agent's yell echoed in the alley: "You motherfuckers!"

Frank's head was bleeding.

"Where are you hurt?" the agent asked.

"I only hit the wall," Frank assured the agent.

"Please leave us alone," Baruch asked the agent in a whisper.

Frank cradled his friend like a newborn, applying pressure to the wound. Frank felt the warm blood of Baruch's mortal being pour from the bullet hole.

"Frank, go to the Bank of Austria in Semriach," Baruch said, handing him a key from the pocket of his bloodstained black linen jacket.

"Oh, Stefan. You're going..." Frank began consoling him.

"Be calm," Baruch interrupted, lifting his bloody hand to speak. "Frank, yesterday that man—the old farmer from

Semriach—came back after my interview at WBG. He said, 'You have served well. You have earned the right to be called the blessed one.'"

Baruch, with a magnificent gleam in his eyes, seemed somehow to subdue the pain in his convulsing body.

"This time, Frank, the old man didn't walk away. Instead, he looked to the heavens and saw a flock of geese more beautiful, more radiant than a field of lilies. Suddenly, I heard a gunshot, and the bird at the peak of the formation spiraled to the ground. After a moment of confusion, a new leader took the point and led the flock into the distance. The old man said, 'The hunter keeps shooting, but the flock reforms over and over, because every one of those geese is willing to lead. Unlike humans, they will not be intimidated.'"

Frank's tears poured onto Baruch's bloody face. In the background could be heard the siren of an ambulance entering the alley.

The agent moved in to help Frank with the deep wound, but Baruch grabbed the agent's outstretched hand.

"I had only my words. Why did they have to shoot me?"

Frank held him tightly. The FBI agent could only swallow deeply and drop his head.

"Be calm, Baruch. God is in you." Frank stroked his thick black hair and clutched his hand.

Baruch gasped for breath. "Go to Semriach, my friend. You have a key to the truth. There is truth."

Amongst the scurrying police and doctors, Frank nestled Baruch's motionless head against his shoulder.

"The world will always remember you. You are the blessed one."

CHAPTER 47

A DOZEN OFFICERS, A JANITOR, AND SEVERAL RECEPTIONISTS ENCIRCLED the large screen in the corner of the Chicago Police Department.

The WBG logo—a globe with a dove—gave way to Todd Zone's taped interview.

"We've all heard the rumors about the spiritual figure of the twenty-first century, Baruch. Rumors have circulated that he was dead, or kidnapped, or belonged to some terrorist group. Despite all the words recently written and spoken about Stefan Mostl—the man we call Baruch—he has escaped this row of accusations unscathed, vindicated of all charges by the U.S. government."

The group listened silently. Marco and Agent Duarte sat alone in the corner, drinking coffee and smoking. Marco looked relaxed as he tried again to explain what had happened.

"Here's the deal. In June of last year, Jim Anderson calls me. I had met him back in 2008 while investigating a case in Baku where I'd done some contract work. He says that 'Baruch is out of control'—asks me to shadow him and get as much info on him as I can. So I'm doing my job, when Jim pulls a switch. About six months ago, he tells me that I'll be officially working for Scott McNally and that our arrangement is confidential."

Marco grabbed a cookie from the desk behind him and continued.

"My guess is that when the Baruch story escalated, Jim

wanted to distance himself from me and the whole situation. Anyway, McNally gets obsessed with Baruch. Tells me and a bunch of other folks he wants Baruch dead. Last night, he asks me to kill Baruch and I explain to him that killing is where I draw the line."

The lanky FBI agent interrupted. "Would you rig an explosion at an oil platform?"

"McNally did send me to Baku to try and get the right results. But by the time I had arrived—in fact, I was with one of WNN's reporters—the insurance guys had already come and gone. I couldn't get close to the evidence. I guess I pissed off a lot of people in Baku when I was with Interpol. And all the crap about Baruch being a terrorist was smoke; hell, they rescinded the story."

Cory Duarte leaned forward. "Were you shadowing Baruch this weekend?"

"No, I was here in Chicago with that cute blond reporter, Amy Laurance. Saw *Carmen*, went sailing..."

The FBI agent sipped his coffee. "Did you call a hit on Baruch?"

Marco slid around the desk and pointed angrily. "I've been tracking this guy for a year. With the exception of this week when he was in hiding, I could have taken him out any time I'd wanted." Marco put his index finger on his temple. "Think straight for a second, Cory: You know who I work for. The only thing I lose if Baruch dies is 50K a month from the AZI-Group!"

Marco reached in his attaché case and pulled out a hefty file.

"Here you go. That's a copy of my reports and personal notes from the last twelve months. Even though I tried a few times, I did nothing illegal. Zero."

Marco grinned and stood up to wish his old acquaintance good-bye. In the corner, the interview was almost over when WBG's Todd Zone broke in live.

"Ladies and gentlemen. It could be called a tragic irony or, more likely, fate. While you were watching this interview—filmed yesterday here in our LA studio—Baruch has been shot and killed in Chicago."

Marco and Cory exchanged glances. Marco shook his head. "Some people just don't make it. You better go find McNally and Anderson."

CHAPTER 48

"THIS EVENING COULD BE THE MOST TRAGIC OF THE CENTURY. Baruch's followers, thought to number in the tens of millions, learned only hours ago that his prophecy had in fact been realized."

Amy Laurance was bundled up in a long, wool coat on this first cold fall evening, shot live outside the Federal Building where dozens of FBI agents combed the outside of the building.

"The Ecumenical Society issued a statement of regret that 'a man of such good spirit who tried to help the greater cause was taken from a spiritually-starved world.'

"Also, the Oval Office has announced that the president will make a statement momentarily.

"Standing beside me is FBI Special Agent Martin Pena. Agent Pena, what can you tell us about the shooting at this time?"

"A vehicle carrying three passengers and a driver entered the alley of the Federal Building at around 10:30 PM. Shots were fired, and Mr. Stefan Mostl and the driver of the car were both mortally wounded. We are using all of our resources to find the person or group behind this attack."

"At this time do you suspect an individual gunman?"

"It's simply too early in the investigation to know that."

Amy and Agent Pena went back and forth, not getting any closer than 'We're doing our best' and 'We're tapping every available resource'.

"The president has ordered all flags to be displayed at half-mast tomorrow," Amy said, wrapping-up what was sure to be one of only many reports throughout the evening.

Frank, sitting in the government-owned Boeing 737 on the runway at Chicago's O'Hare, talked to Amy through his portable screen.

"There you stand, above the fray, the global narrator: a criminal."

Frank flipped to Mike McMillan's WBG.

"The AZI-Group and WNN had a very difficult day. Federal agents seized the tenth floor of the headquarters in Chicago and instructed Interpol agents to raid the company's headquarters in Baku."

Todd Zone appeared on Frank Schleiers portable screen. "Arrest warrants have been issued for three officers of the AZI-Group—CEO, Jim Anderson, WNN President Scott McNally, and, Oiltron President Haig Abku. Mr. Abku, it should be noted, has been charged in Baku, Azerbaijan, of involvement in the BNG/Kirov drug scandal. However, it has been reported that Mr. Abku somehow escaped the country and is unaccounted for."

♦ ♦ ♦ ♦ ♦

The Boeing jet, put at Frank's disposal by the FBI, vectored through the clouds into the dark glow of the night. The copilot, a young army officer, opened the door from the cockpit and saw Frank's brown eyes reflected in the tiny window.

"We will arrive in Graz at 8:30 AM local time, sir," the young man announced.

"Thank you, that's very kind," Frank acknowledged, gazing out the window into the darkness of space. He kept this strangely vacant look the entire flight, except when he closed his eyes and sank into a fitful doze. He was in one of these short dozes when the copilot returned.

"Sir, we'll be landing in ten minutes."

Frank was glad to see Stephanie, his older sister, at the airport. Her embrace reminded him that he was still alive. They stopped shortly at the old farmhouse, where that single, aluminum grain silo would now serve as a memorial to Stefan. He looked at the fall colors dotting the hills in the background—those hills where he and Stefan had played so many times—and was reminded that he still had a family, a place to go, a place where they spoke the way he had learned to speak.

After he had washed up, his sister offered him some coffee and they talked about how Stefan Mostl had changed the world for the better.

"Who would have ever thought that someone from our village would be so important?" Stephanie deliberated.

Frank sat silently and looked at his watch.

"Could you drive me to the bank in Semriach, Stephanie?"

CHAPTER 49

CHARLEY SAT FACING GREG AND MAGGIE AT THE WEST EGG DINER. His eyes were swollen from lack of sleep, a lot of crying, or both. He spoke in an unusually slow manner.

"So like I told Greg, Baruch talked Jim into creating a prophet for the AZI-Group."

Maggie looked confused. "But why did Jim bite?"

"All these New Age prophets had created huge followings, so Jim figured he'd have his own spiritual division. He planned on using his media strength to deliver a *complimentary* message through Baruch."

"And Jim believed he'd pull it off. It's impossible!" Greg said.

"Baruch always possessed that persuasive power that was...unexplainable. Jim's plan was certainly not impossible," Charley contended.

"So did Jim kill Baruch?" Greg asked.

"No, I think it was Marco Van Wels—remember him?"

Greg sprang up in the booth. "Marco killed him?"

"Probably not himself. Marco works for the government, Greg. He's a double agent. It's the capitalistic cold war, the government against the virtual corporation. It seems like the CIA or Interpol arranged for Marco to become Jim's confidant through Haig Abku. Haig worked with the CIA until things got hot in 2008."

"Why would the government want to kill him?" Maggie inquired.

"Because they want to regulate the virtual corporations. Because once they regulate the virtuals, they can get control of the money again. Let me ask you, Maggie: how many times have presidents tried to take the power of the money away from the banks?"

She shrugged her shoulders. "I don't know. Once?"

"Close. Twice. Lincoln tried to create greenbacks to finance the Civil War. And Kennedy signed an executive order to back currency with silver. Lincoln and Kennedy. Get it?"

"But Baruch wasn't controlling the money," Greg added.

"Right—but he was the emotional element that would help the U.S. government to break the AZI-Group. They already had the Kirov drug deal and market manipulation during the Oiltron purchase. That was enough to throw some people in jail. But if they could link Baruch's death to the AZI-Group, think how public opinion would move away from the global corporations. Once Marco found out about Jim and Baruch, the government saw an opportunity to move in for a corporate kill. I've got ten-to-one odds they pin Baruch's death on Jim Anderson before it's over."

"So Baruch was a government invention?" Maggie mocked.

"No, Maggie. This is where the conspiracy people get it all wrong. You see, it wasn't a master plan by the government. The government's scheme was to break the AZI-Group, and Baruch just happened to be there. Marco didn't create the events as much as he steered them."

"My God, Charley. I hope you're wrong," Maggie injected.

"Listen, Mag, this was a set-up from the beginning. Why does Jim have Sharon filter all the stories? Answer: to keep you out of the loop so you don't ask questions and, at the same time, to distance himself. Why does Baruch get linked to the Oiltron fire? Answer: because Jim thinks he's out of control and wants to ruin him."

"But why did that fall through? Who started the fire?" Greg asked.

"The fire was an accident. The oil rigs were too old, just like Human Race claimed! But Marco talks Scott into implicating Baruch. Marco has AZI-Group companies do all the dirty work. Then he turns around and exposes them. He was supposed to set Baruch up, but he actually framed the AZI-Group for Interpol. He never stopped working for Interpol! Do you guys get it?"

"But why try to link Baruch to Human Race?" Greg asked.

"Classic misinformation campaign. Haven't you listened to your own station? They call him a philosopher, a prophet, a guru. They try to confuse the viewers."

Charley had a reluctant look on his face, as he continued his diatribe: "Mag, why does Jim have you sent to Baku? Answer: because you don't know shit about what's going on. If he sends an expert, they ask too many questions."

"Yeah, I wondered that myself," Maggie replied shyly.

Greg leaned close to Charley.

"I just can't believe it. Who knew besides Jim, Baruch, and you?"

Charley sighed, "Listen you guys, this wasn't easy for me, keeping all this stuff from you. Stefan Mostl was my friend. He told me he was going to die...." Charley began sobbing. "... And damn it, I tried to stop them. I just didn't know who 'them' was!"

Maggie moved around the booth and hugged Charley. "But you said you knew Marco was a double agent."

Charley spoke through his tears. "Everybody wanted Stefan dead! I thought Marco was just a seed in the AZI-Group. I really thought Anderson was going to do it. It's so damn complicated, this world!"

Maggie comforted her friend. "Baruch had a plan, Charley. He always had a plan."

Chapter 50

The professor entered the tiny village's small, modern bank and approached the well-dressed young man sitting at the desk.

"Good morning. I'm here to open my safe-deposit box."

Frank offered the young man his encoded key, which the well-trained employee diligently scanned. Frank thought of all the trouble that he and Baruch had gone through—secured lines, the MED II encryption chip, and FBI protection. He felt anger, and a bit of irony, that the only secure place in this 'free' world was a safe-deposit box in a remote corner of Europe.

"You must be Mr. Schleier, sir. I need to see your identification."

Frank pulled out his magnetized, hologram card and handed it politely to the aspiring banker who inspected it carefully.

"Please follow me, Mr. Schleier."

The young man snatched the printout and held it up proudly. "This insures that every time you enter, the code matches the box number you choose."

Frank was trying to figure out the whole time how Baruch had opened a box in Frank's name without his I.D.

"There you go, sir. Number 090913." The boy hesitated and said lightly, "Yesterday's date."

That strange vacancy returned to Frank's eyes. He inserted the key and slowly lifted the lid off the long, narrow metal box.

There were six videodisks and a thick envelope. As Frank stacked the disks together, he noticed they were labeled in order from one to three, with a backup for each disk.

"How did you know?" Frank asked out loud.

He thanked the young banker and joined his sister, who had waited out front.

As the car approached the farmhouse, Frank became uneasy. Less than twenty-four hours ago he had felt the warm blood of his closest friend, who had died on his shoulder. Now he would have to see him alive.

Inside the house where he had grown up, his hands fumbled the disk labeled " No. 1". He clumsily inserted it into the drive and pressed 'enter'. Tears fell on the keyboard when he saw Baruch appear: handsome, dynamic, glowing...alive.

"Hello, Frank. You are the best friend any person could ask for. I do find it ironic that we so often debated the concept of truth and that I never told you the entire truth. I believe now you will understand why."

Baruch paused and grabbed a file from the small desk near the fireplace.

"You may have heard rumors of the 'six spirits' meeting in our little village. Well, there were really only four of us: Charley Hardeway, Dr. Horstmann, and... the one person who implemented this elaborate plan. That person is now the most powerful man on the planet. So why did I work with Jim Anderson? I didn't work with him—I ruined him, because he was systematically destroying the human spirit. You must understand, Frank, that I never believed corporations and governments could destroy faith. I was wrong. The past decade proved that faith could be bought and sold like a pair of tennis shoes. As the virtual corporations raced to perpetuate their global model, they realized that people's faith—their innermost desire to be humans and believe—was an obstacle to mechanized,

*overproductive, nonthinking human beings. And they broke that
faith, Frank. My God, they broke it."*

Baruch, fighting tears, gathered himself and continued:

*"Frank, do not concern yourself with the group that killed me. Not
even they know the depth or nature of what has just happened.
Remember when I used to say that there was only one law of nature—
our desire to live? My only desire was that faith has a new beginning. I
believe I have accomplished this goal."*

Baruch stood up as he spoke.

*"How can I make this world a better place? For years I asked myself
this question. I did not wish to become a cynic; I left that to my good
friend Charley. Intellectual greatness...that is a talent you were blessed
with. Looking for my cause, I formed my academy.*

*"The world of the Old Testament needed people like Jeremiah 'to
rule over nations and kingdoms, to uproot, tear down, to destroy, and
overthrow, to build and to plant'. In my years at the academy, I devised
a way to create a twenty-first century Jeremiah and throw open a new
door, a new path, for a truly New World Order.*

*"The elite virtual corporations regard humans as indistinguishable
from the animals and machines surrounding us. Those in power fear a
human awakening, a human technology. So when I asked how I could
create a new path, I concluded that power had to be redistributed: The
AZI-Group needed to be removed. But I was not going to bring a knife
to a gunfight. I needed adequate firepower and diversions - lots of diversions. In fact, the entire plot was one big diversion.*

*"Ten years ago I spent a year studying philosophy in Paris. I met a
bright twenty-seven-year-old student who was studying economics and
French language. The first time I shook his hand, I had a moment of
insight, that moment of totality I had experienced only on the grain silo
as a child. The student's name was Mike McMillan, the fourth member
of my academy.*

"So when you turn on the news tomorrow, you will see the AZI-

Group tumbling and Bates/McMillan rise to prominence. AZI-Group officers will be arrested and their stock will crash. Ironically, this devaluation will allow Mike McMillan and Jerry Bates to purchase many of the AZI-Group's holdings. Jerry Bates will also help people like Sharon Tucker and your uncle, Werner Kubitz, stage management buyouts of individual companies. Each of these is a sign of a small victory for the human spirit.

"There are some important things I need to go over.

"I want you to understand that Jerry Bates is a good man, but we needed to paint him as ruthless in order to avoid suspicion. Please know that Jerry can be trusted.

"Understand as well that all the public actions by Mike and Jerry were meant to keep the government agencies at bay. WBG, for instance, continued its unconscionable reporting to provide a cover.

"Originally, the coup was to take place in November, after the elections. But we had to work quickly last week when the CIA started to link Mike to me. Mike went to Chicago and bluffed Jim into thinking that the FBI was on to him. Thank goodness Jim went for it.

"Another detail concerns the oil rig. Human Race blew it up. This group is a proxy of the U.S. government. Do not trust them.

"Finally, you were supposed to be included in the plan. But I decided it was safer to have someone we could trust outside the circle.

"God told Jeremiah: 'I have made you a fortified city, an iron pillar and bronze wall to stand against the whole world'. Well, Mike now has his fortified city, and Jim Anderson's empire will no longer be an obstacle.

"Next week, after Jerry Bates takes a controlling position in Oiltron, Mike McMillan will call a conference amidst the 'crisis' and announce a new world compassion. Those are my words. When Mike begins to remove the barriers that isolate individuals and berate the soul, replacing them with an environment of trust and respect, those are my programs. When he balances business, government, and religion in order to give personal liberty a chance, I am the juggler. We are going

to enter an era of true hope and expose the shameless New Age spiritu-
alists who say 'Life is miserable, learn how to deal with it.'

"Frank, I hope you understand why I couldn't accomplish this elaborate plan and remain alive. The world has become too cynical. And
never forget that you are no longer just a professor. With these videos
you could ruin Mike and Jerry. You could topple world markets and
government leaders. Keep the video in a safe place, in case you ever need
to tame an unyielding character.

"In the coming months, you will be offered a professorship at UCLA
in Los Angeles. Thereafter, Mike will fund an institute for the study of
human technology. Mike needs guidance; he needs a man of your intellect. Stay close to him. Nurture him as you nurtured me.

"Frank, the people of the world need only a short reprieve from the
invisible cage that surrounds them. Never lose sight of the goal: faith
and freedom. If anyone jeopardizes our work, you must fight. Learn to
hate slavery, no matter how well disguised."

Weeping, Frank opened the manila envelope and found the
original manuscript of *Apocrypha Truth*. Attached with a paper
clip was a handwritten note that read: "September 10, 2013.
Frank: Please deliver to my father, Dr. Horstmann, with enclosed
letter. Love. Stefan." Behind the note was a photo of Stefan and
Frank playing on a seesaw in the schoolyard.

CHAPTER 51

FRANK DRANK A DOUBLE ESPRESSO AND READ THE PAPER IN HIS favorite hometown café, Kleiner Wirt. The small, brown café was like so many in Europe, and not much had changed in these cafés this century. A union worker with his working-class blue overalls sipped a beer, while two businessmen ate baguettes and drank coffee. And an out-of-place, wiry professor sat alone, thinking. He thought about what Baruch had so often said: "The few are always trying to change the many, but there are always many more than the few."

Frank flipped the page and saw the lead article: 'AZI-Group temporarily delisted, Oiltron under investigation'. He scanned down the page to an editorial: 'Bates/McMillan the real winner'. Frank smiled for the first time in two days, his eyes admiring the relaxed, confident smile of Mike McMillan. The fact that only he knew Mike's real agenda gave him a feeling of omnipotence. Frank thought it dangerously close to playing God.

"Are you Frank Schleier?" a bearded man with a fisherman's cap asked.

"Yes, I am."

"You probably forgot me. I'm Michael Fischer—we went to school together."

Frank's face lit up. "Oh yes, Michael. How are you, my friend? Are your parents still in the cottage up by the caves?"

"Sure are. People around here don't move!"

Frank grinned. He and Baruch had tried moving, but they always ended up in this café in this little village.

"Frank, I know you were very close to Stefan, so I thought you might want to know that we plan to build a little memorial where he used to have his academy."

Frank's eyes filled with enthusiasm. "That's a fine idea. I would love to see it."

As Frank stood up, the simple-looking Michael took off his cap and, looking as if he'd seen a ghost, pointed at Mike McMillan's picture in the newspaper.

"That guy was one of the men we called the 'spirits'!"

Frank closed his eyes and smiled. "Can we keep that our little secret, Michael?"

"Of course. Whatever you say."

The two old friends left the café, and Michael Fischer led Frank past the cows in the open field towards a group of several dozen men.

"Those are all the local builders. We're working on a plan for the academy already."

The two men dodged cow dung and puddles, moving toward the area where Stefan had masterminded his overthrow of the AZI-Group and the rise of his new world compassion.

"By the way, Frank. I heard that your uncle, Herr Kubitz, may take over the furniture factory. They say his son is going to run it."

Frank stood up tall and hugged his old schoolmate. "That's wonderful news, Michael. Wonderful news!"

Chapter 52

October 5, 2013. The narrow street along the Mur River was closed for the special session of the United Nations Spiritual Conference. The mass of well-dressed guests in the majestic lobby of the Grand Hotel in Graz, Austria, the home of Dr. Horstmann, moved towards the doors of the ballroom. The Ecumenical Society had organized this special event to recognize the 'Spirit of Stefan Mostl'. Clerics, a litany of government officials, and corporate leaders packed the modestly decorated ballroom. The president of the United States was scheduled to address the group via satellite, to commemorate Baruch's 'robust spirit' and 'desire for change'. The heads of the Catholic and Lutheran Churches pretended as if Baruch had always been their best friend.

The followers of Baruch, mostly relegated to observing the happenings from outside the hotel, held posters hailing their leader. Other groups, including Human Race, used the opportunity to promote regulations aimed at the virtual corporations or to demand the arrest of Baruch's killer.

Inside the ballroom, Dr. Horstmann, holding the original manuscript of *Apocrypha Truth*, stood next to Frank Schleier behind the podium, as the two Austrians commemorated the life of Baruch. Mike McMillan, the force behind the newly-founded Institute for the Studies of Human Technology, was scheduled to give the final speech of the day. He stood in the back of the hall and watched.

"Well, Baruch got his wish. He's a hero," the voice of Marco Van Wels said.

Mike swung his head around and saw the confident Dutchman standing behind him.

"He was a great man," Mike replied.

"But like all great men, he just didn't quite make it," Marco said sagely.

Mike grimaced. "No, he didn't. It seems the wrong people die...and the wrong people live."

"Yeah, life has a strange way of working out."

Mike gazed deep into Marco's eyes. "I have this feeling that Baruch will live on a very long time."

Ignoring Marco, Mike joined Greg, Maggie, and Charley and said, "Well, is my new staff going to give me a good rating on my speech?"

Greg seized the moment. "Of course. If you give a good speech!"

"You couldn't talk Sharon into joining us?" Mike asked.

Maggie laughed. "No, she's going to write a book about the rise and fall of Jim Anderson."

"She'd better make it fiction or no one will believe it!" Charley jabbed.

"And what about McNally? I heard he's retiring," Greg said.

"Yeah. And Walter's supposedly writing brochures for a travel agency," Maggie said with a smile.

"And Jim agreed to never again run a company in return for a reduced sentence at one of those country club prisons. End of story," Charley added.

Maggie set her hand on Mike's shoulder and theorized in a harmless tone.

"Jim Anderson out. The AZI-Group forced to divest Oiltron. And now, you're on top, Mike. If I were a skeptic like Charley, it would almost appear that this was all planned from the beginning."

"Are you saying a conspiracy, Maggie?" Mike asked lightly.

"Yeah, I guess so."

With an eerie gaze, Mike answered, "Life's a progression of conspiracies. Some are simply better than others."

THE END

To contact Brad Johnson directly, send an e-mail to btjohnson@mindspring.com.

Or visit us at www.rutledgebooks.com.

ACKNOWLEDGMENTS

AFTER TRAVELLING THE GLOBE FOR A DECADE, I CAN'T BEGIN TO THANK all of you with whom I had so many great experiences and from whom I learned so much. I would, however, like to thank those people who, through their direct input, made this book possible: Bill Lewis, Amy Bartle, Pete Cook, Marla Eaton, Ed Richards, Dan Gentges, Tiffany Eason, Clay Sills, Dexter Christian, Trish Ellis, Curt Walor, and Kevin Carr.

A special thanks to Aviva Layton for her keen eye; to Art Salzfass at Rutledge for believing in me; to Aimee Peterson for the beautiful illustration; to John Laub and Teri Boccuzzi for pulling a million details together; and to Rosemary Daniell and the entire Zona Rosa group for their support.

Ray Card, Pastor "PB" Bergen, Cecilia Ornelas, and Professor Fenz—to you I am indebted for providing guidance when I needed it most. I also extend a warm thanks to my friends at Eastern Michigan University for all of the support you have given to me throughout the years. My deepest gratitude goes to my many friends in Austria, who inspired the creation of Baruch.

For my brother, Paul, a special word is in order—it was a great ten years traveling, living, and learning together. Mom, I can never repay your tireless support and endless love. To all my family, thanks for always being there for me! And Nathalie, you deserve the biggest *merci* of all, for understanding my craziness.